Breakaway Creek

Heather Garside

Breakaway Creek

Heather Garside

Yarraman Press, 2026

Yarraman Press,
PO Box 275,
Capella, QLD, 4723, Australia
www.heathergarside.com
Cover Art by For the Muse Design Copyright 2026

Prologue

Central Queensland, 1871

'It shouldn't be long now.'

Sarah wiped the woman's sweating brow with a damp washcloth and hoped to God she was right. They were eighty miles from the nearest doctor with only an Aboriginal midwife and herself, newly married and ignorant. Things were looking desperate. After twenty-four hours in labour, Eliza was exhausted. The hot sun pounded on the tin roof of the maid's tiny room and the heat from the kitchen next door exacerbated the stifling conditions. Sarah fleetingly pressed a hand to her own stomach and vowed her baby would be born in Clermont.

She flinched when Eliza screamed and threw her head back, dusky features clenched in agony as she writhed with another spasm. Sarah watched helplessly as the Aboriginal midwife made an exclamation in her own language and bent between the patient's legs.

'Is it coming, Mary?' The woman didn't answer, but Sarah heard the first tiny cry and her heart leapt in dizzy relief as the baby slid free. She moved closer to check. 'You have a little boy, Eliza. Well done!'

For a moment euphoria pushed aside Sarah's revulsion. She hadn't realised what a messy, terrible business childbirth could be. The midwife grasped the wailing infant and cut the cord with the kitchen knife Sarah had provided, before wrapping him in a blanket and laying him against his mother's breast. Weakly, Eliza fumbled with her nightgown, so Sarah helped her open it and guide the nipple into the child's nuzzling mouth. Then she stiffened. For the first time she noticed the baby's skin through the coating of blood and mucus. Her stomach cramped.

'Missus!'

Her gaze jerked up to the black midwife's frightened face.

'What's wrong, Mary?'

Mary pointed and Sarah stepped cautiously closer, nostrils twitching at the metallic smell; blood. It gushed from the birth canal, staining the bed linen in an ever-widening tide. She grabbed some towels and pressed them against Eliza's body, but they did little to staunch the flow. Mary ran to the doorway and grabbed her dilly-bag, then moved the towels aside to pack handfuls of leaves in their stead. Sarah watched in dismay, wondering if the woman had any idea what she was doing. But who was she to stop her?

A touch on her arm made her look down at Eliza's greying face.

'Missus, will you look after my baby?'

The voice was reduced to a whisper, the dark eyes dull. Eliza was slipping away as surely as the blood poured from her body. Sarah glanced at the suckling infant.

'Who's its father, Eliza?'

Eliza's lips moved and Sarah bent closer to hear the whispered words. She froze, all her suspicions crystallising into grim knowledge. Wave on wave of pain and disillusionment lashed her like the sting of the stock whip her husband used on unruly cattle.

Could she possibly take responsibility for this child? She wondered if she had a choice. Sarah straightened, drew her breath in deep, and said the words – God help her – she knew the dying woman needed to hear.

'Yes, I'll take him for you, Eliza.'

Chapter One

Clermont, 2010

Shelley parked her car in front of the Clermont courthouse and grimaced at the heat shimmering off the bitumen in desolate waves. The street was empty and the entire town seemed lifeless, as if everyone had holed up to escape the burning sun.

She was probably mad coming here. Just because of an old photograph...

Her grandmother would be livid if she knew. Not that she really cared what Nanna Audrey thought. Shelley's mother, Noela, was okay with anything that took Shelley's mind off Jason, but it was her Great-Aunt Edie who'd suggested she come to Clermont.

'Now, there's a puzzle,' Aunt Edie had said. 'Audrey has to know something I don't. All I know is, Grandma was estranged from her own family and Grandpa didn't seem to have much contact with his. Audrey ended up with all the family papers.'

Shelley surveyed the low weatherboard building as she walked up the path and mounted the timber steps. It looked old enough to have existed in her ancestors' day. Perhaps they'd once trod these same boards. She wondered how they'd coped with the blistering temperatures in those long, layered clothes they used to wear.

'I'm trying to trace my great-great grandparents,' she told the young woman behind the counter. 'I was told they were married here in Clermont.'

The girl flicked her long fringe out of her eyes and smiled apologetically.

'I'm sorry, but with current privacy laws the public can't access our records. If you know the dates involved, I can look it up for you, though.'

Shelley dug in her handbag for the photograph. She'd found it last week in one of her mother's old photo albums, and looking at it now still made her scalp tingle. There was something about the dark-haired man and the pretty young woman seated before him, both formally dressed in the fashions of the late nineteenth century, that fascinated her. She held it out to show the girl.

'Their names are on the back – Alexander and Emma Baxter. It's dated 1898.'

'Was that when they were married?'

'I assume so.'

'That's a starting point, anyway. I'll see what I can find.'

She disappeared into the adjoining room, leaving Shelley to wander restlessly, studying the posters and sample birth certificates on the shabby walls. It was a depressing place. She swung around as the girl returned with a sheet of paper, her face beaming with satisfaction.

'I found the entry. They were married here in Clermont on February 25, 1898. She was Emma Watson. There are also records of a child, born in 1898. If you like, I can order copies of the marriage and birth certificates for you.'

A surge of elation sent Shelley hurrying back to the counter. Perhaps this crazy trip would prove to be fruitful, after all.

'Thank you! That's great. Is there any record of Alexander's birth? I think Emma was a Brisbane girl.'

'Do you know when he was born?'

Shelley shook her head.

'No, but he looks to be in his mid to late twenties here. My guess is sometime between 1870 and 1875.'

'I'll check for you, but births weren't always registered that far back, especially if people lived on remote properties.' She bustled away but was back again in no time. 'I'm sorry, but there's no record of Alexander Baxter's birth.'

What a bummer. Shelley smiled to cover her disappointment. She ordered copies of the available documents, requesting they be posted to her parents' address.

'Thanks for all your help. I appreciate it. My aunt told me Alexander was from Breakaway Creek station. Do you know if it still exists?'

The girl shrugged her thin shoulders.

'I've only been in town a couple of years. Why don't you ask one of the agents? Landmark or Elders know all the properties.'

Shelley stopped at the first stock and station agency she found. The shed-like building was filled with an assortment of rural merchandise which included everything from dog food to elastic-sided boots. Drums of chemicals lined the shelves, along with numerous items whose use was a mystery to a town-reared girl like her.

'Breakaway Creek,' the burly man behind the counter repeated, after greeting her with a jovial affability one seldom encountered in the city. 'I know of it. It's a bit out of the Clermont area now, since the mining towns sprung up. Do you know someone there?'

'I'm tracing my ancestors. My great-great grandfather came from there.'

'Hmm, you could be in luck. I think the family's been there for generations.' His eyes lit up with genuine interest. 'I don't suppose you want a job? I know they're looking for a housekeeper.'

Shelley blinked.

'I don't think housekeeping's quite my thing.' Did she look like a housekeeper, for God's sake? She was on leave at the moment, but her admin job in Brisbane was a far cry from mopping floors.

He shuffled through some papers and produced a tattered sheet.

'Here's the job description. "Housekeeper required for central Queensland cattle station: cooking and general house duties for two single males".'

An image of a pair of desperate and dateless types from the back blocks flashed into Shelley's mind.

She winced. 'Sounds scary.'

The man grinned.

'The brothers are decent blokes. One of them was married, but the gossip is his wife left him a few months ago. They must be sick of fending for themselves.'

'Well, I'll pass, thanks. I just want to visit, ask them some questions.'

'I'd ring ahead if I were you. You can try now, but your chances of catching anyone in the house during the day are pretty slim.'

He gave her the telephone number and Shelley returned to her car to use her mobile phone. As the agent had predicted, no one appeared to be at home, but finally an answering machine clicked in with a male voice: "This is Luke Sherman here. Leave your name and number and I'll get back to you."

Shelley left her contact details but didn't elaborate on the purpose of her call. If she didn't hear from him, she'd try again tonight.

She glanced at her watch. Two o'clock, and the gnawing sensation in her stomach reminded her she hadn't eaten since breakfast. She started the car and drove to the main street, where she found a café and ordered a steak burger. When in cattle country, she thought. She sat at a corner table and wondered what to do next.

If she couldn't contact these Shermans before dark, it looked like she was staying in Clermont for the night. Hopefully even one of the brothers would be able to see her in the morning. In the meantime, she could explore the town. It wasn't like that would take her long.

The steak burger turned out to be delicious, with a generous helping of salad including beetroot. She then braved the sun to walk the main street, starting at the top where brightly-painted murals decorated a set of coal wagons. At the other end she stopped to rest on a shady seat, watching ducks and geese swim on a sparkling lagoon amongst purple waterlilies. It was definitely the best spot in town.

She tried the Sherman's number again, but still there was no answer. It looked like finding a motel for the night was in order.

~*~

Shelley shut the door to her motel room and headed for the adjoining restaurant. She fished in her bag for her ringing phone.

'Hello, Shelley Blake speaking.'

'Luke Sherman. I'm returning your call.'

'Oh, thanks. I'm sorry to bother you, but I'm trying to find some information on my great-great-grandfather.' She realised she was rushing and took a deep breath to slow down. 'His name was Alexander Baxter and he once lived at Breakaway Creek. That was about 1898.'

'Well, 1898 was a bit before my time.' The masculine voice sounded vaguely amused and not at all like the bashful bachelor she'd been expecting. 'But he was probably some relation. My mother was a Baxter and the family have been here since the 1870s. She inherited the property from her father, John Baxter.'

'Oh, that's excellent. Do you have any family records I could look at?'

The line went silent for a moment.

'There's a family bible and a box of old photos. You're welcome to go through them. I don't know what else we might have. My mother's overseas at the moment, or I'd ask her.'

Shelley took another deep breath.

'Would it be all right if I visited you tomorrow? To have a look through the papers, I mean. Besides, if my family came from there, I'd love to see the property.'

'Of course. So you're in Clermont now?'

At her affirmative, he gave her directions.

'It's over an hour's drive. What time do you plan to leave?'

'I'll get away about seven in the morning, if that suits you?' As an afterthought she added, 'What's the road like?'

'It's pretty good. A lot of bitumen now.'

What did that mean? If it wasn't all bitumen, Shelley thought, how good could it be?

~*~

As she showered and dressed the next morning, Shelley tried to picture this Luke Sherman, who was possibly a distant relative. He'd sounded much younger than the old, crusty bushie she'd envisaged. Was he the one with the absent wife, or was that his brother? Not that it mattered; she wasn't interested in guys these days, least of all some cowboy.

She pulled on a pair of snug hipster jeans and a knit top with shoestring straps, knowing the outfit flattered her long legs and slim figure. Leaving her dark hair hanging loose about her face, she applied a touch of make-up. Just because she wasn't in the market, didn't mean she shouldn't look her best.

After an early breakfast in her room, Shelley set off in her little blue Mazda. After fifteen kilometres, she turned off the main highway – such as it was – onto a narrow bitumen road. Assuming that was as bad as it would get, Shelley relaxed into the drive just hoping she wouldn't have to pass any trucks. But a few kilometres further on, her relief turned to dismay as the bitumen ran into gravel and her low car scraped on the higher centre of the road. She winced every time the many stones rattled against her tyres.

A four-wheel drive tore past in the opposite direction, enveloping her in dust. What if she got a flat tyre out here, in the middle of nowhere? There was not much chance of anyone stopping if she needed help.

Resigned to taking it slowly, she crept along, avoiding sharp stones and straddling the wheel tracks where necessary. The countryside looked depressingly dry; the grass in the paddocks brown and withered, the sparse grey foliage on the trees drooping in the still, heat-hazed air. The expanse of empty countryside scared her, reducing her to insignificance.

Following Luke's directions, she eventually drove onto bitumen again and passed through a town of tired, generic-looking houses with hardiplank facades. The man at the stock and station agency had told her that the town of Faradale had been built to serve the coal mines thirty years earlier. It had a dirty, neglected air, as if its residents lived here under protest and no one really cared. Clermont seemed charming in comparison.

After a few more kilometres of gravel road, Shelley began to panic. Had she missed the turn? She stopped to consult the directions she'd written down and decided to keep driving. Finally she spotted the sign she'd been looking for, hanging over a brightly-painted oil drum that served as a mailbox. Breakaway Creek. At last, she thought.

Shelley turned off the main thoroughfare and drove up a narrow dirt road through open forest country. The car nudged over a rise and passed a dam of still, brown water. Another bend in the road led her into a cleared paddock, revealing a large, low house, an assortment of outbuildings, and a small cottage hiding behind a hedge of bougainvillea. The open land in front of the house sloped away to a line of trees which appeared to mark a watercourse – possibly the creek for which the property was named.

She drew up in front of the big house, and looked with interest at her surroundings before stepping out and stretching her stiffened muscles. Dogs barked from a row of cages between the house and the sheds as a man appeared on the veranda. She waited at the front gate as he came down the low steps to meet her, the remnants of her preconceptions about bush bachelors evaporating as her stomach tightened in anticipation.

'Hello – Shelley?' Her name was a question, as he looked her over with sharp green eyes, which made her feel absurdly self-conscious.

A few days' growth of whiskers suggested he hadn't placed as much importance on this meeting as she had – unless he subscribed to the 'designer stubble' look. Somehow, she didn't think so. In his faded Wrangler jeans and navy drill shirt he looked conservatively country. Yet the 'yokel' label didn't quite fit. If this guy was a bachelor, it must be from choice – unless he was the one with the broken marriage.

'Yes, that's me,' she said, somewhat unnecessarily. 'So you're Luke?'

He nodded and shook her hand, his fingers strong and calloused against her soft skin.

'Pleased to meet you. Come in. I was beginning to think you'd got lost.'

'Sorry.' Her fingers tingled and she had to resist the urge to pull her hand from his. She wasn't usually this fidgety around men. 'I took it slow. I'm not used to gravel roads.'

'Better safe than sorry. Mitch – that's my brother – isn't here at the moment. He had to check some waters. I've been catching up on office work while I waited.'

'I hope I'm not holding you up from anything important.'

He shrugged.

'Nothing special. We mustered last week and we've got weaners in the yards. I'll have to feed them shortly.'

He ushered her into a large kitchen with shabby timber cupboards and pulled out a chair for her at the laminex table.

'Sit down. I've been looking through some old photos and things since you rang.' He sat opposite her and tapped an ancient-looking bible, bound in battered black leather. 'I'm a bit mystified about your ancestor, Alex.'

Her pulse leapt. There it was again – that reference to a mystery.

'Why's that?'

'Well, I found this photo.' He held up a faded family portrait, featuring a seated man and woman in nineteenth-century dress. Five children of varying ages stood beside the chairs or sprawled on the floor at their feet, gazing solemnly towards the camera. The woman cradled a baby in a long white gown.

'This is Frank and Sarah Baxter, the couple who pioneered this place. There are six kids here, including the baby, and one of them is listed as Alex.' He turned the photograph over to show her the names scrawled on the reverse and then flipped it back again. 'I think that's him here.'

He pointed to the tallest of the children, a boy of about eight, standing at the back. With a quiver of excitement, Shelley took the photograph and looked more closely. It was possible the boy was Alexander – he was dark-haired, like the man in her mother's photo, and the features were similar.

'Yes, that looks like him. But what's the mystery?'

'The thing is, all the other births are listed in the family bible, but not his. The same with the marriages. Who did you say he married?'

'Emma Watson, from Brisbane.'

'It's strange.' He gave a little shrug. 'Perhaps he fell out with the family, which is why they didn't record his marriage. But you'd think the birth would have to be in here.'

Shelley examined the photo with avid interest.

'I wonder … he looks different from the others. Could he have been an adopted child? That sometimes happened in those days. People took in orphaned or motherless relatives and raised them as their own.'

'It's possible.' Luke passed her the bible. 'You're welcome to look at this.'

The family history was inscribed on a few blank pages at the back: the record of Frank and Sarah Baxter's marriage; the births of five children, and their subsequent marriages. The flowing script had been penned with heavy black ink, and in places there were spots where the pen had spluttered. But there was no mention of Alex.

The hair prickled on the back of Shelley's neck.

'It's very strange. I came up against the same lack of info with my mother's family.' She handed over the photo that had spurred her search. 'This is the couple in question, but my grandmother refused to talk about them, apart from calling Alex "a good-for-nothing stockman". She got quite stroppy when I persisted. It was my great aunt – her younger sister – who sent me here.'

'Family secrets, eh?' Luke's smile crinkled the crow's feet around his eyes as he peered at the picture. For the first time there was real warmth on his face. 'Perhaps he was born on the wrong side of the blanket.'

'Perhaps.' Shelley returned his smile, trying to suppress the foolish quiver in her stomach. What had happened to her recently-adopted disinterest in men? 'That's what's got me intrigued.'

'I can ask Mum when I talk to her next. She and Dad are travelling in Europe so we have to wait for them to ring us.' He stood up, casually stretching his long, lean body. 'Would you like a cup of tea or coffee? A glass of water?'

'Coffee would be nice. But I hope I'm not holding you up.'

'No, it's smoko time. I'm sorry I wasn't more help.'

As he filled the electric kettle, Shelley looked around the room. She judged the house to be only about thirty years old – hardly a pioneer dwelling.

'What happened to the original homestead?'

Luke glanced at her.

'It's still here. It's about a kilometre away, closer to the creek. The floods went through it once or twice, so they built up here in the late sixties.'

'So it's still standing?'

'Yeah.' He took mugs from one cupboard and a jar of instant coffee from another. 'It's pretty dilapidated now.'

'I'd love to see it.'

'Sure. I can show you later.' He made the coffees and put them on the table, then sat opposite her. 'So, where are you from?'

Shelley spooned sugar into her mug, willing herself to relax.

'My family's in Rockhampton – I grew up there. But I've been in Brisbane for the last eight years.'

Luke raised his eyebrows.

'The bright lights, eh? What do you do in Brisbane?'

'I work in administration. I'm on leave at the moment.'

'Then you must be good with computers. Mine's playing up this morning. Keeps freezing on me.'

'I can have a look at it if you like. It must be hard to get a technician out here.'

He grinned and sipped his coffee.

'We can't. We have to take it to them. The joys of living in the bush.'

'It's so quiet. Don't you find it lonely?' Apart from the faint hum of the refrigerator and the twittering of a willy-wagtail in a tree outside the window, the silence was absolute. It was a far cry from the hustle and roar of Brisbane.

'You city girls,' he smiled, shaking his head. Then his grin faded. 'That's what my wife used to say.'

That answered one question. Luke was the one with the broken marriage.

~*~

You must be crazy, Shelley Blake, she told herself later while sitting at his cluttered desk. Here she was, in the back of beyond, with a cowboy-type hanging over her shoulder as she ran through the settings on his computer. At least he smelled clean, which only proved he hadn't been working outside today. She just wished he wouldn't stand so close.

She glanced for the umpteenth time at a framed photograph on the desk. It was obvious that the laughing, younger guy in the picture was the same man who now stood behind her. Luke had one arm around a pretty blonde woman, who cradled a baby, and his other arm held a small boy of about two against his hip.

Shelley set the anti-spyware to scan and turned to look up at her companion. From this angle his stubbled jaw looked squarely determined in contrast to his wide mouth and full, well-shaped lips. His eyes looked tired.

'This could take a while,' she said. She pointed at the photo and took a calculated risk. 'Is this your family?'

Pain flickered in his eyes.

'Those are my boys. The photo was taken about three years ago.' He took a deep breath. 'I don't see much of them now. Their mother took off recently.'

'Oh, I'm sorry.' His obvious distress made her wish she hadn't asked. 'Where are they living?'

'In Brisbane. Back where she came from.'

Ouch. His derisive tone indicated he didn't think much of Brisbane.

'How old are they?'

'Ben's five and Jack's three. They're real little bushies. They must hate it down there.' The corners of his mouth tugged down in dejected lines.

A rush of warmth, or empathy, had her sharing more than she'd ever intended.

'I've just been through a break-up, too. Luckily there were no kids involved.'

'Were you married?'

'No, living together. Jason didn't want to get married, and I'm glad of that now.' She abruptly pushed out her chair. No more talk about Jason – he wasn't worth it. 'Well, I'd better leave you to it. It looks like the mystery of Alexander Baxter isn't going to be easily solved.'

He stepped back, giving her room to rise.

'It was a long way to come for nothing. Are you in a hurry to leave? I need to feed the weaners now, but I could take you to look over the old house later.' He hesitated. 'If you'd care to stay a couple of days, my parents usually ring on a Friday night. Mum might know something.'

'Oh, I couldn't impose on you like that.'

For the first time he grinned with real humour. It made him look almost as young as he did in the photograph.

'Did you know we're looking for a housekeeper?'

Shelley stood up and gave him a level stare. His grin was hopeful, boyishly charming – but no, she wasn't falling for it. She glanced around her at the untidy, dusty furniture.

'Nice try, buster. Do I look like the domestic goddess type?''

He shrugged.

'Do they still exist?'

It *would* be disappointing to leave without any of the information she'd come for. It would also be nice to spend a few days on a working cattle property – something she hadn't experienced before. The stock and station agent had given the brothers a character reference and there was a family connection.

'If I stay, I'll pull my weight, but I'm not going to be your slave. Does your brother live here too?'

'Yeah. He used to live in the cottage, but when Miranda left we decided he might as well move back in. He's got a girlfriend in town though, so he stays there a bit.'

'Okay. I'll stay for a few days. Thanks. And I'd love to see something of the property.'

'Of course.' He flashed that quick grin which transformed his face. 'I suppose you want to see kangaroos and koalas, that sort of thing.'

His mildly patronising tone made Shelley's neck prickle. She tilted her chin and looked him in the eye.

'I don't expect to see koalas. I know there aren't many left around here.'

He shook his head.

'True. We have a few roos, though.'

'I've seen the odd kangaroo or two. I did grow up in Rockhampton, remember.'

'I'm glad to hear it. So I suppose you know all about horses and cattle, too?'

She knew he was taking the micky out of her.

'Not much about cattle, no. But I learned to ride as a kid – I went to Pony Club for a few years.'

His grin widened.

'Sounds like you'll fit right in, Shelley.'

Chapter Two

Half an hour later Shelley was bumping up a dirt track in the passenger seat of a Toyota Land Cruiser while Luke drove. She'd changed out of her good clothes after Luke had shown her into a spare bedroom. It was a functional space with two single beds, an old-fashioned wardrobe and not much else. She hoped her old denim shorts, joggers and a short-sleeved polo shirt were suitable attire for a working girl.

The track took them past a dilapidated house of greyed weatherboards.

'There's the old house.' Luke took his hand from the steering wheel and waved it vaguely in that direction. 'It's a bit of a wreck now.'

The branches of a giant bottle tree hung over the house and creepers sprawled on the neglected, tumbledown fence. Broken windows gaped like unseeing eyes, caught in a memory of better times.

Shelley stared at it, imagining it as it had been a century earlier, perhaps with a horse and buggy standing outside and a group of children in pinafores and short trousers playing in the yard.

'I don't suppose there's anything inside? Any old papers, or such like?'

His brow furrowed.

'We'll have a look later. Mitch and I used to play there when we were kids. There used to be some stuff in the roof space. It's probably still there, if the mice and rats haven't got to it.'

'That sounds interesting. I can take myself if you're too busy.'

'Better not.' He glanced sideways at her. 'The place is pretty rickety. I don't want you falling through the floor.'

'Whatever you think.' Noticing one of her shoelaces had come undone, she propped her foot on the dash to re-tie it. Something made her look up and her face flamed as she followed his gaze. Her shorts had ridden up, exposing a lot of bare thigh. She dropped her leg hastily, smoothed down her shorts and brought her knees together to sit so primly her grandmother would have been proud. 'Hey, aren't you supposed to be watching the road?'

He corrected a slight wobble in the steering and grinned.

'Sorry. You make it hard sometimes.'

She made a derisive noise in her throat. 'I thought we were supposed to be related.'

'Oh yeah, thirty-second cousins or something.' His voice had a husky catch to it. 'That's if we're related at all. We haven't worked out who Alexander was yet.'

'I'm not so sure I should be staying, now.' It was a miracle her voice sounded cool when he had her thoughts so agitated. He shook his head.

'I was kidding. I'm not looking for anything, Shelley. Officially, I'm still married. Although she has been gone a while.'

A breathless, involuntary laugh escaped her throat.

'When I heard about the job here, I pictured a pair of desperate and dateless hillbillies. Then I met you and that notion didn't fit. Now you're making me think again.'

He shook his head, a wry smile twisting his mouth as he changed the Toyota's gears.

'Desperate and dateless, that's me.'

Heart thudding, she turned to stare out the window, realising it was sensible to end this conversation right now. The suggestive undertones were too disturbing for comfort, considering she'd met this man only a couple of hours before. A man who, as he'd just reminded her, was still legally married.

Before the silence became too uncomfortable, Luke drew the Toyota up to a set of stockyards.

'Here we are,' he announced. He got out of the vehicle and waited for Shelley to join him. 'These are the calves we've just weaned from their mothers.'

Shelley joined him at the stockyard rails, peering through them at the mob of sleek red animals that fled to the far side of the yard at their approach. Dust floated over them, thick with the acrid stink of cow manure. She looked down at her clothes and grimaced. She'd need a shower after this.

'They're still a bit touchy, but they'll settle down over the next few days.'

'How many are there?' It was a relief to have a safe, unromantic topic like cattle to discuss.

'We counted two hundred and twenty-six. The hay's in that shed over there.' He gestured at a corrugated-iron building a hundred metres away. 'I'll bring it over with the tractor. Can you let me through the gate when I get here? Make sure none of the weaners get out.'

He pointed to several round hay feeders.

'I'll drop the bales of hay into those.'

Surely that wouldn't be too hard, Shelley thought. Except when she opened the gate, which obviously swung inwards, she would have to walk into the yard with the cattle. They weren't very big, but still…

Luke must have noticed her apprehensive glance. His face softened.

'You can get in there. They won't hurt you – they're more scared of you than you are of them.'

She waited beside the gate while he walked over to the shed. The tractor started with a roar and soon came trundling towards her, a huge round bale of hay speared high on the front forks. The noise made the calves retreat to the far side of the yard. This was easy, she thought. Shelley unlatched the chain and swung the gate wide as he drove through, then held it closed as he eased the machine close to the nearest feeder and tilted the forks downwards, dropping the bale of hay neatly into it. When he drove out of the yard, Shelley chained the gate behind him and waited for him to return with the next bale.

When all the feeders were full, he left the tractor and walked back to join her.

'We have to cut the twine off now.' He grabbed a large knife that had been wedged against the gatepost. 'Do you want to help?'

It would have been easy to say no. Already the cattle were crowding around the hay, snatching mouthfuls from the top of each bale above the webbing that encased it. But she didn't want to seem like a complete wuss.

She nervously followed him into the yard, ready to take refuge on the rail if necessary. The cattle moved away at their approach and she began to help him pull the webbing off as he cut it free. Then one bold animal ventured to the opposite side of the feeder, snatching a mouthful of hay. Its companions began to follow and she shouted at them, waving her arms in the air. Startled, they ran to the furthest side of the yard.

'Hey!'

She swung around at Luke's yell, to find him glaring at her.

'Don't frighten the cattle. We're trying to get 'em quiet!'

Chastened, she continued pulling off the netting, watching the cattle all the while. But it seemed the damage had been done. They didn't come close again.

After they'd finished, she sat on the top rail and watched as he spent ten minutes walking amongst the weaners, talking to them in a soothing voice. They soon stopped rushing away from him and began to snatch hungry mouthfuls from the feeders, watching Luke warily but accepting his presence. When he swung to the rail beside her he gave her a rueful look.

'I guess that's my fault. I didn't tell you."

Her face heated.

'I'm sorry – I know nothing about cattle.'

'At least you're willing to have a go. That's something.' He vaulted to the ground. 'Come on, I'm finished here.'

~*~

Back at the homestead, Shelley left Luke in the shed, patching a punctured motorbike tyre, while she returned to the house. She was hot and sweaty and her clothes and skin ponged of the cattle yards. She fetched her suitcase from the car, unpacked a few things and laid them out on the second bed in her room, then headed for the bathroom to shower off the fine layer of dirt.

Once fresh and clean, she checked the computer, which had finished its scan, and did a disc clean up. Then she ventured to the kitchen, looked dubiously at the pile of dirty dishes in the sink and decided it wouldn't kill her to do a bit of washing up. She was just wiping down the table when Luke came in with a young man she assumed was his brother.

He looked pleasantly surprised.

'Thanks for doing that, Shelley. This is my brother Mitch.'

The newcomer was an inch or two shorter and more compactly built than Luke. He stepped forward with an open, easy-going smile and took her hand in his large, calloused one. He looked significantly at the sink.

'Going on the improvement in here, you're welcome to stay as long as you like.'

She smiled.

'Don't get excited. That was an aberration.'

'Can you cook?' Mitch jabbed a thumb in his brother's direction. 'You've gotta be better than him.'

'You should talk.' Luke hung his hat on a hook just inside the door and grinned at Shelley. 'He's the worst cook in Australia. Come on, mate, set the table while I get the food out.'

Luke cut slices of corned beef while Shelley made a salad with lettuce, tomatoes and cucumbers. She voiced her surprise at the well-stocked fridge and Mitch grinned.

'I'm used to fending for myself and Miranda was never at home, so Luke did plenty of batching. It's just the cleaning that gets on top of us.'

Shelley glanced at Luke. His mouth had a grim line to it, dissuading her from any comment. It didn't sound as if Miranda had ever been the settled country wife.

'What'd you find out this morning?' Mitch asked as they sat to their places at the table. 'Any luck with that ancestor of yours, Shelley?'

'Luke found him in a photo.' Shelley passed him the salad bowl. 'But he's a bit of a mystery. His birth and marriage aren't recorded in the bible, like the rest of your family. We're wondering if he was adopted, or something.'

'We're going to look through the old house tomorrow,' Luke said. 'Check out that stuff in the ceiling.'

'Good idea. I hope you find something. You've come a long way for nothing, otherwise.'

She smiled at Mitch.

'Even if I don't, it's a new experience. Feeding weaners, cleaning up after two men…' Her lips twitched with gentle mockery. 'What more could any girl wish for?'

She didn't miss Luke's grin as he helped himself to the salad.

~*~

After lunch Luke headed off to do more repairs in the shed.

'Just make yourself at home,' he said. 'Unless you fancy holding a spanner.'

Shelley looked at his grease-stained jeans and shuddered.

'I've just had a shower. I think I'll stay away from the shed.'

She grabbed her laptop from the bedroom and settled into a wicker chair in a cool spot on the veranda. She experienced a moment of panic about the remoteness of her location when she plugged in her USB modem and the connection registered only one bar. To her relief she managed to spend a few hours checking her emails, catching up with news on Facebook and searching fruitlessly on ancestry sites.

She had no real idea how she was going to occupy herself while she was on leave. Perhaps she'd been a bit hasty. What had happened in Brisbane – the shock and humiliation of finding Jason in bed with another woman – had just made her want to escape. And she'd got away fast. In moments of crisis it was still her Mum and Dad she turned to, back home in Rockhampton. Shelley knew she wasn't ready to go back to Brisbane yet, but eight weeks was a long time.

Christmas was coming up too, and once that was over she'd need to go home. She had other friends in Brisbane after all. Her life hadn't revolved around Jason even though they'd been together for more than five years. Looking back, it was obvious now that they'd drifted apart, but that didn't excuse him from cheating on her. She was still stunned by the turn of events. One moment she thought she had her life mapped out, the next … BAM! She was in limbo.

Jason had kept their flat so she'd need to find somewhere new to live. There was, however, no point in making hasty decisions. She had plenty of time to decide.

Mitch was the first to come in, just before dark.

'Want to help me feed the dogs?'

She jumped up eagerly.

She'd seen the four Border Collie-crosses jump in Mitch's tray-back after lunch, milling excitedly as he drove off to work. Now it was time to shut them back in their pens.

'They wander if we leave them off at night,' he explained. 'Collies tend to be a bit hyperactive, always looking for mischief. They should be kept busy, but we can't do cattle work all the time.'

Shelley stopped to pat the most appealing of the dogs, a little black female with a white muzzle, chest and legs, who sat gazing up at her with dark, trusting eyes. None of them had the long coats she associated with Border Collies, but Mitch explained they'd been bred that way for Australian conditions.

'The long-haired types get their coats full of burrs and they suffer in the heat.'

'So these dogs are bred for the bush? Not like city girls.'

Mitch gave her a quick look.

'Plenty of city girls settle in the bush, but Luke's wife was the exception. Miranda isn't the type to settle anywhere.'

Shelley straightened, surprised at his bitter tone.

'Doesn't sound like you think much of her.' He shook his head.

'She's putting Luke through hell, not letting him have his boys.' His usually affable voice grated like a rusty gate hinge. 'He's only seen them a few times since they left, and it looks like he's got to go to court to get access.'

No wonder Luke looked a bit grim whenever his wife's name was mentioned. Shelley's heart softened.

'That's terrible. I know marriages have their problems, but I've never been able to understand why people don't put the children first. Surely those little boys have a right to know their father.'

'Yeah, they sure do.' Mitch tipped dog biscuits into one of the collie's dishes. 'Luke is a good dad, too. He looked after those boys as much as she did. It was bloody frustrating at times when we had work to do and she took off and left him babysitting.'

Shelley shifted uneasily. Obviously Luke had more things to worry about than some visitor looking up her ancestors. In the circumstances, it was a wonder he could be bothered with her at all. Or perhaps he needed a distraction, just as she did.

When she returned to the house, Luke was in the kitchen, stirring a big pot of minced meat over the stove. The savoury smells of frying beef, garlic and onions reminded her how long it had been since lunch.

'Do you want a hand?'

He turned to smile at her. As long as his absent family wasn't mentioned he seemed relaxed enough. No doubt he was entitled to be prickly in the circumstances.

'You could peel some spuds. I'll throw the rest of the veggies in here, but we like our mashed potato.' He added water to the pot, along with some chopped carrots and cabbage.

'No problem.' Shelley grinned at him. 'Can I help with the weaners again tomorrow? I promise I won't chase them this time.'

'I suppose I'll risk it. I'll show you the old house afterwards.'

~*~

Lying in the narrow bed later that night reminded Shelley of her room in her parents' place in Rocky. But it was even quieter here, without the occasional hum of traffic and, even at 10 pm, it hadn't cooled down. She got up to turn on the ceiling fan and then leant out the window, looking up at the magnificent night sky. Childhood memories of camping out with her grandfather came rushing back.

The stars! She'd forgotten how extraordinary they could be without city lights competing for attention. Shelley drank in the cloudy haze of the Milky Way and a myriad other twinkling pinpoints, including constellations she'd once been able to identify but could no longer remember. Thankfully she could still find the Southern Cross.

She inhaled deeply, enjoying the freshness of the night air. This was something to savour, a memory to take back to the city. Perhaps coming out here was a good thing after all.

~*~

The next day the weaned calves seemed calmer, approaching the hay feeders even as Shelley cut the netting from the bales. This time she summoned the courage to walk amongst them with Luke. She caught him glancing at her in approval and then wondered why on earth his opinion mattered to her. Once he'd had a chance to speak to his mother, she'd have no excuse to stay any longer. She'd probably never see him again.

The old house looked even more dilapidated at close quarters. The front gate groaned as Luke pushed it open, and he ducked to avoid a hanging branch of spiny bougainvillea. Leaves and seedpods from the bottle tree littered the sagging veranda and rotting steps, the debris of years of neglect.

Luke picked his way with care, carrying the stepladder he'd put in the back of the Toyota that morning. He glanced back at Shelley, indicating a broken step.

'Watch where you put your feet. Don't stand on that one.'

He led the way across the veranda, testing each board before allowing it to take his weight. The door resisted his efforts to open it and he set the ladder down before putting his shoulder to it, forcing a protesting screech from it as he pushed it across the warped floor. Shelley grabbed the ladder and followed him, wrinkling her nose at the musty interior. A rusty sink against the wall and a row of cupboards with peeling paint indicated the room had once been the kitchen. A heavy layer of dust covered everything.

Luke took the ladder from her and led the way into the hall, where he positioned it under an access hole in the ceiling. He looked at her and smiled. He'd shaved the night before and the strong lines of his face looked tantalisingly good.

'Now, for the moment of truth.'

A flutter of anticipation winged through Shelley's stomach.

'Let's hope there's something up there.'

She held the ladder as Luke climbed up and pushed aside the cover. When she found herself admiring his denim-clad backside and long legs, Shelley turned abruptly to look out a dusty window.

Why did he have to be married, she wondered, and why did he have to live in the sticks? Why was she even interested? Hadn't she decided she was over men?

The stepladder wasn't high enough to allow Luke to reach into the ceiling space, but he could grasp the edges of the access hole. He hoisted himself the rest of the way into the crawlspace and disappeared.

'Try not to fall through the ceiling,' Shelley suggested helpfully.

'I will do my best. Just wait there, Shelley. If I find anything I'll hand it down to you.' A brief silence was broken only by the bumping noises of him moving about in the roof space. 'Heck, I should have brought a torch. There's one behind the seat of the Toyota. Can you get it for me, please? Just watch where you walk.'

Shelley returned in a flash with the torch and climbed up to hand it to him.

'There's an old suitcase or something up here,' Luke said, dragging something back towards the trapdoor. 'And a bit of old furniture, but we'll start with the suitcase. If I pass it down, can you grab it? Be careful, it's bloody heavy.'

Shelley had to stand on the third rung to reach it as he cautiously lowered the case down through the hole. He was right – it was heavy. She set it on the top step of the ladder as she descended, and then with her feet safely on the floor she reached up to lift it down, almost overbalancing as she took the full weight of it in her arms.

It was a very old suitcase with rusted catches and cracked leather straps, thickly coated with dust. Shelley sneezed several times as Luke climbed down to join her. He laid the case on its side and crouched to unbuckle the straps, struggling for a moment with the rusted catches.

Shelley held her breath, like a child at Christmas about to rip open her presents. Steady, she told herself. It's probably just old clothes or something else totally irrelevant.

At last the catches gave way and Luke lifted the lid and let out a low whistle.

'Bingo,' he said, lifting out a bundle of envelopes, tied together with string. 'This could be interesting.'

He shone the torch on them before flashing it over the rest of the contents.

'Here're some newspaper clippings, too.'

Shelley sank to her heels beside him and reached for the clippings, carefully flicking through them as Luke directed his torch on the brittle, yellowed paper. His breath was warm against her ear and the smell of the cattle yards clung faintly to his clothes. It seemed fitting that one of the clippings pictured a man on horseback, holding a silver cup in his hands.

Jack Baxter on Firefly, winner of the Open Campdraft, the caption read. The paper was the *Peak Downs Telegram*, dated 1933.

'Was this one of your ancestors?'

'Yeah, that was my great-grandfather.' Luke's voice was matter-of-fact. 'He was a top horseman.'

There were others in a similar vein, celebrating family achievements. But right at the bottom of the pile was something that made Shelley draw a deep breath.

MAN GRAVELY WOUNDED IN SHOOTING ran the headline of another issue of the *Peak Downs Telegram*.

A man suffering from a severe gunshot wound to the chest was brought to the Peak Downs Hospital two days ago. He has been identified as Mr Alexander Baxter, of Breakaway Creek Station.

His frantic companion, a Miss Emma Watson, from Brisbane, claimed to be his fiancée. Police have interviewed her regarding the circumstances of the shooting but there is no suspect at the present time. Medical Officer Kent, reported that Mr Baxter was in a serious condition but refused to comment on the patient's chances of recovery.

The couple were married last night from Mr Baxter's hospital bed.

Shelley silently passed it to Luke, who expressed perfectly what she'd been thinking: 'Holy shit! The mystery deepens. I wonder who shot him, or if it was an accident?'

'And they got married from his hospital bed. That seems desperate. I wonder if he survived?'

'He must have, if they had a child. Unless…'

Their eyes met and Shelley finished the thought for him.

'Was she already pregnant when this happened? If so, no wonder they had a hasty wedding.'

'I wonder if there's anything more.' Luke thumbed through the clippings without success and then began to search the remaining contents of the suitcase. 'I can't see anything. We should take this home and look through it all with better light and a cool drink.'

Luke stood up and took Shelley's hand to pull her to her feet. His fingers were hard and strong, reminding her of the physical work he did for a living. She looked up at his face and their eyes met briefly before she lowered hers, alarmed by the thrill of awareness that coursed through her.

Way to go, Shelley! she thought. This man had more baggage than a supermodel on an overseas tour.

She was quiet all the way back to the homestead, trying to keep a bit of distance between them. But once they had the contents of the suitcase spread over the kitchen table and had begun sorting things into piles, she forgot her reservations. It was sad, but this was the most fun she'd had in a while.

They placed the bundles of letters together. The rest of it, apart from the newspaper clippings, appeared to be mostly old bills, some dating back to the 1900s. They were possibly of historical interest, but not helpful to her.

Luke looked at the postmarks on the letters.

'Some of these are hard to read. But this lot look like 18-something, is it 1885?' He untied the string and opened the first envelope.

'This one was written from Halborough Station via Longreach, August 4, 1885. It's addressed to Sarah. Is that the lady listed in the bible?' He scanned the letter quickly. 'Seems like Sarah's sister wrote this. It's full of family stuff, but no mention of Alex. At least this is the right era. If we read all these, we might learn something.'

He passed the bundle to Shelley.

'I'd better get back to work. I'll leave these with you.'

'You don't mind me reading them? It's your family.'

He shook his head.

'If you uncover any skeletons, they're probably to do with Alex. Besides, what's a bastard or two these days? And I mean that in the proper sense of the word.'

Shelley chuckled. 'I know. I must be old-fashioned, though. I still believe in marriage.'

'Yeah, so did I.' Luke pushed back his chair and got to his feet, grimacing. A scathing note crept into his voice. 'More fool me.'

Shelley watched his retreating figure in silence, surprised at the empathy his words evoked in her. But was she being too quick to judge his faithless wife? After all, she'd only heard one side of the story.

Chapter Three

Brisbane, 1897

'You're mad, wanting to go out there,' Fanny Watson declared. She tilted her silk fan in soft white fingers and wafted hot air on her face. 'Nothing but dust and flies and smelly cattle – I can't think of anything worse. I don't know how Lucy puts up with it.'

Emma gritted her teeth.

'She loves Breakaway Creek, Mother.'

To Emma, even the name of the property was romantic, conjuring images of wild cattle, campfires and dusty stockmen. Her cousin's invitation to visit had been the most exciting thing to come her way for quite some time. Surely her mother wouldn't be so cruel as to stop her going.

Lucy had married a grazier from Central Queensland six months before and wrote glowing reports of life on a remote cattle station. Her only regret was the distance separating her from family and friends in Brisbane. Emma missed her too; the girls had practically grown up together and she considered Lucy the sister she'd never had.

'I'm not happy about you travelling alone,' Mrs Watson persisted.

'But I won't be alone, Mother. Mrs Dexter's on the same steamer and will chaperone me. Lucy said they would meet me in Rockhampton. And I'm twenty-one, hardly a school-girl.'

'You needn't remind me of that.' Her mother tossed the fan onto her lap with an impatient air. 'I know you're no beauty, but you've had your admirers and you should be settled by now. Besides, Mrs Dexter's a common woman. If she wasn't a particular friend of Sarah Baxter I wouldn't consider it. I'll have to see what your father thinks.'

Emma looked the other way, smarting. She knew she wasn't beautiful but she'd had plenty of compliments. When it came to dealing with her only child, her mother seemed to think tact was unnecessary. And she was such a snob! Personally, Emma liked Mrs Dexter, appreciating her down-to-earth manner and absence of airs and graces.

Fortunately, Emma's merchant father was too engrossed in business affairs to be bothered with her mother. Henry Watson looked up from his papers long enough to take but a fleeting interest in Emma's plans.

'The girl's your cousin – I can't see any objections to the visit. A change of scenery may help you appreciate what's been offered to you here.'

Emma recoiled inwardly. Her father was referring to his intention to marry her to the son of a business associate. It didn't matter to him that she cringed every time Cyril Timms came near. Money and position in society were important, not girlish fancies about marrying for love.

She was determined not to marry Cyril Timms, but so far she hadn't found the courage to tell her father. Most of the time he seemed remote, even disinterested, but she knew from experience how quickly he could erupt into a rage if crossed. At least this visit to Central Queensland would postpone the inevitable confrontation.

~*~

A month later her ship entered the muddy Fitzroy and steamed up-river, finally dropping anchor at the port of Rockhampton. She hung over the rail, her stomach a flurry of nerves as she took in the hive of activity on the wharf. Piles of sacks, barrels and wooden crates lined the dock and a host of wagons, buggies, sulkies and gigs waited to meet the steamer.

Emma anxiously scanned the crowd for a familiar face, wondering what she'd do if Lucy wasn't there. Her cousin had promised to meet her but it was a long journey by train from Breakaway Creek. Emma's companion, Mrs Dexter, had been kind, but was leaving her to travel on to Mount Morgan with her husband.

'Of course it's no trouble to meet you. I seize any excuse to come to Rockhampton for shopping,' Lucy had written. 'George is wonderfully indulgent. He knows I find it lonely on the property at times.'

Stepping onto the wharf, relief made Emma light-headed as she spotted her cousin clutching her husband's arm. Lucy's petite figure was dwarfed by a wide-brimmed straw hat with a cluster of pink fabric flowers stuck in the crown. With his drooping, fair moustache, George was ruddy and good-natured, the silver watch-chain across his waistcoat glinting in the bright sunlight.

'Emma!' Lucy enveloped her in a warm hug, her face flushed with excitement. 'It's so wonderful to see you.'

She stepped back and surveyed Emma's dark green travelling dress.

'You look so pretty in that colour. You remember George, don't you?'

'Of course.' She'd been bridesmaid at their wedding after all and she liked George. Emma extended her hand. 'How do you do, Mr Baxter?'

He pressed her hand, smiling broadly.

'I'm so pleased you could come, Miss Watson. Lucy's been looking forward to it for a long time.'

'We're staying at the Criterion Hotel,' Lucy informed her. 'We catch the train back to Clermont tomorrow evening. That will give us time for shopping tomorrow. I know you'll find the stores here rudimentary, but please indulge me. They're the best I've had access to for a while.'

Still reeling from her latest shopping expedition with her mother in Brisbane, Emma was inclined to think the pastime overrated, but she wouldn't disappoint her cousin. Of course, Lucy was a much more congenial companion than her mother, who was too concerned with creating the right impression to be able to enjoy clothes for their own sake.

'I'm sure we'll have a splendid time,' Emma replied. Her enthusiasm was only partly feigned.

That evening, Lucy came to her hotel room before they went downstairs for dinner.

'I just had to come and tell you my exciting news.' Her round face beamed but she lowered her voice, even though they were alone in the room. 'I'm expecting a happy event in January.'

A little thrill ran through Emma.

'Oh Lucy, how wonderful!' She glanced at Lucy's middle and knew she was blushing. 'I thought you'd put on weight – I should have guessed. What does Mr Baxter think of this?'

'He's delighted, naturally. Only our family know, at this stage – I've written to Mother and Father. But I had to tell you.'

Emma didn't like to ask if her cousin was concerned at the prospect of motherhood in the bush, so far from medical help. At least Lucy had her mother-in-law for support.

'George is hoping for a boy,' Lucy prattled on. 'To inherit Breakaway Creek after him.'

Emma looked at her sharply.

'Doesn't he have an older brother? I remember meeting him at the wedding.'

It was hard to forget him. Alexander Baxter, or Alex as everyone had called him, had made an impression with his quiet manners and steady dark eyes. She had spoken to him only briefly, but she'd found herself wishing she could get to know him better. Hopefully she would remedy that during her visit with the Baxters.

'Oh, Alex.' Lucy sounded dismissive. 'He's not really George's brother. He's some sort of cousin, I think. He was orphaned and Mr and Mrs Baxter raised him as their own.'

That explained why Alex didn't physically resemble the other fair-haired Baxters. Lucy had been struck by his almost-black hair, dark brown eyes and smooth, tanned skin that bore none of the freckles that characterised his siblings. He was also a few inches taller than his brother.

'So he's not really a Baxter at all?'

Lucy shrugged.

'I'm not sure. He's known as Alexander Baxter and everyone treats him as one of the family, but George assures me he'll never own Breakaway Creek. He's the overseer now, and George is happy for things to stay that way once he takes over from his father.'

In other words, Alex didn't have prospects, Emma thought, conscious of her parents' ambitions for her. What a shame.

The train journey to Clermont was hot, tiring and dirty. Coal dust blew in the open windows, stinging their eyes and leaving a fine gritty layer on their skin and clothes. The leather seats grew hard and more uncomfortable as the night wore on. Emma barely slept, but she was too excited at the prospect of visiting her first cattle station to mind.

She and Lucy had spent a pleasant day shopping in Rockhampton's East Street. Although the town's amenities compared poorly to Brisbane's, they'd found several decent stores, James Stewart and Co. in particular. Emma had enjoyed helping Lucy select fabrics and wool to make garments for the coming baby and maternity clothing for herself.

They arrived in Clermont in the early morning. From the railway station Emma was able to look down the hill to the centre of town, which appeared to be built on both sides of a large lagoon. When she voiced her surprise at the size of the town, George informed her that the surrounding goldfields were booming, leading to an influx of people and increased prosperity for business.

After a breakfast of steak and eggs in the railway refreshment rooms, George left them to wait while he fetched the double buggy and horses from the livery stables. On his return, he loaded their luggage, stowing it with the three swags that already occupied the space under the seats.

'The trip to Breakaway Creek takes two days,' Lucy said as Emma looked apprehensively at the swags. 'We'll camp beside the road tonight.'

Emma had not expected to be forced to sleep outdoors, although she supposed that had been naive of her.

'I haven't camped out before,' she admitted nervously.

Lucy laughed.

'Don't worry, you'll love it. There's nothing like sleeping under the stars.'

Once they were all aboard, George drove them down the street, stopping at the bakery to purchase bread and at the general store where Lucy selected tinned meat and packets of dried fruits.

'We get a wagon-load of stores brought out three or four times a year but everything is soon infested with weevils,' Lucy said. 'It's a pity we haven't room for any fresh supplies.'

Emma shuddered inwardly, wondering how long it would take her to become accustomed to eating food flavoured with weevils. The buggy was loaded to capacity, with everything piled under the seats and beside Emma at the rear.

Although it was only September, the sun beat down on them in the open vehicle. Emma was shocked at the state of the road, which was nothing but a dirt track through the bush, filled with potholes and wheel ruts from the last rains. She felt for her cousin, who didn't complain but must surely, in her delicate state, feel every bounce. As they left the black-soil downs behind they encountered patches of bulldust into which the buggy wheels dug deep, forcing the pair of horses to heave into their collars. The dust floated up over them in a haze as fine as talcum powder, painting their faces and clothing a dirty shade of grey.

That night they pitched camp beside a creek. George filled their billy and waterbags from a muddy waterhole before allowing the horses to drink. Later, as Emma lay in her swag close to the dying campfire, she tried to convince herself this was an exciting adventure and refused to think of snakes, spiders and other insects. Just as she relaxed an eerie howling jolted her upright, prickling the fine hairs on the back of her neck.

George, rolled in his own swag on the other side of Lucy, chuckled softly.

'It's a dingo, Miss Watson. Don't fear; they rarely attack people.'

She tried to feel reassured, taking her cue from Lucy who appeared unconcerned. But her anxiety, combined with the discomfort of lying on the hard ground, made sleep elusive. At last she slipped into a fitful doze and awoke some time later to crackling flames and the sting of smoke in her nostrils. Surely it couldn't be morning already. But apparently it was, for birds were twittering and an orange glow lit the eastern sky.

Looking towards the fire, she could see George's dark figure hovering over it, stoking it with fresh wood. She scrambled out of her swag, yawned and stretched her stiff muscles. After a second night of little sleep her head ached, and the thought of resuming their journey in the buggy was uninviting. But she resigned herself, knowing that the sooner they got it over with, the sooner they'd be at their destination. She busied herself filling the billy from the muddy creek, saving the clean water in the waterbag for the remainder of the trip.

Late in the afternoon they arrived at Breakaway Creek. George drove the buggy on past a large house, which was his parents' home, and drew up in front of a new weatherboard cottage a hundred yards away.

'It's only small,' Lucy said cheerfully. 'But George has assured me we'll build more rooms as the children are born.'

'It looks charming.' Emma eyed the flowerbeds that bordered the veranda. 'You've been busy in the garden.'

Lucy smiled in obvious pride and pointed to the line of trees in the near distance. 'There's a permanent waterhole in the creek, so there's some water to spare for my plants.'

She showed Emma to a small bedroom, which had been made homely with white lace curtains at the windows. The tongue-and-groove walls were painted pale yellow.

'This will be the nursery when the baby comes,' Lucy told her. 'But for now, I hope you'll be comfortable.'

Emma gazed at the white damask counterpane on the bed.

'It's lovely. The bed looks tempting. I hope you'll excuse me early tonight.' She eyed Lucy's face, which was drawn with fatigue. 'You must be exhausted.'

'I am,' Lucy admitted. 'Unfortunately I don't think I'll be travelling again before the baby's born.'

The next morning, Emma woke to birds calling outside her window. For a moment she lay still, enjoying the familiar warbling of a butcherbird and the twittering of a willy wagtail. A decent night's sleep in a soft bed had restored her and made her eager to face the day.

Lucy also seemed to have recovered and at breakfast described her plans for Emma's entertainment.

'We must go for a picnic one day, Emma. What a pity I can't ride anymore. But we can take the sulky.' She smiled persuasively at her husband. 'What do you think, George?'

George's brow furrowed.

'I think you should be resting, Lucy. You've had a strenuous few days. If you're well enough, we can think about a picnic on Sunday.'

'Mr Baxter's right,' Emma said firmly. 'It's important for you to rest, and there's all your shopping to unpack. A picnic sounds delightful, but only when you're ready for it.'

'You're a pair of fusspots,' Lucy pouted. 'I'm not an invalid, you know. I'm perfectly well.'

'And we want you to stay that way,' George said calmly.

Emma spent a pleasant day with her cousin, unpacking and chatting. Late in the afternoon while Lucy rested, she decided to go for a walk.

She followed a well-worn track to the creek. Tall river coolabahs lined its steep banks and were mirrored in the dark, still water that lay six feet or more below. Emma walked along a twisting path that followed the top of the bank, under the welcome shade of the trees. A flock of drab brown birds flew up in front of her, shrieking noisily. "Happy Jacks", George had called them. She kept a careful eye out for snakes, remembering Lucy's warning that the deadly brown was prevalent in this area.

Intent on watching where she placed her feet, the snort of a horse brought her to an abrupt stop. Her gaze jerked up, flickering over the startled animal to meet its rider's amused brown eyes, shaded by a broad-brimmed hat. He steadied his mount and for a moment Emma stared at him in silence. He was the first to speak.

'Miss Watson.' He swung out of the saddle and turned to face her, politely doffing his hat. 'How d' you do?'

'Mr Baxter,' Emma nodded, recovering her equilibrium. She moved forward and held out her hand. 'I was in a world of my own.'

Alex Baxter took her hand briefly in his hard, calloused one.

'My apologies for startling you.'

The smell of horse and saddle leather assailed her senses as she took in his tall, lean figure and deeply tanned skin. At the periphery of her vision she was aware of his mount watching her with nervous, pricked ears.

'This is a beautiful place, Mr Baxter.' She heard herself gushing in her need to fill the awkward moment, and winced inwardly. 'The creek is so peaceful. Is the water deep?'

Alex nodded.

'Over ten feet in places. Me and George used to swim here a lot when we were kids.' He grinned. 'Still do sometimes, when it's hot.'

She noticed the lapse in grammar with mild surprise. She'd hardly conversed with Alex at the wedding, but she knew George had been educated in Brisbane and his speech was without reproach. Had his adopted brother been given the same advantages? Though not roughly spoken, Alex's choice of words seemed less refined.

'How is Lucy?' he asked. 'Did the trip to Rockhampton knock her about?'

Emma shook her head, smiling. The warmth in his voice indicated he was fond of his sister-in-law.

'Not really. She's resting under sufferance.'

'Would you like me to walk you home?' He hesitated, seeming suddenly unsure. 'Unless you planned to go further?'

'No, I'd like to walk with you.' They fell into step on the narrow path, the horse following behind while Alex loosely held the reins.

'I've been shifting cattle,' he told her. 'One of the waterholes has gone dry and I've had to move the stock onto the creek. We're usually dry here at this time of year, but I hope the storms come soon.'

'I love riding. Perhaps I'll be able to help you with the stock work. Lucy tells me she used to go mustering.'

'She's a game little thing. She won't like being left at home if you come with us, I reckon.'

Maybe it wasn't such a good idea, Emma thought, feeling suddenly discouraged. She didn't want to upset Lucy. Alex's spurs jingled on his boots as he walked. Emma glanced covertly up at his profile, thinking there was something elemental and earthy about him, as if he truly belonged to the dry, dusty land. Her head reached only up to his shoulder, and in her crisp white blouse and dark skirt she felt feminine and fragile in contrast to his masculine strength. His white moleskins were saddle-stained and, like his striped Crimean shirt, covered with a fine layer of dust. But instead of being repulsed Emma was overly conscious of his presence, and her pulse raced.

Making conversation with the opposite sex had never troubled her before, but now words flitted just beyond her reach. She mentally searched for a suitable topic, thinking of the domestic details she and Lucy had chatted about. Even the shopping they'd done for the baby seemed an indelicate topic to share with a man, and hardly of interest to him. Her life in Brisbane was so far removed from his world. Would he care to hear the latest city gossip when he probably didn't know the people concerned? She thought not.

'Do you have any other brothers?' she asked, at length. 'I remember meeting your sisters at the wedding, but obviously none of them still live at Breakaway Creek.'

'No, me and George were the only boys. We have four younger sisters who have all married and moved away.' By the time he'd finished telling her about his nephews and nieces, they'd arrived at the horse yards. She watched as he unsaddled his sweaty bay mare, who still eyed Emma warily.

'Will she let me pat her?'

He glanced at her as he slid the saddle onto a rail.

'If you take her quietly. She's a bit of a one-man horse.'

He held the bridle as she cautiously approached the mare and stroked her smooth neck.

'What's her name?'

'Doll.'

'That's short and to the point.'

He flashed the quick grin she was already beginning to know and like.

'I don't go for highfalutin names.'

Doll sidestepped and tossed her head, ears pricked in the direction of her paddock. Emma gave her one last pat.

'She wants to go. I suppose I should do the same. I'm sure I'll see you soon, Mr Baxter.'

He touched his hat.

'Too right. Thank you for your company, Miss Watson.'

Emma turned away and retraced her steps to George and Lucy's cottage, a new anticipation humming through her veins. Would she be seeing a lot of Alex Baxter in the coming days? If so, the prospect pleased her.

As she entered the kitchen Lucy moved away from the window.

'I was watching you.' There was something cautious about her expression. 'You were with Alex.'

'Yes.' Emma smiled, pretending not to notice the guarded look on her cousin's face. 'I was walking by the creek and almost bumped into him. He's charming.'

Lucy's eyes softened.

'I'm extremely fond of him and I'd love to see him marry some nice girl. But remember your parents, Emma. I don't think Uncle Henry and Aunt Fanny would approve of him as a suitor for you.'

'Goodness.' Emma kept her tone deliberately light. 'It was just a chance meeting. I hardly know him.'

Lucy said nothing more on the subject. Of course he was not the sort of man her parents expected her to marry, Emma told herself. But away from her mother's eagle eye, there was nothing to stop her from indulging in a little light flirtation. She had enjoyed Alex's company and saw no reason to keep him at a distance.

A couple of days later Lucy took her to the big house and she renewed her acquaintance with George's parents, whom she had met briefly at their son's wedding. George's mother, Sarah, was a small yet formidable woman. Her wiry frame hinted that hard work was the core of her existence and her stern face suggested she had forgotten how to smile. Frank, her husband, was gnarled and wiry with fair, freckled skin that the years of Queensland sun had not been kind to. He made little effort to converse with the two young women, and Emma thought his pale blue eyes were the coldest she had ever seen. Here, perhaps, was the key to his wife's unhappy expression.

Sarah, who seemed to do the talking for both of them, invited them to stay for morning tea. Aided by Molly, her Aboriginal maid, she served them a feast of fresh scones with jam and cream, a fruit cake and biscuits.

'These scones are delicious, Mrs Baxter,' Emma said as she spread one lavishly with thick strawberry jam and whipped cream. 'I didn't expect to eat so well in the bush.'

Sarah's lined face relaxed slightly.

'Ah, but we're nearly self-sufficient out here. Mr Baxter milks the cows every morning and I skim the cream and churn it into butter. I even grew the strawberries to make this jam.'

'I'm surprised strawberries will grow in this hot, dry climate.'

'Only in the winter. It's the best time for gardening here. I grow vegetables and preserve them to see us through the summer. And of course I have my own hens to keep us supplied with eggs. I bake bread and we kill our own meat. The only things we buy are staples like flour, tea and sugar.' She passed around steaming cups of tea. 'What do you think of the bush, Miss Watson?'

'I'm enjoying it. It's quite different from Brisbane.'

Mrs Baxter pressed her lips together.

'It can be hard for a city girl to adjust, especially if she's not used to working hard.'

Emma glanced quickly at Lucy, who stared silently at her plate. It seemed obvious where that comment was intended, but she couldn't think what had provoked it. In her opinion Lucy had embraced the harshness of bush life with remarkable cheerfulness.

After that, conversation was stilted. When Molly brought in a fresh pot of tea Emma watched the maid curiously, thinking she wasn't as dark-skinned as the two stockmen she'd seen riding out with the men. Perhaps Molly wasn't fully Aboriginal.

The Aboriginies had a camp further down the creek but there appeared to be only half-a-dozen who lived there, including women and children. On afternoon walks Emma had observed them from a distance, intrigued by the way they cooked and socialised around open campfires. With regret she noted the rough shelters of corrugated iron dotted amongst their bark gunyahs, and suspected European influence was perhaps spoiling their traditional culture.

Emma was relieved when they were able to take their leave of the senior Baxters. Reluctant to criticise her cousin's in-laws, she waited for Lucy to comment on the visit.

'Mrs Baxter makes me feel inadequate,' Lucy confessed. 'She works so hard – I don't think she ever stops to indulge herself in any way. She never reads, apart from the bible, and when she sits at night she's always busy with needlework.'

'It sounds a dull way to live.' Emma slipped her arm through her cousin's. 'You don't need to be like that, Lucy. Don't lose your ability to laugh and enjoy life.'

Lucy stopped in mid-stride, turning surprised eyes to Emma's face.

'You know, you're right. Too bad if she thinks I'm a flibbertigibbet – I don't want to be like her. It's as if she's martyred herself for her house and family.'

That summed her up precisely, Emma thought. Had Sarah always been that way, or had life sapped the joy from her? She'd found the visit disheartening and she wondered how Alex endured living in a house that seemed full of unhappy undercurrents. Being an adopted son must make it even harder for him.

~*~

The afternoon had made Emma appreciate just how lonely Lucy's life must be. There was so little friendship to be had from Lucy's mother-in-law, so Emma set out to compensate. The two girls occupied their time with housework, sewing, and walking by the creek. Their enjoyment of each other's company made mundane tasks pass pleasantly. On Sunday, with George at last free to join them, the picnic came to fruition as promised. When he drove the buggy up to the house to collect them, Alex accompanied him on horseback.

'Look who I talked into coming with us,' George indicated his brother with a grin. 'Thought I could do with some male support. A chap gets tired of all this girlish chatter.'

Lucy tossed him an indignant look.

'That's hardly fair, George. You spend so much time working, we seldom see you.' But she welcomed Alex, who swung off his horse to greet Emma with a warm smile. 'Of course we'd love to have you, Alex.'

As he took the picnic basket from Emma's hands, Alex touched his hat in his gentle, courteous way. He smiled as his brother and sister-in-law exchanged their banter. Then he turned away to place the basket in the buggy, all without speaking. With fingers tingling from the brief contact, Emma wondered how a man could be so quiet, yet command so much of her attention.

George drove the buggy down the creek to a waterhole Emma hadn't visited before. The men lit a fire and set the billy to boil while the girls laid out the food on a large checked tablecloth. George twisted a leafy branch from a tree and used it to brush away the flies. He seemed to be in a teasing mood.

'It's been jolly rough, Alex. I don't know what these women find to talk about all day, but they're still at it when I get home at night. I warn you, cobber – when you get married, don't let your wife's relatives come to stay.'

'George!' Lucy tapped her fingers sharply on his arm. 'Don't be so mean to our guest.'

Alex smiled and rubbed his clean-shaven chin.

'I don't like to side with the ladies, George, but Lucy's spent a lot of time with no one to talk to.'

'There you go, George.' Lucy flashed him a triumphant smile. 'See, Emma. I told you Alex was a darling.'

Alex coloured and looked down at his boots. George muttered something good-natured about traitors and added some wood to the fire. Though it hadn't been exactly what Lucy had said, Emma didn't correct her. Lucy was right: her parents wouldn't approve of Alex as a suitor for her. But the more she got to know him the less inclined she was to care.

Chapter Four

Alex waited at the creek bank as Emma walked down the path towards him. The afternoon sun reflected off her pale blouse and straw hat and glinted gold in the brown hair that tumbled down her back. Little clouds of dust puffed about her feet as she walked, soiling her trailing hemline. She looked almost pretty, her face soft with anticipation, her trim waist defined by the snug band of her skirt. His body stirred, reminding him of all the reasons why he shouldn't be doing this.

From the first he'd known it would be unwise to spend much time with her. But Emma hadn't been easily discouraged. It had become her habit to stroll outdoors when the worst of the heat was over and she'd seemed to take a fancy to him. She had sought him out as he unsaddled his horse after work, or joined him as he fed the working dogs and chained them to their kennels. And then, fool that he was, he had asked her to meet him at the creek each afternoon when he'd finished work. He preferred the privacy here, away from the watching eyes of his family. He wasn't being deliberately secretive, he told himself, but why attract their attention?

Even so, he'd caught a few worried glances from George. Perhaps he was making fools of himself and Emma both, but for now he wasn't prepared to put a stop to their friendship. He wasn't sure of Emma's feelings towards him, but her presence here was all the encouragement he needed.

The first time he'd seen her at George and Lucy's wedding he had liked the look of her, but expected they'd have nothing in common. It turned out he was wrong. Her fascination with the bush seemed to draw him out. He loved sharing his knowledge of animals, not only the horses and cattle he worked with but also the native creatures which lived around them. She'd learned to recognise various bird calls and the tracks left in the sand as the animals came to the creek to drink. He showed her a wood duck's nest amongst the reeds and together they watched when the tiny ducklings hatched. Today, as they sat on the bank he pointed out the ducklings swimming behind their mother, one of them hitching a ride upon her back.

She watched in rapt enjoyment before giving him a smile that made his skin grow warm.

'You see so much. How did you learn all these things?'

He shrugged.

'I live with them every day. The Aborigines taught us, too. We all spent a lot of time at their camp when we were kids and the women took us hunting with them.'

'I thought the men were the hunters.'

'For big game like kangaroos, yes. But the women catch snakes and goannas, find grubs and eggs, dig up yams – things like that.'

Her eyes widened.

'Did you ever eat their food?'

He laughed.

'What do you think? We were game to have a go at anything. Besides, you accept what you grow up with.'

'I'm not sure I could stomach it,' she shuddered. 'Do the Aborigines still hunt?'

He shook his head.

'Not so much these days, except when they go walkabout. White fella tucker is easier to come by. We give them rations of flour, tea, sugar and tobacco. And meat, of course. Mother tries to keep them all clothed, which is easier said than done.' He grinned. 'Unless it's cold, they'd sooner go without.'

Emma blushed a little, reminding him how sheltered her life had been.

'My father says the Aborigines are a mob of useless savages.'

Alex cringed inside. She was only repeating the sentiments of much of the white population, he told himself. They were her father's words, not hers. But suddenly the day seemed less bright and he wondered what he was doing here with this cosseted city girl. She didn't seem to notice his sudden silence, prattling on innocently.

'But Lucy tells me Mick and Billy are good stockmen. She plans to have one of the girls come to help her when the baby's born.'

He focussed on her last remark, remembering his mother's exasperation when she'd been training Molly to do housework.

'I hope Lucy doesn't have too much trouble with her. You have to think of it from their point of view. It's a bit different to living in a gunyah with a dirt floor.'

She gave him a warm look.

'You seem to understand them very well. Most people aren't so tolerant.'

He scrambled to his feet and held out his hand to help her up. She brushed down her skirts and then he froze when she mentioned that she'd like to visit their camp sometime.

He looked away as the old anger and denial rose up to lodge in his throat.

'I don't go there these days. Not since I went to boarding school.'

Emma went pale and looked down at her hands.

'I'm sorry. I didn't realise … I've seen you talking to the stockmen as if they were your friends.'

Her obvious confusion shamed him.

'Of course, they are my friends.' He made his voice deliberately gentle. 'I work with them every day. But it's one thing to hang around their camp as a boy, and another altogether for a grown man.'

'Oh.' She blushed again, making him think she wasn't totally ignorant of why some white men visited Aboriginal camps. Her change of subject was a relief. 'Where did you go to boarding school?'

'Brisbane Grammar, the same as George. I didn't stay as long as he did, though. I never liked the city – all that noise and bustle.' The call of the bush had been too strong. He hadn't been able to settle into his studies or enjoy the Brisbane social scene as George had. George had met Lucy at a party there, but even the wedding had been an ordeal for Alex.

Emma smoothed her skirt, her movements quick and nervous. He cursed himself for upsetting her.

'I know what you mean about the hustle and bustle,' she said. 'It's so peaceful here. But don't you ever get lonely?'

'I used to.' He didn't say any more, but her startled glance told him she read his meaning perfectly well. She looked away, her colour heightening again.

'I should go back to the house. Lucy will be starting dinner.'

He didn't ask if he would see her tomorrow. That was up to her. If he'd frightened her away, that was probably a good thing. But as watched her walk away, despondency weighed heavy on him.

~*~

Emma's mind was in turmoil as she returned to the house. She could no longer pretend that it was just a light-hearted flirtation. Alex was obviously interested in her and she must decide if she should continue to encourage him. His strength and gentleness irresistibly drew her, but today there'd been a disturbing intensity in his manner.

She doubted the match would be a problem, if it weren't for his lack of prospects. She loved it here at Breakaway Creek and she could imagine making her life here with him. But did his future include the property? According to George he was only the overseer and would never be anything more. Her parents would never agree to such a union.

It was hard to face Lucy's questioning glance when she walked into the kitchen. Lucy and George knew she'd been seeing a lot of Alex. But something in Emma's expression must have warned her cousin not to comment.

George surprised her with an invitation over dinner.

'We're mustering the Five-Mile Paddock tomorrow, Emma. It won't be a long day. Would you like to come with us?'

'I'd love to!' But caution swiftly tempered the thrill of anticipation. 'Lucy, do you mind? It doesn't seem fair to leave you alone.'

Lucy smiled generously.

'Of course you must go! I'll feel madly jealous, but I couldn't ask you to stay at home on my account.'

Emma hesitated.

'No, go on,' Lucy insisted. 'I've had my opportunity to enjoy the mustering. Why shouldn't you?'

Early the next morning, dressed in her riding habit and boots, Emma carried a borrowed side-saddle to the horse yards. She and Lucy had cut lunches for George and herself and the sandwiches, wrapped in newspaper, were stowed in her saddlebag. Lucy's blackened quart-pot was strapped to the d-rings of the saddle.

A pair of blue cattle dogs ran to greet her, tails wagging as they drooled in excitement. While she stooped to pat them, George led up a little brown mare.

'This is Lucy's horse, but she's happy for you to ride her. Her name's Fortune.'

He picked up the saddlecloth as if to saddle her, but Emma reached out to take it from him.

'I can do that, George.' During the course of her visit, they had come to be on first name terms. If Lucy was like a sister, she was beginning to think of George as a brother. 'I don't believe women should be helpless.'

'Oh yes.' George grinned but let her take over. 'I'd forgotten you were such a bluestocking.'

Alex, who seemed extraordinarily quiet, looked up from tightening his horse's girth and smiled. As his eyes met Emma's, something seemed to flash between them and her pulse quickened. When he turned back to his horse she watched him covertly while she positioned the side-saddle on the mare's back, her eyes lingering on the breadth of his shoulders and travelling the length of his moleskins.

She brought herself back from her daydream suddenly and busied herself with the reins, her face heating. What was she doing, staring at him like that? Hopefully George hadn't noticed. She didn't quite understand the subtle longing within her, a craving to be close to Alex's quiet strength and good looks.

They set off with Mick and Billy, the two Aboriginal stockmen, and old Mr Baxter who sat on his horse with an easy grace despite his age. He'd muttered a brief greeting, his cold eyes flickering over her with an indifference that stung. Emma hadn't exchanged more than a dozen words with him, and she didn't think that was about to change. Not for the first time she marvelled that such a man had fathered a son as warm and outgoing as George.

It was early enough to be pleasantly cool. The sun shone brightly with only a promise of the day's heat. Fortune, walked briskly, her ears pricked as if anticipating the day's work. Her mouth was soft; she seemed quiet and well mannered. It felt good to be back on a horse again.

Mr Baxter took the lead, alone. George and Alex rode abreast behind him, discussing their plans for the day. Emma followed while the stockmen brought up the rear. When they entered the paddock they were to muster, Mr Baxter gave instructions from his horse as Alex put up the slip rails that served as a gate.

'We'll split up to cover the paddock. Mick and Billy can come with me. Miss Watson, you go with George and Alex.'

Twenty minutes later, Emma was beginning to wonder if they'd ever find cattle when George pointed out a mob in the distance.

'You be careful, Emma,' he warned. 'Stay back if they start to run.'

'I'm a competent rider,' she protested.

'I'm sure you are, but I won't have you galloping through the timber in a side-saddle.'

Alex checked his horse and fell back beside her.

'He's right, Miss Watson. I've seen plenty of men come to grief.' He paused. 'If you get lost, stay where you are and cooee until we find you.'

It was the first time he'd spoken to her since they'd left the yards and Emma was feeling his neglect. She seethed inwardly. Of course mustering was a new experience for her, but it wasn't fair to judge her by Lucy's abilities. Her cousin had never been a particularly good rider.

As the men had obviously expected, the cattle set off at a fast rate through the box timber. George and Alex gathered up their reins and their horses leapt into a gallop. Fortune tossed her head and danced sideways, loath to be left behind. Emma put her into a cautious canter, startled at the sudden transformation of her mild-mannered mount.

Threading her way through the trees at speed was tricky. The cattle and men were soon out of sight and, afraid of becoming lost, Emma relaxed her tight hold of the mare's head. Fortune immediately increased her speed and Emma rode with grim concentration, guiding the mare through the timber with heel and hand.

Suddenly a bird flew up in front of Fortune's hooves, making the horse jump sideways. Thrown partly out of the saddle, Emma battled to bring the mare under control, but was unable to turn her away from the tree that loomed ahead. Emma's left shin slammed against its trunk. In a haze of pain she felt herself become dislodged. As the panicked mare raced out from under her, the ground rushed up to meet her.

The brutal impact knocked the wind from her body. Agony consumed her as she tried to suck air into her lungs. It seemed like minutes before she was able to drag herself to a seated position and gingerly move her arms and legs. Her left leg protested and she pulled up the skirt of her habit, revealing a bleeding graze on her shin and an already egg-sized lump.

She staggered to her feet and moved to the shade, where she leant against a tree trunk for support. Fortune was nowhere in sight. What should she do? Wait until the men came looking for her, she supposed, remembering Alex's instructions if she got lost. She flushed. How humiliating to have come to grief at the first bit of action!

She was wondering if she should start cooeeing when Alex rode out of the trees, leading Fortune from his own horse. His anxious face made her immediately forget her fear of his derision. He swung out of the saddle without a word and dropped both sets of reins, moving to grasp her hands in his.

'Emma! Are you all right?'

She nodded. She was so conscious of his touch it was difficult to frame a sensible reply.

'I hit my leg on a tree. I'm sorry to be such a nuisance to you. What's happened to the cattle?'

'Hopefully George has them under control. But you're all right – that's what matters.' He pulled her close and pressed his lips against the top of hair, which she suddenly realised was uncovered. She must have lost her hat in the fall. 'I got such a fright when your mare came galloping up.'

Hardly believing she was actually in his arms, she savoured the strength of them around her. The closeness of his hard-muscled body was even more thrilling than she'd imagined. The pain in her leg receded as she moved closer, forgetting decorum and usual reserve in the excitement of the moment.

Alex drew an uneven breath and bent his face to hers. Their kiss seemed to happen by instinct. He was gentle at first, and then increasingly urgent. Her heart thudded wildly as she learned the taste of him and the feel of his hot breath on her cheek and ear.

'You're beautiful,' he murmured. 'I think the world of you, Emma.'

'And me of you,' she whispered, realising it was true.

He kissed her again. It wasn't a chaste kiss such as she'd expected from him; it made her blood race and her body turn to butter. She sank against him, understanding, for the first time, why women were tempted to surrender their virtue to men. It was Alex who finally put distance between them.

'I don't want to stop this. I wish we could stay here all day.' He smiled down at her, his eyes tender. 'But we've got cattle to muster. Do you think you can ride?'

Emma had momentarily forgotten her leg, but now she realised it was throbbing painfully.

'I'll manage, but I'll have to ride slowly.'

'Good girl. George will be wondering what's happened to us.'

He helped her to her horse and hoisted her into the saddle. Unfortunately it was her sore leg that took all the weight in the stirrup and she winced with pain.

'Are you all right?' The concern in his dark eyes made her want to sink back into his arms.

'Yes, I'm all right, really.' She curled her right leg around the horn and adjusted her skirt. He retrieved her hat and she settled it on her head, thankful for its shade.

He frowned at her restlessly sidling horse.

'Fortune's a bit excited. Once we find George I can take you home if you like.'

'No, of course not.' She sat up straighter in the saddle. The thought of being a bother to them dismayed her; she'd see the muster through if it killed her. 'I won't be responsible for ruining the day's work.'

He grinned at her, a wicked gleam in his eye making her breath come faster.

'Even if we don't get any cattle, you haven't ruined my day, Emma.'

They found George waiting with a mob of cattle at a waterhole in the shade of the trees. His face furrowed with concern as he came to meet them.

'Are you all right, Emma? Did you get lost?'

Alex explained what had happened, but to her relief George didn't say "I told you so".

'I'll be in trouble with Lucy,' he said, instead. 'She told me to look after you. Would you like me to take you home?'

'Thank you. Alex has already offered. But I'm determined to see the day out.' She noticed George's horse was dark with sweat, indicating he'd had to do some hard riding before he got the cattle settled. Already she'd taken Alex away from his work. She resolved to make up for it.

The stock seemed to have expended their excess energy. The cows and calves walked out meekly as the two men herded them towards the place where they'd arranged to meet the others. Only one big calf was recalcitrant, rushing out of the mob at a gallop. Alex's horse leapt after it with no noticeable signal from its rider, quickly gaining ground until it raced neck and neck with the calf.

Emma watched in admiration as Alex turned the animal back to the mob. He sat his saddle effortlessly, as if he belonged there. Remembering the way he'd kissed her earlier, her body heated. She mentally listed his attributes: competent and physically strong, yet gentle, kind and honourable. Perhaps he didn't have money or possessions, but he was everything she wanted in a man, and the miracle was he seemed to feel the same way about her.

She took the position at the back of the herd. Her job involved urging along the smallest calves and trying to coax their hovering, protective mothers to follow the mob. One of the cows came back to find her offspring, bellowing anxiously and sniffing calf after calf until she found the right one. Then she stood over it, facing Emma and tossing her head at her. Nerves leaping in apprehension, Emma quickly retreated, unsure how to deal with the situation.

Alex must have witnessed her dilemma and cantered back.

'Don't let her get the better of you.'

Yelling at the belligerent cow, he spurred his horse aggressively towards her. Intimidated, the beast retreated into the depths of the mob, her calf at her heels.

'You make it look so easy.' Feeling at once chagrined and grateful, Emma made an effort to smile. 'I thought she was about to charge me.'

'She probably would, if you let her. The trick is to let her know who's boss.' Emma supposed her face reflected her doubt, for he returned her smile. 'I'll handle her. You're doing well for your first muster.'

It was a day Emma wouldn't forget in a hurry. As the hours went by they met up with the remainder of the party, who added cattle to the mob until it seemed huge to her inexperienced eyes. When they stopped at a shady waterhole and boiled their quart-pots for lunch, the break was a welcome chance to ease her stiffening muscles. The men were chivalrous, allowing her to rest while they took turns to check any wandering stock.

As they set to pushing the mob towards the homestead, Emma became immersed in swirling dust, heat, flies and bawling cattle. By the time they finally reached the stockyards she drooped with exhaustion and her throat was harsh and gritty with thirst.

Sitting at the kitchen table with Lucy, she slaked her craving with several glasses of cool rainwater from the tank and realised nothing had ever tasted so delicious. Her cousin was full of questions and, as Emma recounted the day's adventures, the myriad discomforts retreated to the background. She decided that she definitely wanted to do it again. The experience had been challenging and at times uncomfortable, but ultimately far more satisfying than home chores.

A soak in a warm bath, to which she'd added a handful of soothing Epsom Salts, made her feel ready to face the world again. At dinner she had only to deal with George's teasing as he told Lucy about the cantankerous cow. But even then George didn't taunt her about her fall.

She tried not to think about Alex at dinner, instead waiting until she was alone in bed to relive her memories. The image of him on his horse, looking tough and capable and handsome, thrilled her. But it was his tenderness and passion as he'd held her in his arms that totally disarmed her. Her blood pounded as she recalled their kisses and when she remembered his flattering concern, she decided that she no longer cared for her parents' approval.

Chapter Five

Breakaway Creek, 2010

After lunch, Shelley settled in a comfortable chair in the lounge room. They'd already read the letter on the top of the bundle, dated 1885, and the rest appeared to be in chronological order. She went through them systematically.

The day-to-day detail about life on a sheep station near Longreach fascinated her. Sarah's sister spoke of baking bread, making soap and candles from tallow, her isolation from medical help when one of her children fell ill, and numerous other details that brought home the hardships of pioneering life. Interspersed through it all were references to her faith and obviously well-meant comments about the station Aboriginals that would today be considered racist.

She found no direct mention of Alex. But one letter said:

My dear sister, the Good Lord above is your witness to this trial that you have been forced to bear. You have done your duty, like the good Christian you are, and more besides. Taking the child in was more than could be expected of you, but you have done it and raised him as your own. When the day of judgement comes, that will not be forgotten.

Her heart beat faster. Was she referring to Alex? It seemed likely. It gave credence to the theory that he'd been adopted into the family. But Shelley wondered why had he been such a trial to Sarah.

There was nothing more of significance until Shelley reached the earliest letter, dated 1871. Its tone was highly sympathetic, her sister obviously indignant on Sarah's behalf.

The burdens we women are forced to endure for the sins of our men must, for the most part, be suffered in silence. But such an imposition is beyond what could be expected of anyone. Of course, it is not the fault of the child, as you have pointed out. If you feel you must do your Christian duty, it is not for me to dissuade you. I only hope you will not be forced to regret your generosity.

Shelley put the letters in a neat pile beside her chair and stared vacantly at the blank television. Was she about to unearth something that would be better left buried? She remembered Luke's comment on illegitimacy in the context of modern-day morals. But the reference to "the sins of our men" suggested something more sinister. Shelley wondered if Sarah's husband had fathered the child, and if so, who was the mother?

She got up and went outside, deciding a brisk walk would help to clear her head. The still, humid air drained her energy so that every step was an effort. The sun had disappeared behind a cloud that took away the full bite of its heat. An ominous bank was building low on the western horizon. It looked like a storm was heading their way. The seared brown countryside cried out for rain, and she guessed Luke and Mitch were watching the sky with hopeful eyes. Flies buzzed about her face and she brushed them impatiently away.

Heading towards the creek, she walked into a stand of tall trees with pale trunks and long, narrow leaves. The fresh tang of eucalyptus told her they were some type of gum. She tried to recall what she had learnt from her grandfather, during their bush-walking and camping trips, but tree names eluded her. Crows cawed harshly from the branches as she scrambled down the creek bank, her shoes sliding on the leaf-strewn soil. At the bottom of the watercourse a shrunken pool remained, black with tannins and speckled with floating debris.

Shelley sat on a fallen log and stared into the water, letting the peace and quiet seep into her. It was a different world from the roar and fumes of Brisbane. She pictured Alexander playing here as a young boy, along with his brother. Perhaps the waterhole had been deeper and more pristine then, before the ravages of men and cattle had filled the creeks with silt. For a moment she could almost hear their childish calls ringing down the years, and see their thin bodies skimming through the water. A sense of belonging infused her, as if some spiritual connection with this place had been passed on through the legacy of her ancestors.

~*~

As they ate their dinner that night, she told Luke and Mitch what she'd found in the letters.

'I'm a bit worried about what I might dig up.' Shelley looked at Luke. 'Do you think I should keep going? If you'd sooner I didn't, that's okay with me.'

Luke shrugged.

'What does it matter? I don't imagine you're planning on telling the world. You've got me interested now – I'd like to know what was behind it all.'

'Me too.' Mitch gave her one of the cheerful grins that came so easily to him. 'We'll trust you to keep it quiet. It's your family too.'

'That storm's getting closer.' Luke got to his feet and walked to the window, peering out into the darkness. 'I don't think we'll get much out of it, though. Looks like it's going to the south of us.'

Lightning flashed in the west and a strong, cool breeze blew through the windows, carrying the scent of rain. A frog croaked in the garden, spurring others to join in sympathy. The telephone's shrill ring made him turn.

'That could be Mum.' He hurried towards the office to answer it. Rain pattered lightly on the roof, but as Luke had predicted, the centre of the storm seemed to be bypassing them. By the time he returned Mitch and Shelley had finished the washing up.

Luke's face was grey with fatigue, as if the last ten minutes had sapped the life out of him.

'That woman!' he fumed. 'She wants to do me for everything I've got. I hoped we could settle it ourselves, but she's determined to fight me all the way.'

Mitch gave him a worried look.

'So it was Miranda, not Mum? Did you talk to the boys?'

'She said they were in bed.'

Shelley left them to it, not wanting to intrude on their private conversation. She went onto the veranda and sank into an old-fashioned squatter's chair, enjoying the breeze as raindrops spattered across the corrugated iron roof and the frogs continued their hopeful chorus. Lightning flickered and thunder rumbled, but the image of Luke's drawn face kept returning to disturb her. He may not have been a perfect husband – how could she possibly judge? – but he seemed a decent guy and didn't deserve to be denied access to his children.

'It's definitely going around us.'

She started and looked around quickly to locate Luke's shadowy form.

'I didn't hear you come out.'

'Sorry. I won't be able to sleep after that phone call, so I may as well watch the storm.'

It was hard to know how much to say when really it was none of her business, but the lonely note in his voice urged her to try.

'I'm sorry. Not seeing your children must be devastating.'

He walked over to the railing and stood with his back to her, looking out at the storm.

'It sure is. I was a fool to marry her. My family never liked Miranda. By the time she left I didn't like her much myself. That hurts as much as anything.'

She deliberately softened her voice.

'She must have some good qualities.'

He gave a short, bitter laugh. The wind whipped away his words so Shelley had to strain to hear them.

'I used to think so, but the Miranda I married and the Miranda who took off with the boys seem like two different people.' He turned to face her so his next words were much clearer. 'She had problems and I blame myself for not realising it sooner.'

'What sort of problems?'

'For a start, she never really liked it here. It got worse when she had the kids. She hated being stuck at home with them. I think she was depressed.'

'Ah.' A light bulb went off in her head. 'Post natal depression?'

'Probably.' He hoisted himself up to sit on the railing. 'She used to shout a lot, and when she wasn't shouting she was crying. Her solution was to leave the kids with me and go party.'

'Must have been tough on you.'

He nodded.

'Especially when she got in with a rough crowd. She'd always been a bit wild and I guess I didn't mind that at the start. I thought she'd settle down. I didn't think she'd go off the rails.'

'How could you know? You must have been so young yourself. We all make mistakes.'

'Were you a wild teenager, Shelley? You don't seem the type.'

Was she so easy to read? Good girl Shelley, she thought, with nothing worse to blot her record than a couple of bouts of teenage drunkenness and a speeding fine.

'You've guessed my guilty secret. I'm actually quite staid and boring.'

He laughed again, but this time with a warm, intimate note that made her shiver.

'Certainly not boring. I don't think staid is the right word either. But I've only known you a couple of days.' He paused, and continued in a different tone. 'So, if home's in Rocky, what made you move to Brisbane?'

She thought back to her nineteen-year-old self, remembering her restlessness, her need to experience life away from the big country town.

'I did a course in business admin at TAFE in Rocky. Then one of my best friends from school moved to the city and was looking for a flat mate. I joined her there and was lucky enough to find a job I liked.' She shrugged. 'After I met Jason I never thought about going back.'

'Until now.'

'Yes, but this is just temporary.' She smothered a yawn and rose, smiling at him. 'I have a job to go back to. I'll see you tomorrow.'

~*~

In the morning the sun was shining. Already the heat and humidity had made the air thick and cloying. In the kitchen Luke stood at the stove tending bacon, which sizzled and spat in a blackened frypan. The usual jeans and work shirt were not evident; instead he wore knee-length shorts and a short-sleeved polo shirt. His legs were a paler shade of brown than his arms, which suggested they saw daylight only occasionally. He turned to smile at Shelley.

'Since it's Saturday and we didn't hear from the oldies last night, I wondered if you'd like to go to Clermont and check out the newspaper archives.'

It was good to see him smiling and apparently upbeat.

'That'd be excellent. Are you sure you're not too busy?'

'No, it's okay. Gives me something else to think about. They might have done a follow-up story to the one we found.' He cracked eggs into the pan. 'How many for you?'

That was something else they had in common, Shelley thought – the need to use this ancestor hunt as a distraction.

'One, please. I don't usually eat a cooked breakfast.'

'It's nice to have once in a while. I thought we could take the boat, go out to Theresa Creek Dam afterwards. Do you like fishing?'

She nodded and Luke looked up as Mitch came in the door.

'You wanna come, Mitch?'

'What, to the dam? What are you going over there for? No, I'd planned on spending the day with Julie.'

'I'm taking Shelley to Clermont to do some research at the library. We might as well take the boat and make a day of it.'

Mitch gave him a quick look.

'You're really getting into this ancestor thing, aren't you?'

Luke didn't respond and Shelley busied herself with setting the table. Was Mitch worried about his brother spending too much time with her? He needn't be – she'd be gone in a few days.

~*~

After breakfast Shelley changed into her bikini and pulled a singlet-style top and board shorts over it. She grabbed sunscreen, a hat and towel and found Luke in the shed, fuelling the outboard engine of a good-sized dinghy. A couple of fishing rods lay in the bottom of the boat.

'What do you catch at this dam?'

He grinned.

'Nothing, probably. But it's been stocked with barra and perch. We can only try.'

He reversed the Land Cruiser into the shed and connected it to the boat trailer. In a few minutes they were driving up the road, retracing the route to Clermont.

They commenced their search at the town library, which had archived issues of the Clermont Telegram and its predecessor. The Telegram had been incorporated into the Emerald newspaper more than twenty years before. The plump, moon-faced librarian produced a large plastic box full of reels of microfiche and helped them search for the dates they wanted. She threaded the reel into the viewing machine, switched on the screen and showed them how to move the film backwards and forwards, up and down.

'The newspapers must have been in tatters,' Luke muttered, pulling up a chair beside Shelley as she scrolled up and down a front page of The Peak Downs Telegram and Copperfield Miner, dated February 14, 1898.

'Just as well they didn't leave them any longer,' Shelley agreed, trying hard to focus on the screen and not the man beside her. 'Doesn't look like we're going to find any news on the front page. It's all ads.'

They chuckled over some of the articles inside the paper, one of which included references to "the Chinese invasion" on the goldfields. Racism obviously hadn't been so politically incorrect in the nineteenth century. Interestingly, world news had an important place in The Peak Downs Telegram; one story from Spain depicted a fight between a bull and a lion in grisly detail. Shelley shuddered and Luke shook his head.

'Imagine what animal rights activists would do if something like that was printed these days,' he said.

In the next Saturday's paper, they came on the article they'd found the previous day. Shelley's chest tightened with anticipation.

'Surely there's something in the next paper!'

But the following issues were frustratingly silent.

'What does that mean?' Shelley rocked back in her chair, barely resisting the urge to pound her fist on the table. 'Did he survive, or not?'

'You'd think it would have been reported if he'd died. When was the baby born?'

Shelley rubbed her nose, trying to remember.

'I don't think I was given a date. Only the year: 1898. But I've ordered the birth certificate, so when that arrives we'll know more.'

Luke moved his chair back from the desk.

'What about tracing Emma's family? There might be relatives who know something. Didn't you say she came from Brisbane?'

'Yes. I suppose I could try to trace the family when I go back.'

'I'm driving down soon.' Luke raked his hand through his hair, looking distracted. 'I want to see my boys.'

'Of course.' Shelley gave him a sympathetic look. 'You must be missing them.'

'You can say that again.' He removed the microfiche from the machine and switched it off. 'Come on, let's go and have lunch.'

They ate a counter meal at one of the hotels. Luke seemed determined to put his family worries out of his mind by asking Shelley about her own family.

'So why did you take leave from work?' he asked, when she'd filled him in on her mother and father in Rockhampton and her married older brother in Townsville. She hated talking about it, but he'd been upfront with her. It was time to give him something in return.

'When I split with my boyfriend, I just had to get away.' She hated admitting this part. 'I caught him with someone else.'

'Really?' Luke sipped from his beer glass, looking reflective. 'That makes two of us, then.'

'Your wife was having an affair?'

'Yep. It wasn't the first time, as I discovered later.' His voice sounded indifferent, almost detached, but she noticed his fingers tightening on his glass. 'He was a miner with plenty of money to splash around, so perhaps they'll suit each other.'

'They're still together?'

'Apparently.'

'You must hate that, having another man in your boys' lives.'

Luke winced.

'You know, that's the hardest part. I hate to think of that scummy bastard as their male role model.' He looked down at his beer and sighed heavily. 'I feel like I've failed them, letting this happen.'

'The sooner you can sort out this custody issue the better.'

'I know. That's why I've decided to go down there next week. Mitch can look after things for a while.'

After they'd eaten, they drove to the Theresa Creek Dam. It was obviously popular with the locals; the grassy picnic area crowded with people and vehicles. A couple of speedboats towed water-skiers behind them and there were a number of dinghies further out on the water.

'I wonder if they're catching anything?' Shelley mused.

Luke shrugged.

'Some of them will have put in redclaw pots, but they only get them when the season's right.'

'Do you come here often?'

'I used to take the boys.' His tone was clipped. 'In the early days, Miranda came with us, too.'

Oops, she thought, shouldn't have asked.

He reversed down the boat ramp and soon had the dinghy launched. As he waded through the water, pulling the craft close to the edge, her nostrils twitched at the rank smell of mud and water weeds.

'Are you okay to park the Toyota?'

She swung to look at it, alarm quickening her pulse. That ramp looked steep and slippery.

'I haven't driven a manual for years.'

'Do you want to hold the boat then, while I do it?'

The mud squelched around her bare feet as she waded in. She imagined it lodging under her toenails and guessed a good scrubbing would be on the agenda when she had her shower. As long as there was nothing in here that bit…

Luke was soon back and held the boat while she clambered in. It was hard to do gracefully. In contrast he leapt in as if it was no effort at all. Before long they were chugging across the cloudy surface towards the far reaches of the dam.

It was blisteringly hot in the sun. Clouds gathered in the western sky, promising another evening storm. Shelley was glad of her shady hat as she slathered sunscreen on her face, arms and legs, although her olive-toned skin she didn't burn easily. Luke wore his usual Akubra, pulled low to shade his face.

'I wish the water looked cleaner. I'd love to cool off.'

Luke put his hand over the side of the boat and splashed her with a teasing grin, his good humour apparently restored.

'It won't hurt you. Dive in if you like, while I throw a line in.'

Shelley looked dubiously at the brown water. But already her clothes were sticking to her and sweat was running into her eyes. Before she could change her mind, she pulled off her singlet top and shorts. A quick glance assured her that Luke was busying himself with his tackle box. He didn't even look as she lowered herself over the edge of the boat. The water was pleasantly cool as she swam a few strokes and floated, watching Luke attach a lure to his line and throw it in. At last he turned her way.

'How's the water?'

She grinned up at him.

'Lovely. Why don't you try it yourself?'

He shook his head.

'I'll stick to the fishing. When you've cooled off enough, hop back in and I'll troll the line behind us.'

When she swam to the edge of the boat, he reached over and grasped her hand to pull her in. Shelley struggled over the side, laughing and dripping water. She noticed his eyes on her breasts and realised the wet, clinging fabric of her bikini didn't conceal much. Heat rushed through her. She wrapped herself in her towel, not looking at him. She felt the sexual current as strongly as if he'd touched her. Shelley longed to feel those strong brown hands on her skin, to kiss that sensual mouth, to feel the press of his body against hers. But this was madness – she wasn't ready for a new relationship, especially the transient kind. And she was kidding herself if she thought he might want more. He'd made his cynicism about marriage clear.

Quickly Luke restarted the motor and set off across the dam, trailing a line in the water behind him. Shelley could see the brightly coloured lure flashing through the water, darting along like a live fish. But nothing bit.

He stopped the boat long enough to attach a lure to a second line which he cast out and gave to Shelley to hold. As their hands brushed, his eyes met hers briefly before he turned to his seat at the stern. They traversed the upper reaches of the dam for some time without success. At last he looked up at the rapidly building clouds and began to reel in his line.

'I think we'd better call it a day. Sorry. It's a bit boring when the fish don't bite.'

'No, I've enjoyed it,' she hastened to assure him. In truth, she hadn't been bored. She enjoyed being on the water and Luke's company made her feel curiously alive. Her senses were fine-tuned to her surroundings – the fresh air on her face, the muddy tang of the water and the mellow chug of the dinghy's motor.

Shelley waited with the boat while Luke reversed the Toyota down the ramp and helped him winch the dinghy onto the trailer. She pulled her clothes on over her damp bikini and joined him in the cab once they'd tied down the boat. They stopped at a service station on the other side of Clermont to buy an ice-cream each and Luke turned the ute for home.

The storm caught them just after Clermont. Rain drove against the windscreen in sheets, pooling on the gravel road and making the Toyota slip and slide on the muddy surface. Luke changed down to four-wheel-drive and third gear, driving with grim concentration. The Land Cruiser ploughed through the splashing mud and water. Shelley clutched the handlebar in front of her, caught between nervousness and excitement. Sporadic lightning flashes lit paddocks of grey grass that were buffeted by wind and rain. The day had turned dark.

'I'm worried about the creek near the house,' Luke muttered. 'It comes up pretty quick.'

As he'd predicted, when they reached the deep creek on the other side of Faradale, the headlights picked out a rushing torrent of brown water. The rain was still falling in sheets. Luke didn't even leave the vehicle.

'It's too deep to drive through.' He sighed. 'We'll have to wait it out.'

He switched off the ignition and turned to Shelley with a resigned smile.

'Welcome to the bush, Shelley.'

'This has become quite an adventure.' She shivered a little in the cool air, thinking how quickly the temperature had dropped. She drew her damp towel around her shoulders, glad of its slight protection. 'I'll have a story to tell everyone when I get home.'

'Yeah, about some half-smart ringer who took you fishing and didn't even catch a fish. Then got you stuck on the road on the way home.' He reached across to touch her towel and his voice softened. 'That thing's still wet. Here, lean forward and pull the lever beside the seat. I've got a coat behind there somewhere.'

Shelley took a deep breath, trying to slow her suddenly racing heart. After some groping, she found the lever in question and sat up as the seat tipped forward. Luke rummaged behind it, pulling out a dusty denim jacket.

'Been there since winter. It's not too clean.'

He handed it to her but she shook her head, clearing the thickness in her throat to speak. 'It's yours – you wear it.'

'No, I'm not cold.'

Shelley happily obliged him, discarding the towel in favour of the grimy jacket, which smelled faintly of diesel.

'We could've gone back to town, but I think the last gully will be flooded by now. So we're stuck.'

'Will this rain break the drought?' she asked.

'No, we'll need follow-up.' He reached across her to the glove box, groping inside in the darkness. As his arm brushed against her he drew in a sharp breath and retreated quickly, dumping a heavy packet in her lap. 'Do you want a lolly? I'd sooner a good steak, but that's all that's offering.'

The husky note in his voice betrayed him, fanning Shelley's simmering lust into a burning flame. A rush of recklessness and longing washed away her good sense.

'No, I don't want a lolly,' she said, leaning towards him.

Luke must have read the decision in her voice because he moved half-way to meet her, gathering her in with his right arm while his mouth found hers through the darkness with unerring accuracy. There was no fumbling; just an overwhelming sense of urgency. As they tasted each other's mouths, Shelley became conscious of his hard shoulder under her hand and his arms pulling her against him. As the kiss deepened she strained to be closer to him, frustrated by the confines of the ute's cab. She couldn't remember when kissing a man had ever felt like this.

If his heavy breathing was any indication, he was just as overpowered as she was. Shelley murmured encouragement as his fingers slipped inside her borrowed jacket, cupping her breast through the clinging top. Then his hands slid down her sides and he pulled her hips towards him, pushing her backwards on the seat. He held his hungry, seeking body above her in the cramped space.

As they kissed their fingers fumbled with clothing, baring skin to touch. Luke's mouth trailed down to her breasts and Shelley moaned, arching against him while she clasped his head to her, her fingers threading through his hair.

Luke's hands drifted lower, tracing her belly and hips. Shelley tensed in anticipation, but then he lifted his head so they were face-to-face. He kissed her again and moved his hips against hers.

'Shelley,' he whispered hoarsely. 'I don't have anything – any protection.'

His words took a moment to penetrate the haze in her brain. Then she realised what he'd said, and the haze quickly dissipated. In a moment she realised how close they'd been to doing it anyway – with or without protection.

'Bloody hell.' She pulled away from him, struggling out from under his body, swearing as she banged her shin painfully on the steering wheel in the process. 'What am I doing?'

Luke eased himself away, silently letting her retreat to one side of the vehicle.

'I'm not in the habit of sleeping around, you know.'

He laughed shakily.

'Well, that makes two of us. If I was, I'd carry rubbers in the glove box instead of lollies.'

'I'm not even on the pill. I stopped taking it. I thought I was done with men! God, that's responsible for you!'

'Shelley.' His voice was gentle. 'We didn't do it, okay? So don't give yourself a hard time.'

'But I would have, if you hadn't said anything.'

'We've been around each other too much, the last few days.' He gave a soft, self-deprecating laugh. 'And I don't know about you, but I'm desperate and dateless, remember.'

She should have been able to laugh, but it wasn't funny. His words were like a dash of cold water, reducing it to a purely physical thing. She'd been around other men, but she'd never wanted any of them the way she wanted Luke. Perhaps he'd be like this with anything in a skirt. He was a man, after all. Was she kidding herself when she thought the chemistry between them was something special?

She fumbled with her clothes, struggling to tie the strings of her bikini top under the jacket. Once she had herself back together she huddled in her corner of the vehicle, pulling the jacket closed for warmth. The last thing she needed now was a one-night stand with a married man.

'I should head off in the morning,' she said. 'You don't need me complicating your life. You can let me know what you find out from your mother.'

'There's a problem with that.' His even voice betrayed nothing of his feelings. 'Until the road dries out, I don't think you'll get far in your little car.'

She hadn't thought of that.

'How long will it take?'

'Another day, if it doesn't rain again.'

It looked like they were stuck with each other for the time being. At least once they got out of this predicament she didn't have to stay in his pocket.

'I wonder what happened to those lollies,' he murmured, flicking the light switch on the roof of the cab.

The packet had fallen at Shelley's feet and the paper-wrapped caramels had spilled over the floor. Shelley bent to pick them up and withdrew hastily as Luke did the same. She caught the clean scent of his hair as it brushed her cheek and longing swept through her again, making her insides clench. He gathered the lollies and straightened, glancing briefly at her. Silently he passed her a handful, which she mutely accepted.

With the light still on he searched the cluttered dashboard, coming up with a CD that he slipped into the Toyota's player.

'I hope you like country music.'

'Anything else would seem out of place right now,' she said drily, as Lee Kernaghan's country twang filled the cab. Outside, the rain had nearly stopped, but she could hear the rushing creek even over the music. This was an experience to remember, Shelley thought as they sat in the cramped cab of the ute, listening to lyrics about rodeos and country girls. The atmosphere of frustrated sex lent a poignant edge to the moment.

Once she was back in the city she'd probably laugh about it, but right now it scared her just how much she was enjoying the outback lifestyle and everything it entailed. Even being stranded in a vehicle on the wrong side of a flooded creek was strangely exhilarating. If only Luke was a free man and wanted something more than a one-night-stand ... her thoughts trailed off. That was dangerous thinking. And she was a city girl. She had to remember that.

By the time Lee Kernaghan had sung his way to the end of the CD, time was beginning to drag. The lollies had taken the edge off her hunger but made her feel slightly sick. They could have talked to pass the time, but she was too annoyed with herself to make idle conversation. Luke seemed to have retreated into his own space. Was it purely a man thing? She wondered if frustration made him grumpy, as Jason had always been like that whenever she denied him sex. But in this case Luke had raised the issue of protection, so surely he hadn't expected her to continue regardless.

At last he opened his door and peered into the night.

'The creek's not roaring as much. I'd better check it.'

He switched on the headlights and picked his way down the bank with bare feet. Although Shelley couldn't read the numbers on the depth marker in the middle of the stream, she was sure the level had dropped. Luke rolled his shorts halfway up his thighs and waded carefully into the water. She could see the current tugging at him, swirling about his legs, and wanted to call to him to be careful. But she was silent.

With water lapping at his crotch and the centre of the flow still ahead of him, he turned back. He wrung out the bottom of his shorts and climbed back in the vehicle.

'It's still over a metre deep and running pretty strong. We could drop off the boat and try driving through it, but I don't think it's worth the risk.'

'No, of course not. It won't hurt us to stay here. At least we're safe,' she assured him. In the dark she sensed he was shivering and she shrugged out of his jacket. 'Here, you have this. You're half-wet.'

He pushed it back at her.

'You keep it. I'll be all right.'

'No, at least I'm dry. I can always use the towel.'

'I think we'd better share it.' She heard the amusement in his voice and realised with relief that he wasn't sulking as she'd thought. 'I promise I'll behave myself – as long as you do.'

He pulled her close and draped the jacket over them both, like a shield. For Shelley the pleasure was bittersweet as she relaxed into the closeness of his lean, muscled body. His heat enveloped her and she rested her head against his shoulder, feeling his breath stir her hair, knowing from the quickened rhythm that their proximity affected him as much as her. She longed to turn her face to his and lose herself in another of those mind-drugging kisses. If only they had a condom between them, she thought. If only she wouldn't feel a heck of a lot worse in the morning.

Eventually she slept. She woke with a start, conscious of headlights flooding the cab and someone knocking at the window. As she straightened, Luke grunted and stirred beside her. He wound down the window to reveal the face of his brother. Mitch regarded them with a mocking smile.

'This is a great place to spend the night.'

'We sure didn't pick it for the fine food and five-star accommodation.' Luke yawned. 'The creek was up, in case you haven't noticed.'

'Looks like it's gone down again now.'

They both looked at the creek. The headlights of the vehicle behind them reflected off the water, which had dropped to a shallow flow across the causeway.

'I thought you'd have spent the night with Julie.'

'She's got family there at the moment. Kinda spoilt the mood.' Mitch gave Shelley a penetrating glance, no doubt taking in her dishevelled appearance. 'So, are you two gonna cross this thing, or do you want to let me pass?'

'We'll head home, with pleasure.' Luke turned the key and the engine of the Land Cruiser roared to life. 'See you there, little brother.'

Shelley shifted across to her side of the vehicle as he drove slowly through the water and accelerated up the bank. Lee Kernaghan was singing again, negating the need for conversation. It was just as well, for Shelley couldn't think of a single thing to say.

Chapter Six

Luke woke late the next morning. Given the events of the previous day he wasn't surprised. He peered out the window at the rain-washed world, noticing the pools of water by the edges of the road. The brown grass looked flattened and dispirited, but in a day or two he knew the new green shoots would poke through, transforming the paddocks. His spirits lifted. With this much rain there'd soon be green feed everywhere.

He found a clean pair of jeans and shirt and made his way to the bathroom for a shower. As the warm water ran over his body he found himself recalling images from yesterday: Shelley in shorts and clinging top, helping him hook up the boat; Shelley in a bikini, water beading off her breasts as he hauled her into the dinghy; Shelley kissing him in the ute and responding with a gratifying enthusiasm. He fired up at the recollection.

If he hadn't stopped to think about condoms, they'd have been past the point of no return in another few moments. While his body was aching in regret that it hadn't happened, his head was plain relieved. She'd said she wasn't even on the pill. What a pair of fools that would have made them if she'd ended up pregnant. And he still hadn't visited the doctor since Miranda had left. Although his recent sexual history was chaste enough to satisfy his own grandmother, he couldn't be totally sure he was safe since his loving wife had cheated on him. He'd have to get that checked.

Shelley and Mitch were already in the kitchen preparing breakfast when he walked in. In response to his greeting she gave him a tentative, awkward smile. His pulse quickened. What was this fatal attraction he had to city girls? Not that Shelley and Miranda seemed to have much else in common. Although he hadn't realised it at first, Miranda had the morals of an alley cat. Shelley, on the other hand, seemed genuinely mortified at the way they had behaved last night.

'Mum and Dad tried to ring last night,' Mitch informed him. 'They left a message, said they're in Greece. They mightn't get a chance to try again for a few days.'

Luke gave Shelley a wry look.

'Looks like we'll be kept in the dark a bit longer.' He turned back to his brother. 'Did you measure the rain?'

'Four and a half inches.' Mitch, busily buttering toast, gave him a sideways glance. 'The dam's nearly full.'

'Wow, that's good. Let's hope the rain keeps coming.'

'Not until I've got away from here,' Shelley muttered.

Luke looked at her quickly. It stung that she wanted to leave so badly, even though he acknowledged she was being sensible. She'd said that she hadn't wanted to complicate his life. And anyway, who'd want to get involved with him at the moment? But the thought of her going and the possibility that they'd never get to finish what had nearly happened left a yawning space inside of him.

'The road's a bit wet today, but with the sun on it you'll get out tomorrow.' He grabbed mugs from the cupboard and gave Shelley a questioning glance, trying to pretend it didn't matter to him what she did. 'Coffee?'

She turned from setting the table, flicking back her long dark hair which she'd left hanging free.

'I'd love one. So what's planned for today?'

'I've got some bookwork to catch up on this morning. After lunch, when it's dried out a bit, I want to do some work with the weaners.' He paused. 'Would you like to go for a ride?'

Her face brightened but she hesitated. Was she uncertain about getting on a horse? Or wondering if spending more time with him was a good idea? Apparently she decided it was worth the risk.

'I'd love that. I told you I used to do Pony Club, didn't I? But I haven't been on a horse for years.'

~*~

Shelley didn't know whether to be glad or sorry when Mitch said he was spending the afternoon in Faradale with his girlfriend. It was obvious he guessed there was something between her and Luke, and she wasn't sure how he felt about it. Was he afraid of another city girl messing with Luke's life? Well, he needn't worry, she thought. She was out of here tomorrow.

Luke herded the horses into the yard with his motorbike and found some spare tack in the shed. As they each carried their gear to the yard she tried not to watch him. She'd thought him attractive in boating clothes yesterday, but that couldn't compare to how he looked in jeans, work shirt and riding boots. It was funny, because when her friends had been drooling over the guys in *The Farmer Wants a Wife*, she'd barely looked twice.

He helped her catch a little chestnut mare with a narrow blaze on her face.

'She's a quiet little thing, nice to ride,' he told her. 'Her name's Tess. She's part Quarter Horse.'

Shelley stroked the mare's velvety nose, inhaling that familiar horsey scent with a pang of nostalgia for her Pony Club days. Nerves fluttered in her stomach. It had been so long and this wasn't her safe, fat pony. Tess nudged her gently, watching her with a steady, trusting eye as Shelley heaved the heavy stock saddle onto her back. She looked askance at the string girth and the leather lacing that hung from a surcingle on the saddle. She'd only ever ridden in an English saddle with a buckled girth.

'I think I need help here.'

She stepped back a little as Luke deftly laced the girth, torn between her desire to learn and her ridiculous reaction to his proximity. Those same brown hands had been just as deft and sure last night as they touched her body in ways that turned her on. His tense expression made her wonder if his thoughts were travelling along similar lines.

Once her mount was ready, Shelley leant against the rail and watched as he caught and saddled a big brown gelding, admiring the quiet, proficient way he handled the horse. Then he held Tess's head as Shelley mounted, heaving herself laboriously into the saddle. Luke looked at her uncertainly.

'Do you want to ride her around the yard a bit first?'

'Yes please.'

Shelley shifted her seat in the saddle, uncomfortable with the high kneepads and the strange horse between her knees. Although Tess wasn't tall, the ground looked a long way down. Luke led his horse out of the yard and shut the gate behind them.

'Just ride around and get the feel of her.'

Gingerly Shelley nudged the mare into a walk. Tess felt light and sensitive under her hands and heels, so different to her old pony. She wondered if she should urge her into a trot, but she wasn't quite brave enough.

'I think you'll manage,' said Luke, eyeing her critically.

He opened the gate for her and then swung into his own saddle with grace and ease. He turned his gelding towards the stockyards.

'Let's go tackle these weaners.'

'I hope that's not going to involve hard riding.'

Luke turned and grinned.

'Don't worry. We'll just ride amongst them so they get used to the horses. We might let them into a bigger yard, but they won't be able to get away from us.'

When they rode into the muddy, steaming yard, the weaners milled anxiously, thickening the air with acrid scents of manure and urine. Tess pricked her ears, watching the cattle as if she knew what was expected of her. The calves seemed to accept the horses with a readiness that surprised Shelley. She sat her mount near the rails and watched as Luke turned them away from his horse.

'I'll let them into the bigger yard now,' he said at last. 'Ride in front of them with me and we'll steady them when they run.'

The young cattle seemed reluctant to leave their familiar pen at first. Then a more adventurous steer cautiously led the way. One or two followed and suddenly the rest surged through the gate in a rush. Tess broke into a trot and Shelley bounced in the saddle, grabbing at the pommel for support.

'Pull her up!'

Pulling on the reins and holding onto the saddle were difficult to do simultaneously. The next moment Luke was beside her, leaning from his saddle to grasp her rein and drag the mare to a halt.

'I thought you could ride!'

Tess tossed her head and sidled in agitation, increasing Shelley's discomfort.

'Sorry. I panicked.'

'It helps to hang on with your legs, not your hands.' He gave her an encouraging smile.

'I'll try to remember that.'

'Okay. Just follow what I do.'

Luke released her rein and rode towards the end of the yard where the cattle were now milling, having run past them while he was busy helping her. He must be wishing he'd left her at home, Shelley thought.

For the next twenty minutes or so he rode amongst the mob, herding them from one end of the yard to the other, using words like "whoa" and "steady" in a soothing voice. Shelley did her best to follow suit, realising that her mare relaxed as soon as her focus returned to the cattle. By the time Luke announced it was time to go home, she'd gained her confidence with the horse and had even managed a trot once or twice.

Luke nodded his approval.

'We'll make a ringer of you yet.'

'I could probably learn to enjoy this.' She was absurdly pleased at the faint praise, although she knew all credit was due to Tess, who obviously knew a lot more about cattle work than she did.

'I'll get Mitch to help me tail them out of the yard tomorrow. It's a pity you're leaving – you could've lent a hand.'

Don't encourage me to change my mind, she thought, neither of us needs that.

Back at the homestead, she felt unaccountably bereft as she removed Tess's saddle and, following Luke's example, hosed her down. She slipped off the bridle and scratched the sweaty place behind the mare's ears, and stood silently watching as the horses trotted off with their heads up as they searched for the rest of the herd. Looking around her at the soaked paddock, she thought the trees' foliage had already brightened in response to the rain.

Until now, she hadn't realised how much she missed horses and riding. Shelley remembered how devastated she'd been when she'd outgrown her pony at the age of twelve. Her father, who had been establishing his business as a builder, had said they couldn't afford to buy her another horse. She'd soon filled the void with friends, clothes, shopping and school. Would her life have been different if her parents been in a position to indulge her?

~*~

Shelley set off after breakfast the next morning, careful to ensure that the car straddled the rutted wheel tracks on the dirt road. Luke had given her directions for a direct route to Rockhampton which he assured her was much shorter than driving through Clermont. He estimated she should be home within three or four hours.

Home, Shelley thought, where was that these days? She'd lived away from her parents for too long to consider their house her home any more. It was just a temporary refuge – she hoped. She certainly didn't feel like someone returning to the fold; instead there seemed to be an unseen force tugging her heart and mind back to Breakaway Creek. It was more than her foolish attraction to Luke. She'd sensed a spiritual affinity with the place, with the very earth and rocks and trees, which she'd never known before. Did it have something to do with her ancestor who had possibly been born there?

Her mother was home to greet her when she arrived. Because Noela Blake worked in the family-owned business, her hours were flexible and she'd obviously taken time off to spend with Shelley.

'This is exciting.' Noela hugged her warmly. 'Tell me all about these Sherman brothers. And what did you find out about our ancestors?'

Shelley filled her in with the little she'd learned about the Baxters, but evaded most of the questions about Luke and Mitch. It wasn't like her not to confide in her mother, but she didn't want to talk about Luke. If only it was that easy to stop thinking about him.

When her mother went to make a phone call, Shelley booted up her computer and distracted herself by searching the rental market in Brisbane. She'd need somewhere to live when she went back to work. But as she read each property description, nothing jumped out. City living had excited her once, but her memories of Brisbane were tied up with Jason. He'd soured it for her. The thought of travelling on a crowded train to work each morning and sitting all day inside four walls behind a computer now seemed vaguely depressing.

Fortunately there was no interrogation from her father when he arrived home. Peter Blake looked hot and tired from a long day on a building site and was happy to relax in front of the television with a cold beer. Shelley had never been as close to him as to her mother, but she knew he loved having her at home, even if he didn't actually say so.

A few days later, the arrival of an official-looking envelope stirred her out of her lassitude. She ripped it open find the marriage and birth certificates she'd requested at the Clermont courthouse. Shelley scanned them eagerly. The first recorded only the bare facts of Alexander and Emma's marriage on the February 16, 1898, but it was the birth certificate that intrigued her.

William Alexander Baxter was born on the November 20, 1898, in Clermont. The father was listed as Alexander Baxter, a stockman of twenty-seven years, his birthplace Breakaway Creek, Clermont. The mother was Emma Anne Baxter, née Watson, twenty-two years, born in Brisbane.

Shelley did a quick calculation. That put the birth at almost exactly nine months after the wedding. But if Alex had died, wouldn't he have been listed as deceased?

'You should apply for Emma's birth certificate,' Noela suggested. 'That'll help if you want to trace that side of the family.'

'Yes, I'll do that,' Shelley agreed, inwardly wincing at the thought of another twenty-five dollar fee. Her funds would be stretched by the time she went back to work.

Later that night the phone rang.

'It's for you.' Her mother beckoned her over, covering the mouthpiece with her hand. 'It's that Luke Sherman.'

Shelley's pulse leapt. She took the receiver, her heart thudding so loudly she was almost sure Luke would be able to hear it over the phone.

'Hi Luke,' she managed in a casual tone.

'Hello, Shelley. How're you going? I couldn't get you on your mobile.'

'Sorry, I left it in my bedroom.' After a brief exchange of pleasantries she decided to cut to the chase. 'Have you heard from your mother yet?'

'Yeah, that's why I'm ringing.' He paused. 'She knows the whole story, Shelley, but I don't want to tell you over the phone. I'm driving to Brisbane tomorrow to see the boys. Is it okay if I drop in to see you on the way home?'

'Of course.' Her heart was hammering. She wasn't sure if it was from her anticipation at finally solving the family mystery, or the thought of seeing Luke again. 'I'd better tell you how to find us.'

Halfway through her garbled attempt to give directions – Shelley had never had much aptitude for it, and right now her brain wasn't working at all – he cut her short.

'Just give me the address and I'll find you.'

'Sorry.' She gave him the information. 'It's a low brick home with a Poinciana tree in the front yard.'

'I'll let you know when I'm coming. I'm not sure how long I'll be in Brisbane.'

'I hope everything works out for you, Luke.'

There was a momentary pause, and when he spoke again his voice had softened.

'I hope so too. I'll see you soon, Shelley.'

~*~

It was early evening when Luke reached the outskirts of Brisbane. The ten-hour drive had left him gritty-eyed and yawning, so he decided to find himself a motel. After tea he planned to ring Miranda and arrange to see the boys – hopefully tomorrow. She hadn't answered the phone when he'd tried to contact her the night before, but he had mentioned the previous week that he was coming down.

He went into the drive-through at a Red Rooster and bought a chicken dinner before checking in at the first motel he saw. He ate his lonely meal sitting on the bed with the television tuned to a game show. When he'd finished eating the last of his chips, he turned the sound down and dialled Miranda's number on his mobile phone.

His spirits rose when a childish voice said hello.

'Ben! How's my little mate?'

'Daddy?' The child hesitated, breathing loudly into the mouthpiece. 'Is that you?'

'Yes, it is.' His heart twisted with the familiar love and longing. 'How are you?'

'Where are you, Daddy? I want to see you.'

'I'm here in Brisbane, little mate. I'll see you soon. Is something wrong?'

'I'm scared.' Ben's voice trembled. 'There's a monster under my bed.'

'Are you sure? Ask Mummy to chase it away.'

'But Mummy's not here.'

'What do you mean?' He heard his voice sharpen and tried for a softer tone. 'Where is Mummy?'

'Mummy and Bevan have gone somewhere.'

'Where have they gone?' He tried to keep the rising panic out of his voice. 'Is Jack there?'

'Yes, Jack's here, but he's scared of the monsters too.'

'How long have Mummy and Bevan been away?'

'I don't know. Mummy bought us a pizza, an' she said we had to eat it and go to bed.' The little voice broke into a sob. 'But I'm too scared to go to bed.'

'Don't worry, Ben. I'm coming over to see you right now. Is the front door locked?'

'Yes, Mummy locked it.'

'Well, when I come, I'll knock on the door three times, like this.' He held the phone close to the bedside table and rapped on it. 'You can open the door then, but don't open it to anyone else. I'll see you soon, Ben. I love you.'

'I love you too, Daddy.'

~*~

He had Miranda's address in Petrie. She'd moved since the last time he was in Brisbane. Thinking of his little boys alone and scared in the house made him clench his fists with fury. That bloody woman! She'd never been a careful mother, and the distraction of a boyfriend like Bevan wouldn't help. She was keeping the boys only for the maintenance payments, and to spite him.

The house turned out to be a weatherboard cottage in a poorer area of the suburb. In the headlights the garden looked neglected; a few tired shrubs straggled against the front wall. Miranda hadn't exactly come up in the world. Cynically, he wondered what Bevan was doing for work since he'd left the mines.

Luke jumped out of the four-wheel-drive wagon and locked it, almost running up the path. He paused to steady himself, drawing in a ragged breath as he knocked three times on the front door.

He heard a shuffle inside, and then a small, frightened voice.

'Is that you, Daddy?'

'Yes, it is. Open the door, Ben.'

The door opened to reveal his elder son, his eyes wide and tearful. Luke made a muffled exclamation and stooped to gather him into a tight embrace. The child's soft hair tickled his cheek as Ben flung his arms around his neck, clinging desperately. Then Jack was there beside him and Luke scooped him up with the other arm, carrying both boys to a sofa and sinking down with them on his lap.

'Are you both all right? You poor little buggers. Has your mother left you on your own before?'

'Once,' Ben told him solemnly. 'On her birthday, she and Bevan went out.'

'Did she now? And what was her excuse this time?'

'She said we'd been naughty. She needed a break.'

Luke made a disgusted sound.

'Well, she can have a good, long break this time. Come on, we'll go and pack your clothes. I'm taking you home with me.'

Jack's face lit up.

'Can we really go home? To our proper home?'

'Yes, you can. Not tonight, because it's too far. But tomorrow we'll go home.'

Ben clapped his hands.

'That means I can see Biddy and Buttons and ride Rambo again.'

He got the boys to show him to their bedroom. It was a mess of unmade beds, scattered toys and dirty clothes on the floor. He bundled clothes into two suitcases, instructing the boys to add their favourite toys.

'Hey, that's enough,' he protested, when both cases were threatening to overflow. 'Anymore and your bags will burst. You'll be too busy outside to play with this lot at home.'

In the kitchen he found a notepad and scribbled a note for Miranda.

I rang to find the boys on their own, so I came straight over. They were terrified. I'm taking them home with me. It's obvious you're not looking after them properly. I'm going to contact my lawyer and I'd advise you not to challenge me on this. Your track record speaks for itself. Luke.

He cast one final glance around. A pile of dirty dishes filled the sink and a pizza carton sat on the table. He sniffed the air suspiciously, detecting a tang of something that wasn't stale food and swore under his breath. He knew that smell and it wasn't cigarette smoke.

'Did you boys finish eating your pizza?'

Ben shook his head.

'We weren't very hungry.'

Luke compressed his lips, containing his anger. No wonder they were so scared. He lifted the carton lid to find a nearly untouched pizza inside.

'We'll take this with us. You might want it later.' He glanced at the boys' bare feet. 'Where are your shoes?'

Ben shrugged. 'In the laundry, I think.'

'Show me where that is and we'll get them.'

Ben pointed to a small room beyond the kitchen. As he bent to gather up two small pairs of joggers, he noticed a tall potted plant in the corner. It had long, pointed leaves with serrated edges and he had no trouble recognising it. His lips thinned even further.

'Daddy, did you get my medicine?' Ben asked from the doorway.

Luke looked down at his son.

'What medicine is that?'

'I have sore ears. The medicine's up here.' He led the way back into the kitchen and pointed to the high cupboard above the sink.

Luke opened the cupboard door and found a bottle of prescription antibiotics with Ben's name on it. Then he noticed a plastic zip-lock bag pushed to the back of the cupboard and pulled it out. The hairs on the back of his neck stiffened as he saw the white powder inside. He opened it and sniffed, then swore under his breath and pushed the bag back in its hiding place.

'Come on boys, let's go.'

Stuffing the medicine bottle into Ben's bag, he carried the luggage out and bundled the boys into the back seat of the wagon. In less than half an hour they were back at the motel. He lifted Jack into his arms and took Ben's hand, relinquishing it only to unlock the door. The boys stared at the big double bed inside.

'Where will we sleep, Daddy?'

'You can sleep with me. Just for tonight, mind. No getting into bad habits here.'

'Jack needs a nappy,' Ben informed him importantly. 'Otherwise he wets the bed.'

'It's lucky I got some nappies from your cupboard, then.' Luke let his face rest against the silky softness of his youngest son's hair, drinking in the childish smell of him. He'd missed the boys so much. They were so precious, and it tore at his gut to think of that selfish bitch neglecting them.

He didn't sleep well that night. Both boys clung like limpets in the bed, and their incessant wriggling and tossing would have been enough to disturb his slumber even if his mind hadn't been seething with worry and anger. He knew taking the boys was a risky move. It would antagonise Miranda and she was likely to use it against him. But in all conscience he couldn't have left them there. He would fight her every inch of the way if she tried to take them back.

In the early hours of the morning he eventually dozed off. Jack's cries woke him and it took ages to settle him again. Consequently, Luke slept until seven, long past his usual waking time. Groggy and disorientated, he revived himself with two cups of strong coffee before setting out on the road to Rockhampton.

Fortunately for him the boys were excited at the prospect of returning to Breakaway Creek and were on their best behaviour. When they became restless he dug out an old Wiggles CD and cajoled them into a sing-along.

When they stopped at a roadhouse so the boys could use the toilet, Luke let them run around a grassy area. He took out his mobile, glad he had his lawyer's number. When he explained the events of the previous night, there was a brief silence.

'You realise you haven't helped your case here, Luke?'

Although he'd expected to hear as much, Luke's stomach churned.

'But how could I leave them there? What about the drugs?'

'Why don't you report them? If they're up on drug charges it should improve your chances.'

Could he dob in his own wife? The thought repulsed him.

'Let's wait and see. I don't know what she's going to do, yet.'

'A file for custody has to go through a dispute resolution process first. I'll try and set something up. You should be able to do it by phone or video link. Your wife might even agree to you having the boys.'

'Perhaps.' He doubted it.

'The problem for you is the courts usually favour the mother. But if you can prove that there are drugs involved…' the lawyer paused. 'Let me know what happens. Ring me as soon as you've talked to her.'

After lunch the boys slept for a couple of hours. When they stopped for fuel at Gin Gin he dialled Shelley's number.

'I wasn't expecting you back this soon,' she said when he told her where he was.

'Is it all right if I come and see you tomorrow? I'll tell you all the news then. I've got the boys with me.'

'Of course! But where are you staying tonight?'

'I'll find a motel when I get to Rocky.'

'There's a bull sale on and the town's pretty full. Why don't you stay with us?' She hesitated. 'Mum and Dad won't be home until late, though. They've got some bowls do on.'

'Are you sure? I wouldn't be putting you out?'

'No, it's fine. There are two spare bedrooms. I'll cook you some dinner.'

He found the house easily enough and pulled the wagon partly onto the grass verge, doing his best to ignore the boys' irritating squabbling in the back seat. As they tumbled out of the car, he put one each side of him to separate them.

'Come on, your best behaviour, boys. If you can't be good I'll have to put you back in the car and find a motel.'

Shelley opened the door at his knock. The sight of her made him forget how weary he was. Her dark hair was twisted up on top of her head and just a few tendrils hung loose about her face. She was wearing brief denim shorts that made his eyes keep drifting to her long, shapely legs. A clinging singlet top emphasised those breasts he'd once kissed and hadn't been able to forget. With an effort he focussed on an appropriate greeting and introduced the boys.

She bent down to them with a natural charm that warmed him.

'So these two big boys are Ben and Jack. I'm so pleased to meet you. I saw your photo, you know.'

'Shelley stayed at our house for a few days. She's a relation of ours.' Luke explained. He smiled at her. 'I really appreciate you having us like this.'

Shelley gave him a questioning look.

'So you decided I'm a relation?'

'Yeah.' He grinned. 'A thirty-second cousin, or something. I'll tell you all about it later. But if I can get this pair of rascals bathed and fed first, that would be great.'

Shelley ran a bath for the boys and went to fetch Luke a cold beer while he helped them undress. When he had them both in the tub he looked up to find her standing in the doorway.

'Sit in the lounge room,' she told him. 'If I stay near the doorway I can watch the boys in the bath.' She poured a glass of wine for herself and positioned her chair.

'Do you want to tell me what happened in Brisbane?'

'I hadn't planned to take the boys.' Luke settled himself in a leather recliner and sipped his beer. 'I found them alone in the house so I just grabbed them. The poor little buggers were terrified.'

Shelley's eyes opened wide.

'You mean Miranda had gone off and left them?'

He nodded.

'She was out partying with her boyfriend.' His teeth clenched with renewed fury and he took a deep breath to calm himself. 'Not the first time she's done it, apparently.'

'Poor little kids.' Her face creased with concern and he found himself contrasting her to his wife. Miranda thought of herself first and only noticed other people when it suited her. 'Do you think she'll make trouble?'

'She'd bloody better not. I spoke to my lawyer and he told me we have to go through a dispute resolution process before anything else happens.'

'So meanwhile you're left in limbo. Are you going to divorce her?'

'Yeah, but we have to be separated for a year, first.' Ben called from the bathroom and he rose, putting down his beer. 'I'll be back in a minute.'

Ben's skinny body bobbed amongst the frothy bubbles Shelley had let them use.

'I'm clean now,' he informed his father cheerfully.

Jack piled bubbles on his chin and looked up at his father, giggling. 'Look, Daddy. I've got a beard.'

'So you have.' Luke smiled down at them, grabbing one of the clean towels Shelley had provided. There was a catch in his voice when he spoke.

'Come on, who's first out?'

~*~

After dinner, when the boys were tucked up in bed, Shelley and Luke took their drinks onto the front porch. Memories of the last time they'd been alone in the dark tantalised Luke, so that when Shelley spoke he had difficulty focussing on her question.

'Have you found a housekeeper yet?' Or at least that was what he gathered she'd asked.

He shook his head, as much to clear his thoughts as to reply.

'A housekeeper? No one wants to come to the bush. You'd think there'd be lonely women lining up to look after a couple of blokes like Mitch and me.'

She laughed.

'Have you got tickets on yourself, or what? But you'll need help even more now. How do you think you'll manage with the boys?'

'It's going to be a challenge. I can take them with me sometimes, but not when we're mustering. I'll have to leave them in day-care in town sometimes.'

She took a deep breath. The words came out in a rush, as if she was afraid she'd change her mind if she stopped to consider.

'I still have a few weeks of leave. I can help you out for a while, until you find someone else.'

His pulse missed a beat and he turned to stare at her, wishing he could read her expression better.

'This is a change of heart.'

'The boys need stability after what they've been through. I think they're gorgeous and I'd enjoy looking after them. Besides, I'm getting bored here.'

'I really appreciate this, Shelley.' In truth, the pleasure and surprise was tinged with caution. As far as the boys were concerned, it was a wonderful solution, but what was he getting into? His hormones were cheering her decision, but that was enough reason for his brain to signal a warning. He made a resolution to go shopping for certain personal items before he left Rockhampton.

Of course there was the information his mother had told him about Alexander Baxter. Would it make a difference to how Shelley felt about Breakaway Creek or her relationship with him?

'Before you commit yourself, I'd better tell you what my mother had to say about your ancestor.'

'That sounds ominous.' Her eyes scanned his face anxiously. 'I've been on tenterhooks about this since yesterday.'

Luke drew in a deep breath, strangely reluctant to speak now that the time for disclosure had come.

'Mum and Dad will be home in few weeks and I guess we'll find out more then. But this is what she told me over the phone.' He raised his glass and swallowed a mouthful of beer. 'I hope this isn't going to upset you.'

She stared at him with narrowed eyes.

'You're worrying me. Is it that bad?'

'I don't think it is. I hope you don't either. It's not what I expected, though.' He paused, searching for the right words. 'I'd better start at the beginning.'

Chapter Seven

Breakaway Creek, 1897

Emma waited nervously at the creek for Alex to join her. Even in the shade it was hot, and he was late. Sweat dampened her palms and trickled between her breasts, making her chemise stick to her skin.

Perhaps he couldn't come. Perhaps he'd changed his mind and no longer wanted to see her, she thought. Perhaps the way she'd responded to him yesterday had disgusted him. He hadn't proposed marriage, after all. What if he was only amusing himself with her?

When he finally appeared her pulse leapt. She tried to appear unconcerned as she sat on the grassy bank, her knees drawn up and her feet tucked under her skirt, but her fingers restlessly twisted of a stalk of grass and wouldn't be still. As he came closer she noticed his bleak face and trepidation accelerated her heart rate. She hadn't seen him look so troubled before.

'Emma.' He took off his hat to reveal tousled dark hair and sank down beside her. 'I'm glad you came. I need to talk to you.'

'This sounds ominous.' She tried to keep her tone light, even though her heart thudded against her ribs. Stealing a quick glance at his face, she noted a fine sheen of sweat on his brown skin. Was it the heat, or was he just as uneasy as she? She wound the grass stalk around her finger, then dropped it quickly when she saw it stained red with her blood. Sucking the stinging cut, she fumbled in her sleeve for a handkerchief and looked up to find him watching her, his dark eyes intent on her face.

'Emma, I meant what I said yesterday.' His throat rippled as he swallowed and she realised he was nervous. 'I think the world of you. I haven't been toying with your affections – never think that. I want to ask you to marry me, but George has warned me your parents won't approve. And there's something you need to know.' He took a deep breath and stared over the water, not looking at her as he continued. 'I don't expect you'll still want me, but I have to take a chance. If I don't tell you, you'll find out anyway.'

Her corset seemed to constrict her breathing. His very manner alarmed her – this sounded far more serious than his lack of prospects.

'What are you talking about, Alex? I know you're adopted. That doesn't matter.'

'But I'm not, really.' He still wasn't looking at her and his face was set in grim lines. 'It's not like you think. You see, I'm only half adopted, if that makes sense. Sarah's not my mother but I am the old man's son.'

She stared at him, trying to understand.

'You were born to another woman.'

'Yes. Soon after he married Sarah. I don't think things have been good between them since.'

Emma's face flamed and she looked down at her hands, hardly knowing what to say or think. She knew she'd led a sheltered life, but she hadn't heard of a situation like this before. The silence pressed down on her until she had to break it. She asked the obvious question, even though she wasn't sure she wanted to know the answer.

'Who was your mother?'

'That's the hard part.' Glancing up, she saw his face contort as if with a painful memory. 'My father brought her to Breakaway Creek when he first came here in 1870. She was supposed to be his housekeeper, but she was his paramour as well. He was still carrying on with her even after he was promised to Sarah.' Alex took a deep breath and turned to Emma, his eyes intense and staring into hers. 'She was a half-caste Aboriginal.'

The breath rushed out of her and she stared at him in disbelief. Had she heard him properly? He looked nothing like the stockmen, or even Mrs Baxter's half-caste maid, Molly.

'W-what did you say?'

'I'm a quarter-caste, Emma. I know I don't look it, but it's the truth.'

The blood roared in her ears and everything seemed to spin around her. She remembered him talking about the Aboriginies at the station camp and there'd been no clue. He'd spoken of them as any settler would, and even when he mentioned the time he'd spent with them, he said it had been in the company of his brother, George. But it did explain his affinity for the land and the particular camaraderie he seemed to have with the Aboriginies.

Nausea churned her stomach. With dismay she remembered her father's sneering references to the few Aboriginies who remained around Brisbane. The way he'd spoken of them had seemed cruel to her, but she'd dismissed it from her mind. She'd never imagined that one day she'd discover the man who'd kissed and courted her shared their blood. If her father knew, he'd be more than furious!

Alex was watching and waiting for a response, but she couldn't think what to say. All that came to her were the details that didn't seem to fit. She cleared her throat, but her voice still croaked.

'Why did Mrs Baxter take you in? I can't imagine any woman doing that, in the circumstances.'

He sighed.

'My mother died when I was born but before she did, she asked Sarah to take care of me. I looked white and my mother didn't belong to the station tribe, so they wanted nothing to do with me. What was she supposed to do? If she'd handed me over to the authorities, there would have been a lot of gossip. Besides, she's always had a strong sense of obligation and I think it suited her to make a martyr of herself.'

Oh yes. That fitted Emma's impression of Mrs Baxter.

'She must have resented you.'

'I suppose so, but to her credit she treated me well enough. They told everyone, including me, that I was adopted. I was supposed to be some sort of cousin to the family. I just accepted that and didn't expect equal status.'

'But…' it was difficult for Emma to form coherent thoughts. 'You don't look black. I'm sorry, that sounds insulting.'

'My mother was only a half-caste. And my father is very fair.'

She found herself studying him, knowing she was being rude, but unable to help herself. His lips were full and his nostrils were wider than average, but she saw nothing of the broadness about his features that characterised the station Aboriginies and even Molly, who was a half-caste like his late mother.

Suddenly it was all more than she could deal with. Try as she might, she couldn't forget her father's derision. She jumped to her feet.

'Heavens, what am I supposed to do? If my parents knew about this …' their horror defied imagination. Her eyes smarted with unshed tears. 'I was so happy! I thought it didn't matter that you didn't have prospects! I thought I could tell them their approval didn't count. But this…'

He stood up, facing her. His face had whitened under his tan and she thought he was trembling, but it was hard to tell when she was shaking so much herself.

'It's my fault. I should have stayed away from you. I shouldn't have led you on.'

'No, you shouldn't have.' The anguish on his face cut her to the core but she couldn't tell him what he wanted to hear. Her voice shook. 'I have to think. I can't just say it doesn't matter.'

With an effort she met his pleading eyes.

'I have to go now, Alex.'

She walked away; conscious that he stood watching her. Knowing she was hurting him only added to the overwhelming mix of shock and pain, and, perhaps in self-defence, her feelings turned to anger. He'd kissed her yesterday and left her wallowing in foolish dreams, and now he'd destroyed them all. It wasn't fair.

'Emma.'

She paused and turned, her movements jerky and uncoordinated.

'Lucy doesn't know. I just thought I should warn you, in case you were going to talk to her.'

Well, that made sense. If Lucy had known she surely would have warned her of more than his lack of prospects. Emma nodded and resumed walking back to the house, wondering what she should do. Should she share the story with Lucy and risk upsetting her marriage? She would no doubt be as shocked as Emma. It was probably best to keep the knowledge to herself. It was the devil's choice, whichever way she looked at it.

In the end she couldn't bear to talk to anyone. When Emma found Lucy in the kitchen, she told her she felt ill and went straight to her room. As she lay on her bed the past few days revolved in her mind, reducing her to a trembling morass. She hadn't thought herself a prejudiced person. But it was one thing to accept a person of different race as a friend; to marry one was something else again. And the Aboriginies were scorned by European society. Her father was not alone in expressing contempt for their race.

Of course, Alex was no savage. He'd been raised a white man and he had more European blood than Aboriginal. But that wouldn't stop people shunning him if they knew the truth and her with him if she was his wife.

Supposing she married him, how would that affect any children they might have? She'd heard of babies who looked like throw-backs to their Aboriginal ancestors. If one of their children were born dark-skinned, Emma's parents – and society in general – would never accept the infant. Could she knowingly put her offspring at risk of being shunned and rejected by society?

She was no closer to an answer when Lucy knocked on the door and peered anxiously around it.

'How do you feel, Emma? Can you I bring you some supper?'

The thought of food made her stomach churn.

'No, thank you. I might make myself a cup of tea later.'

'I'll bring it to you.'

She struggled up on the bed.

'I appreciate your concern, Lucy, but I don't want you running after me. Please, just leave me be. I have a shocking headache.'

But she couldn't feign illness indefinitely. The next morning she waited until she knew George would have left the house before she came out for breakfast. He must know the truth about Alex and she couldn't bear to face him just yet, knowing he'd probably guess what had happened.

~*~

Alex was glad he was on his own that day. In no mood for anyone's company, he had taken his lunch and ridden off to check cattle at the far end of the property.

Just thinking of Emma's reaction made him heartsick. He'd been a fool to expect anything else. She was a city girl, not someone who'd grown up with the Aborigines. Even people who had were often far from accepting. Not many knew of his mixed blood, but of those who did only George treated him without discrimination. Even his father, who was responsible for him, acted as if he was somehow inferior.

No, he couldn't blame Emma, he thought. When he'd first found out the truth he'd been devastated. He'd been just as full of prejudice.

All through his childhood and the years at boarding school, he'd lived in happy ignorance. He'd always been shy, but he supposed that wasn't surprising given his upbringing. He'd known he was adopted and his father had largely ignored him. Mrs Baxter, to her credit, had treated him fairly but had never shown him any affection.

He'd felt like an outsider, hovering on the fringes of the family group. The only person he felt close to was George, who'd accepted him as a brother and a friend throughout their lives. In early childhood Alex had looked after his younger, smaller brother, and as they grew into adulthood their roles often had been reversed. George's outgoing, friendly nature made up for Alex's reserve.

Alex would never forget how he'd learned the truth about his parentage at just seventeen. He'd been home from boarding school for a couple of years and George had still been away. Their mother had recently taken a new maid into the house.

Molly, a half-caste, was a year or so younger than he. She'd grown up with the station Aborigines. Her father had been a white stockman who'd left Breakaway Creek years before without bothering to take his lover and child with him. She was no more used to life in a civilised house than her full-blood relatives, and Alex had watched in amusement as Sarah battled to train her to cook and clean. He'd thought her full, high breasts and skin the colour of chocolate attractive, but though he'd watched her he had no intention of pursuing her. He despised men who took advantage of Aboriginal women.

Possibly Molly had sensed his latent interest. She began to waylay him, deliberately attracting his attention and trying to talk to him. Alex had backed right off, aroused and repelled in equal measure.

Sarah had given the girl a little room at the back of the kitchen to sleep in. It wasn't close to his bedroom, but nor was it distant enough to keep her out of his way. One night when he had gone to the room he usually shared with George, he'd lit the kerosene lamp to reveal Molly lying in his bed.

At his shocked exclamation she'd sat up, letting the bedclothes fall to her waist. He'd drawn in a deep breath. In the soft lamplight she appeared completely naked. He'd seen the Aboriginal women's bare breasts plenty of times, but theirs were mostly sagging and unattractive. Molly had always been buttoned up tight in the cast-off dresses his mother had given her, and her breasts certainly didn't sag. Her nipples were high and puckered, and at that moment they had pointed right at him.

'Molly! Get out of here!' His blood pounding, he'd retreated until his back pressed against the wall. He hadn't dared stay closer for fear he'd lose control. 'I'll have you fired if you don't behave yourself.'

She'd only giggled.

'I know you want me, Boss. We can have a real good time. I won't tell no one.'

He hadn't doubted she could show him a good time and it became harder and harder to deny her.

'You're behaving like a slut, Molly.'

Her eyes had narrowed.

'You think you're too good for Molly? What's so special 'bout you? Growin' up in this house don't change nuthin'. You still black like me!'

Black like me! Her words had echoed in his brain, obliterating his awareness of her nakedness and crushing his desire. He'd stared at her, taking in her smirking satisfaction.

'What are you talking about?'

'Ha! You thought I didn't know! Your mumma was a different mob, but she was half black fella too. My mumma told me so.'

A tide of anger had risen in him, shocking him into fury.

'Shut up!' Alex had yelled. He'd snatched her clothes off the floor and threw them at her. 'Get out of here before I throw you out!'

She went without bothering to dress first. He'd slammed the door behind her and sank onto the bed, his face buried in his hands. When he sprang up, he'd walked to the mirror and held the lamp to his face. Wild eyes had stared back at him and his hair stood on end. He had examined himself: dark brown, almost black hair and dark brown irises, a nose that broadened at the nostrils, a wide mouth with full lips. He'd looked down at his burnt brown arms and unbuttoned his shirt, looking at his chest where the sun seldom touched; it was brown, too – not as dark as his arms, but brown nevertheless.

He hadn't been able to stand it. He had to know, one way or the other. He'd marched out to the sitting room, where Sarah sat on her rocker, knitting needles clacking in her busy fingers. Frank had smoked his pipe in another chair. Both of them were silent. They had looked up as he had swung through the door.

'What's going on?' His father had looked annoyed. 'Someone was shouting.'

Alex had ignored the question, looking at them both in turn.

'Who was my mother?'

Sarah blanched.

'You're a cousin to George. Your father was a Baxter. Your parents died in an accident when you were a baby.'

He'd turned to look at Frank. Frank had watched him carefully, saying nothing.

'That's not what Molly said.'

'What were you doing talking to Molly at this hour of the night?' Sarah's eyes had darted from Alex to Frank, her expression wary and defensive.

He'd just ignored her.

'Who was my mother? Molly told me she was Aboriginal.'

He'd expected angry denials, but instead there was a long silence. At last Sarah had made an angry sound and turned accusing eyes on her husband.

'I told you to tell him. I knew he'd find out. Well, this is your mess. You deal with it.' She'd dumped her knitting in the basket beside her chair and left the room without another word. Her chair had rocked wildly for a moment before slowing to a gentle rhythm and finally stopping.

Alex's stomach had churned. He'd stared at his father, willing the taciturn man to speak. His legs had been trembling, but he wouldn't sit down. Somehow he'd thought he could deal with the truth better on his feet.

'Molly was right,' Frank had said at last. He'd sounded almost indifferent. 'Your mother was a half-caste like Molly. I brought her here as my housekeeper. She died when you were born. Because she didn't belong to the local tribe, there was no one else to take you. Sarah decided it was up to her.'

'Who was my father?'

Frank had cleared his throat and looked down before meeting Alex's eye. Something had flickered in his face, but his voice never changed. 'I am.'

Perhaps, subconsciously, Alex had already begun to suspect it, but the words had still shocked him. Yet it had been the coldness in Frank's voice that had really stung. Alex had never before appreciated the depth of his callousness.

Frank had puffed at his pipe, outwardly unconcerned.

Alex had gaped.

'But I was born after you were married.' He hadn't been sure of the dates, but he knew that much.

'I stopped seeing the gin when I married Sarah, but I didn't know she was in foal until later.'

It had been too much. Hatred for his father's immorality and apparent lack of remorse had threatened to choke him. Alex had swung away from that hard face, strode out of the house, grabbed his swag and spent the night a couple of miles away in the horse-paddock. He hardly slept during that time, staring up at the distant stars while the events had replayed in his mind like a particularly vivid nightmare. When he awoke the torment was still with him.

It had taken Alex a long while to make peace with his heritage. He'd spent a lot of time with the Aborigines as a child. Although he liked them and respected their knowledge of the bush, he had realised that he subconsciously shared the sense of superiority most Europeans felt towards them. He didn't like knowing there were many who'd look down on him if they realised his mother was a half-caste. Worst yet was having to accept his father's cruelty. He hadn't even referred to Alex's mother by name. His offhand reference to "the gin" was the ultimate insult.

For a while Alex had sought the company of those who judged him the least. At the time his father employed two white stockmen at Breakaway Creek and Alex moved into the men's quarters with them. They took him to Clermont when they had time off and introduced him to liquor and gambling. One night at the station, heavily influenced by rum, he had finally taken Molly up on her offer.

Sarah had seen what was happening and cared enough to intervene. He still wasn't sure if she knew about Molly, but the influence of the stockmen had been obvious.

'I didn't bring you up so you could sink to that level,' she'd told him. 'You'd better move back to the house while you still can.'

Her stinging rebuke was all the encouragement he had needed. Never really comfortable with the stockmen, he moved back into his old room and told Molly it was over. When she married one of her own tribe a few months later and vacated her room, he had felt nothing but relief. Then George had come home from Brisbane and Alex had confided the whole sorry business to him. Good old George had taken it in his stride. It seemed that their father's part in the story had shocked him more than Alex's mixed blood.

~*~

Alex had come out of it with a new appreciation of Sarah. Whatever her motives, she'd done a brave thing by taking him in and raising him with her own children. He often caught her watching him with concerned eyes and realised she cared, in her undemonstrative fashion. He made an effort to talk to her in an attempt to show his thanks, understanding, now, what marriage to his father must be like. Although he and Frank hardly spoke, it was because of Sarah's loneliness that he still lived in the house.

One day he'd found the courage to confront his old man about his mother.

'What was her name?' he'd asked. 'Don't you think I'm entitled to know that?'

Frank had looked at him as if he couldn't understand why.

'Her name was Eliza,' he'd muttered. 'Don't you think you should forget about her?'

Alex had ignored him.

'Where was she from?'

'Her mother was from a Hunter Valley tribe. That's where I worked before I came up here. I doubt she ever knew who her father was.'

'Why did she die?'

Frank never met his eyes.

'She bled to death. Don't ask me why. They don't usually have that sort of trouble.'

Alex had challenged him with a hard stare.

'She was all alone, away from her people, and you sound as if you didn't give a damn.'

Frank had shrugged.

'It was a pity. She was a good type, for a gin.' He must have seen the disgust in his son's eyes, for he'd added, 'Not that I touched her after I got married.'

That was all Alex ever found out about her. He didn't want to upset Sarah and he was too proud to ask the tribesmen. He did discover where she was buried – on a rise above the creek with only a piece of sandstone marking her grave. He erected a wooden cross and carved her name into the timber along with the words: Rest in Peace. Occasionally he visited the site, determined that his mother's short life would not be completely forgotten. She was his mother and he would honour her, whatever the colour of her skin.

Chapter Eight

Emma needed to talk to someone. Perhaps if she spoke about Alex's revelations, she'd be able to sort her jumbled feelings. But she couldn't betray Alex to Lucy. Her cousin had already quizzed her and Emma had fobbed her off with a half-truth.

'Alex asked me to marry him, but I don't know what to do,' she'd said. 'Mother and Father would never accept him.'

Lucy looked at her anxiously.

'I warned you this was going to happen. Do you love him?'

Emma hesitated. She'd thought she did, but now she wasn't sure of anything. If she really loved him would his mixed ancestry matter?

'I'm very fond of him. I just don't know if it will be enough. He doesn't even have a home to offer me.'

'George will never ask him to leave Breakaway Creek. He loves Alex like a blood brother. There's plenty of room for another house here.'

If only you knew, Emma thought, that he really is a blood brother. But much as she loved Lucy, she wondered if living in such close proximity to her cousin and her husband was a good idea, especially given Alex's circumstances. However good George and Lucy's intentions were, there would always be a divide and the potential for resentment that it could create.

That afternoon Emma went for her usual stroll by the creek, but didn't see Alex. She hadn't expected to. She supposed he would wait for her to make contact now. On her way back to the house, George fell into step with her as she passed the shed, his day's work over. He gave her a searching look.

'You've looked miserable the past day or so.'

Emma coloured.

'Is it that obvious?'

'Something to do with Alex?' The question was gently probing. 'He's been wretched, too.'

Emma hesitated, but then came to a quick decision. In the circumstances, George was probably the best person to talk to. Her words came out in a breathless rush.

'Alex wants to marry me. But he also told me who his mother was.'

For a moment, George didn't speak. Emma gave him a sideways, apprehensive glance as she tried to gauge his reaction. He didn't look surprised, merely worried.

'I guessed as much,' he said at last. 'And you're having trouble coming to terms with it.'

She flushed.

'Do you think I'm narrow-minded? Are you thinking that if I really loved him it shouldn't matter? This has shocked me to the core. And then there are my parents.'

'As far as your parents go, I think you'll have to decide who's more important to you. From what Lucy's let slip, they'll never accept a son-in-law with mixed blood. Of course, if you don't tell them they may never find out.'

'That's true. But it would be disastrous if they did. It's a difficult decision. I thought I loved Alex, but I'm not sure if it's enough.'

He stopped and took her arm, turning her to face him. He looked very serious.

'Be very certain if you decide to marry him, Emma. Because it will be difficult. If you're not sure, you'd best forget him.'

George's last words stayed with her for the next couple of days. She knew she wasn't being fair to Alex. She couldn't just keep him in limbo, and she owed him more than the angry words of their last meeting. But the chance to speak with him alone didn't present itself.

As she worked in the garden one morning she spotted him leading a horse towards the blacksmith's shop. Quickly she ducked out the front gate, hastening to make the most of her opportunity.

He'd tied the horse at the front of the shed and was inside, raking the smouldering coals in the forge and turning the handle of the blower to make them glow and crackle. As she entered the shed the heat of the fire met her in a shimmering wave that was oppressive in the confines of the iron building. Alex looked up, apparently sensing her presence although he couldn't have heard her above the whir of the blower. His features tensed, the pain in his eyes making all her emotions crowd to the surface, like the perspiration already beading on her skin.

'Emma. I didn't expect to speak to you again.'

His matter-of-fact words stung.

'You insult me if you think that.' Her voice shook. 'I came to apologise for what I said. It wasn't fair.'

'Why not?' He set down the blackened poker and turned to face her fully. 'You were right. I should have stayed away from you.'

'No, Alex. Your Aboriginal blood doesn't repulse me and you don't need to shun women because of it. But I can imagine lots of difficulties for us and my family's not the least of them. I've been agonising for days and I've finally decided what's best. I'm going back to Brisbane.'

He swallowed and looked away. His lids dropped as if to conceal his thoughts, but she sensed his distress as strongly as if it was her own. Perhaps it was.

'I expected that.' His voice sounded resigned, almost defeated.

'I'm sorry, Alex.' A dreadful finality swept her; it was the realisation that she'd closed a door that wouldn't open again. Her eyes stung with threatening tears. 'I have extremely strong feelings for you. I just don't know if it would be enough.'

'I can understand that. Thank you for coming to tell me.' He turned back to the forge, spinning the handle on the blower and sending sparks flying from the glowing charcoal. Fine ash blew from the forge as he stirred the coals. Then he picked up a rasp and walked over to the horse, bending to pick up one of its front hooves.

Emma watched him for a moment, noticing the way his muscles moved under his shirt as he rasped the chipped edges of the hoof wall. He didn't look at her again and she realised their conversation had ended. Numbly she moved around the other side of the gelding, pausing to run a caressing hand down its neck. It switched its tail and bent its head to sniff her arm, then resumed its stance. She didn't want to leave, but she had no excuse to stay. Feeling ignored, she retreated to the house.

She had to break the news to Lucy, she realised. Staying here wouldn't be fair on Alex or her. And yet, she desperately did not want to go. Lucy was ironing clothes in the kitchen. As Emma walked in, her cousin returned a flatiron to the stove's hotplate, released the wooden handle and picked up another. The wood fire made the room unbearably hot and perspiration stuck loose strands of hair to her face.

Emma took the iron out of Lucy's unresisting hand.

'Let me do this. Sit over there, please. I need to talk to you.'

Lucy gave a relieved sigh and did as she was bid, pulling up one of the wooden chairs at the kitchen table. She took a handkerchief from her sleeve and mopped her face.

'Why do I feel so tired?' She patted the gentle mound of her stomach. 'I'm only six months gone.'

Then she gave Emma a second look and her expression changed. 'What's wrong?'

'I've decided it's time to go home.' Emma looked up from the shirt she was ironing and saw the protest forming on her cousin's lips. She put up a hand to forestall her. 'I need to get away from Alex. I've decided I can't marry him, and it's too painful to keep seeing each other.'

'What a shame.' Lucy's mouth drooped. 'I don't want you to go, but I know that's being selfish. Promise me you'll come back when the baby's born?'

'I promise.' Emma wondered if she was being rash, but the baby was still three months away. In three months' time she and Alex would be over this infatuation. She hoped.

George took her to Clermont a few days later to catch the train. Saying goodbye to Lucy had made Emma feel as if she was deserting her cousin, and her stomach churned with the need to see Alex again. But he had kept himself well out of sight; her last memory of him was as a distant figure riding away with the two stockmen.

As the buggy trundled through the horse paddock gate she looked back at the homestead, her eyes drawn to the line of trees marking the creek. Inside her was an aching void that even Lucy's and George's cheerful friendship hadn't been able to fill. The prospect of returning to the house in Brisbane with only her harping mother and autocratic father for company was bleak indeed. She could merely hope Mr Timms had found another female to pursue in the meantime.

~*~

Brisbane was more frenetic than Emma remembered. After the unhurried pace of the bush, the hustling, crowded streets intimidated her. For the first time she truly appreciated how Alex must have felt when he visited the city. She found herself missing the animals, the trees and the open spaces. But most of all she missed Alex. It was one thing to have made a decision not to marry him, but her heart didn't seem to be listening.

Her mother interrogated her about her time away, making disparaging comments about the primitive conditions at Breakaway Creek until Emma refused to listen. Her father showed little interest, but took every opportunity to sing the praises of Mr Timms. When she attended a dinner party with her parents, he was obtrusively present, hovering around her like a lovesick puppy. He repelled her more than ever, and after Alex's natural sincerity his attentions were unconvincing.

With his fair hair, soft hands and flabby body he presented a complete contrast to Alex's dark and work-hardened good looks. Mostly Mr Timms was all affability, but on occasion he make sneering remarks about his colleagues, which made Emma wonder if his easy-going manner was a charade. He never lacked for conversation since his favourite topic was himself. Emma found herself longing for Alex's quiet dignity. Time and again she relived her time spent with him and their kiss. She had hurt him badly, and now she feared she'd made a grave mistake.

Christmas came and went in the usual manner. On New Year's Eve her parents hosted a party, inviting many of her father's business associates as well as a few friends and family. Of course Mr Timms was present. Emma did her best to keep him at arm's length but he was not easily rebuffed. Feeling stifled in the hot, airless drawing room, she escaped to the garden. The night breeze brought pleasant relief, drying the film of perspiration on her face and bare arms. She looked up at the stars, searching for Southern Cross while the babble of voices and a tinkling piano wafted from the open windows.

She swung around when someone spoke her name.

'Miss Watson, my dear. I saw you slipping out. Aren't you enjoying the party?'

'Mr Timms.' She tried to keep the dismay from her voice. 'It's so hot inside.'

'Indeed it is.' He came up beside her and she saw the glint of teeth as he smiled. 'You look beautiful tonight.'

She almost laughed.

'I'm not beautiful, Mr Timms, and you know it.'

'I know no such thing.' He sounded indignant. 'I admire you greatly.'

'Mr Timms, I –'

'I've spoken to your father, Miss Watson, and he's given me permission to ask you to marry me.'

'No, please!' She didn't attempt to hide her consternation any longer. 'I realise my parents are pushing for it, but I don't love you, Mr Timms.'

He snorted.

'What is love? We are well suited, which is more important. And as I said before, I think most highly of you.'

She wished she could be blunt but instead she declared: 'But I love someone else.'

'Who?' His voice had a sudden sharp edge. 'I wasn't aware you had another beau.'

'It's someone I met in Central Queensland.' Silly fool, she chided herself. She shouldn't have mentioned this.

'What, some squatter with cattle dung on his boots?' He laughed harshly. 'I thought you had better taste than that.'

Emma stared at him, her stomach churning with anger and disbelief.

'How dare you speak so crudely! He is ten times the gentleman you are, for all your rich clothes and fancy manners!' She heard his sharp intake of breath and, in the dim light coming from the windows, she saw his face contort.

'Did he kiss you, this country gentleman?'

'That is none of your business!' She suddenly craved the safety of bright lights and the company of others. Emma went to push past him but he reached out and grasped her arm, pulling her close. His free arm slid around her waist, drawing her hard against his body. The smell of brilliantine in his hair mingled with the more elemental reek of stale sweat.

She pushed ineffectively at his chest, her heart thudding. This couldn't be happening! When he bent his head down to hers she averted her face, but he grasped her chin with flabby fingers and held her captive as he ground his mouth against hers. Emma twisted in his arms, caught between fury and revulsion as she tried to escape his whiskey-flavoured kiss. But he was stronger than he looked. He released her chin and moved his hand over her collarbone to her breast. Her stomach churned as his fingers closed around the soft flesh, squeezing painfully.

She gave an outraged cry and stomped hard on his foot. He released her with a soft curse that made her ears burn. Then she ran back to the house, too frightened to compose herself before she burst into the room full of people. Fortunately no one seemed to notice her hasty re-entry or flustered appearance. She moved through the room without speaking to anyone and poured herself a glass of punch with trembling hands. Standing alone in a corner, she surveyed the room warily, looking out for Mr Timms and wishing she could escape to her bedroom. She was suddenly afraid to leave the security the crowd offered.

He didn't appear again. Emma could only hope he had left, but fearing that he lurked in a dark passageway she wasn't confident enough to retire. Somehow she got through the rest of the evening. Her mother looked at her critically as the final carriage drove away from the door.

'What was wrong with you tonight? You were barely civil to Mrs Guthrie.'

'I'm sorry.' She put her hand to her head. 'I have a shocking headache. If you'll excuse me, Mother, I must go to bed. Goodnight.'

'What happened to Cyril?' her father asked. 'He disappeared early in the night.'

'I don't know. Goodnight, Father.' Emma escaped before he could pursue the subject, but as she lay in bed sleep refused to claim her. Her heart hammered in remembered fear as she relived the man's brutal assault. It was a world away from Alex's gentle kisses.

The night had brought the truth home to her more forcibly than anything else could have. Money and fine clothes did not make a gentleman. It was something more intrinsic than that. Despite Alex's mixed blood, he was superior to Cyril Timms in every way that mattered. She ached inside, wondering how she could have discarded something so special.

~*~

A few days later the post brought a letter from Lucy. Her earlier notes had assured Emma all was going well with her pregnancy, but this one referred to her approaching confinement and reminded Emma of her promise to return. There was nothing she wanted to do more, but when she broached the subject with her mother, Mrs Watson looked indignant.

'Why must that girl keep calling on you? She has a mother and sisters, for Heaven's sake.'

'Aunt Lydia can't leave her family. You know that. And Mary is too young to travel to on her own.' The oldest of Lucy's sisters was only thirteen and her youngest sibling was little more than a baby.

'What about her mother-in-law? She lives on the station, doesn't she?'

Emma remembered Sarah Baxter with a little shudder of sympathy for Lucy.

'Mrs Baxter is a stern sort of woman. She doesn't seem very encouraging towards Lucy. That's not the type of company she needs just now.'

Mrs Watson threw up her hands.

'Ask your father! I'm not sure he'll agree to a second visit.'

Mrs Watson was right. When she approached her father in his study, he summarily vetoed the idea.

'No more gallivanting up north, Emma. It's time you accepted your responsibilities to this family.' He swung in his chair to face her, pausing to glower at her as he puffed acrid fumes from his cigar. 'Cyril spoke to me again today. I'd hoped your time away would make you see sense, but it doesn't seem to have had the desired effect. He said he'd proposed to you, but your response wasn't encouraging.'

He wagged the cigar emphatically in her direction.

'I told him I'd speak to you. He wants you to attend the theatre with him on Saturday night. If you know what's good for you, you'd better accept him.'

Emma stared at her father. Revulsion made her stomach churn. A net was closing around her, snaring her in its tangling threads.

'But I don't want to marry Mr Timms! I've told you so often enough!'

Henry Watson's eyes bulged. He thumped his fist hard on his desk.

'You won't defy me, girl! I won't have my business partners offended!'

She glared at him, her anger at his presumption and her new aversion to Mr Timms fuelling a fresh defiance.

'This is the end of the nineteenth century, Father! You can't just marry me off to further your interests. I'm of age and I refuse comply.'

His florid face flooded an even deeper shade of red.

'You'd better agree, or you'll find out what trouble is!'

Emma stormed out of the room, seeking refuge in the garden. She sank onto a cushioned seat in the shade of a sprawling Moreton Bay

Fig, taking deep breaths to calm herself. A ginger cat from next door meowed and rubbed against her skirt, Emma lifted it to her lap with unsteady hands and pressed her face against its silky fur. She'd known it would be difficult to defy her father, but this was worse than she'd imagined. How could she accept Mr Timms after his crude advances at the party? The thought of having to submit to him horrified her.

Could her father really compel her to marry against her will? Probably not, the voice of reason responded. But he could make her life miserable, or turn her out of his house. But if staying in Brisbane meant marrying Mr Timms, she was even more determined to return to Breakaway Creek. Since her parents had refused permission, she would have to leave without it.

Her desire to be with Lucy was strong, but even more urgent was the need to see Alex again. Everything she'd told herself against marrying him no longer seemed important. What did it matter if her parents approved of him, since they cared so little for her? It seemed obvious now that her father wouldn't consent to her marriage to any man he hadn't personally chosen.

Coming to a quick decision, she set the cat down and entered the house through the back door, going up the stairs and to her bedroom without encountering any of her family. She checked her purse, put on her hat and gloves, and crept out the front door.

After walking for three blocks she managed to hail a hackney cab, and instructed the driver to take her into the city. In the shipping office she booked a berth for Rockhampton on a steamer leaving port in two days' time. She would be sharing with another single girl. Whether that girl would be what her mother considered a suitable companion was doubtful, but that was too bad. From now on she refused to allow her parents to dictate to her.

When she returned to the house, Mrs Giles, the housekeeper, was coming down the stairs.

'Have you been out alone, Miss?' Mrs Giles looked surprised. Emma smiled at her, feigning nonchalance. Mrs Giles had been a member of the household since she was a child, and Emma was fonder of her than of her own parents.

'Just a quick errand, Mrs Giles. What's for dinner tonight?'

The housekeeper was distracted to a safer topic. After a short conversation Emma was able to escape and collected a small trunk on the way to her bedroom. She set it beside her bed and begun packing, listening all the while for any approaching footsteps, ready to thrust the trunk under the bed if necessary.

It was difficult to decide what to take. She would have to carry it all herself, and, if her parents were as furious as she expected them to be, there would be no chance of collecting more things later. But her ball gowns could be easily left behind, for she doubted there would be any occasion to wear them if she married Alex. She couldn't imagine him attending society functions.

Of course, she couldn't assume Alex's proposal of marriage still stood. If he wasn't prepared to forgive her earlier rejection, she might be forced to return to Brisbane with her tail between her legs. The idea strengthened her resolve: no, never that, she decided, thinking of Mr Timms. She would find employment in the Clermont district and make her own way. Even a life of comparative poverty would be preferable to marriage to a man like him.

Chapter Nine

That night Emma sat in her room, composing a letter to her parents. She didn't mention Alex, only that she refused to marry Mr Timms, who had behaved improperly to her. As a ruse she mentioned that she planned to visit a school friend, who lived an hour away by train. The lie made her cringe, but if she told the truth her father would intercept her before the boat sailed. She consoled herself with the thought that the alternative to lying was marrying Cyril Timms. The ink dried on the nib as she sat staring at the paper, trying to decide what else to write. After she had listed the essentials, she signed her name and blotted the page before slipping the note into an envelope.

She had to wait for the servants to retire in order to carry her luggage to the hall. At last, when all was quiet and she was sure her parents were asleep, she crept down the staircase with a lamp in one hand and her trunk in the other. The steps creaked alarmingly and she froze, her heart racing, when her heavy case bumped against the wall. But no one stirred. At the bottom she opened a seldom-used cupboard under the stairwell and pushed the trunk inside.

She slept fitfully that night, her thoughts spiralling through anticipation and dread. In her dreams she took the wrong ship, finding herself bound for Sydney with no way off. Alex stood at the wharf and watched her leave, deaf to her pleas for rescue. She awoke with her nightgown drenched in sweat, her distress as real as when he had turned away from her at Breakaway Creek.

Only a dream, she consoled herself, and forced her memories to happier times. If Alex really loved her, she thought, then he'd forgive her.

At first light she dragged herself out of bed, and dressed in a travelling outfit consisting of a brown skirt, jacket and matching hat. She made a quick breakfast of some bread and cheese she'd smuggled into her room and made her way down the stairs, stopping to listen for any activity before descending the second flight. It was too early for her parents to be up and none of the servants seemed to be around. She was on her hands and knees pulling her case out of the cupboard when she heard a voice behind her.

'Miss Watson! What are you doing?'

Jumping up in fright, she banged her head on the top of the cupboard.

'Ouch!' Nausea swamped her as she rubbed the sore spot and repositioned her hat. Her words came out as a croak. 'Mrs Giles! You startled me!'

The housekeeper looked her up and down suspiciously.

'You're going out again. What's going on, Miss? Do Mr and Mrs Watson know?'

'Please keep your voice down, Mrs Giles.' Emma's stomach writhed as she realised her only hope was to take the woman into her confidence. Perhaps she could be persuaded to silence. She spoke in a low voice. 'I have to leave here, I'm afraid. Father's forcing me to marry Mr Timms but I can't abide the man! He practically attacked me on New Year's Eve.'

'Oh, dear! I never liked the look of that fellow! But where are you going?'

'To my cousin, Mrs Baxter, at Breakaway Creek. She asked me to visit to help her with the coming baby.'

'You're travelling all that way alone?'

'I'm sharing a cabin with another young woman. I'll be all right, Mrs Giles. I've done the trip before so I know what to expect.'

'Your parents will be furious. Heaven knows I don't like what I've seen of Mr Timms, but this seems a bit drastic.' Mrs Giles looked worried.

Emma shuddered.

'I can assure you; it's not as drastic as being married to him. Besides, Lucy needs me and they won't let me go to her.' She saw Mrs Giles's hesitation and pressed her advantage, allowing the full extent of her desperation to colour her voice. 'They needn't know you saw me. I certainly shan't tell them. This is my chance for happiness. Please don't ruin it for me.'

'Have you met another man up there?'

Emma nodded.

'He's a true gentleman, so different from Mr Timms. But nothing has been settled between us.'

'I take it your parents don't approve?'

'They don't know about him, Mrs Giles. He's George Baxter's brother. But he's not wealthy and you're right – they wouldn't approve.'

'If he's Mr Baxter's brother…' Mrs Giles frowned and pursed her lips. 'I assume he's respectable. I won't call your parents, but I wish you hadn't put me in this position. If anything dreadful happens I'll feel responsible.'

'Nothing bad will happen to me, I promise.' Almost crying with relief, Emma clasped the woman in a warm hug, something she'd never done before. 'Thank you. I won't forget this.'

The housekeeper briefly accepted the hug before pushing her away. Her voice sounded gruff.

'You'd better go quick, before I change my mind.'

~*~

The trunk was heavy and Emma made slow progress as she walked to the end of the block and around the corner where she was less likely to be seen by anyone who knew her. There she waited for the cab she'd arranged to collect her.

The driver threw her trunk inside with an ease that made her shake her head. In no time the carriage drew up at the wharf and she requested the driver to carry her luggage to the office of the Australasian United Steam Navigation Company.

Once on board the ship, the stewardess directed her to her intermediate cabin. It turned out to be tiny in comparison to the saloon room she'd shared with Mrs Dexter on her first voyage to Rockhampton. But it would have to do. Although she had money in her own bank account, she hadn't liked to fritter it on a first class cabin. She thought briefly of her parents, who must have discovered her absence by now, and were hopefully pursuing her to her friend's house. She could only hope the ship had sailed before they realised she wasn't there.

Her travelling companion was already settled and lay on the lower of the two narrow bunks with a tattered issue of The Young Ladies' Journal in her hands. The woman sat up, hunching to avoid hitting her head on the bunk above, and swung her legs over the side of the mattress. Emma paused uncertainly in the doorway as her cabin-mate rose slowly to her feet. She looked to be a few years older than Emma, plump and untidy, with brown hair that straggled out of its bun.

'So you're me cabin-mate?' She indicated the room with a laugh. 'I hope you don't snore. There's hardly room to swing a cat in 'ere.'

Choking back her dismay at the woman's unkempt appearance and coarse speech, Emma stepped forward and held out her hand.

'How do you do? I'm Emma Watson.'

The woman laughed again, but took Emma's hand in her damp, fleshy one.

'Oh, we have a la-di-da one here, do we? I'm Betsy Phillips. On me way to a job as cook at Berrinbah Station. The manager paid me fare an' all.'

'Where's Berrinbah Station?' Emma asked politely.

'Between Longreach and Aramac, dearie.' She winked broadly. 'Lots of stockmen out there, I reckon.'

'Are you hoping to find a husband?'

The woman chuckled.

'I've already had one of them, and he wasn't much good. Bugger took off with another woman. But I'm open to any reasonable offers.'

Emma looked away, uncertain how to respond. Feeling horribly out of her depth, she turned to her luggage that had already been brought to the cabin. She took out her nightgown, a towel, and her little wash bag. There was nowhere to store clothing, so it was impossible to unpack anything else.

'So, where are you headed, dearie?' Betsy asked.

'A property near Clermont,' Emma said, setting out her belongings on the closed lid of her trunk. 'I'm going to stay with my cousin who's expecting her first baby.'

'Won't that be lovely for you? Have you been there before?'

Emma straightened and looked at the other woman. Betsy's eyes were alight with what looked like genuine interest. Perhaps that rough manner concealed a kind heart. Emma briefly described her previous visit to Breakaway Creek. She omitted all references to Alex but mentioned her excitement about the baby.

'I'm very fond of children, meself,' Betsy said. 'Though the Good Lord hasn't seen fit to bless me with any. P'rhaps it's just as well, seein' as Dick turned out to be such a swine.'

Emma decided against asking any questions. She had a feeling the details Betsy was likely to reveal might be more than she could handle. She'd thought that after Alex's revelations she wouldn't be easily shocked, but a few minutes in the presence of this bluntly-spoken woman was enough to make her realise just how sheltered her life had been.

Even without encouragement, Betsy shared many particulars of her life and failed marriage over the next three days. Emma's ears burned as her companion described – in sordid detail – how she'd caught her "swine of a husband" in bed with another woman. Emma knew little about the conjugal aspect of marriage, except that babies were the usual result. Her mother had only hinted that decent women weren't supposed to enjoy it, and certainly didn't discuss it.

Betsy spoke of her relationship with her absent husband with a good deal of relish, and if she realised the embarrassment she was causing her young companion she didn't let it deter her. Emma gained the impression Betsy had enjoyed that aspect of marriage a great deal, and suspected there'd been other men since faithless Dick's departure.

Her mother would be aghast at the company she'd found herself in, but in the midst of her discomfort she had to admit to finding Betsy's honesty and lack of guile refreshing. There was no pretence about her and no false modesty.

At the same time Emma began to appreciate the reason for her mother's protectiveness. Betsy's talk of men made Emma think of Alex in a way that was no longer girlishly innocent. What would it be like, doing *that* with Alex? Ashamed of her impure thoughts, she took a book of poetry from her trunk and tried to distract herself. But Yeats's eloquent stanzas couldn't compete with her fantasies of passion ignited by a flesh-and-blood man.

In spite of Betsy's disconcerting frankness, Emma was grateful for her company. When they disembarked at Rockhampton she was pleased to discover her cabin-mate would be accompanying her on the train as far west as Emerald. After that Emma had only to travel the short northern leg to Clermont, and then overcome the challenge of finding transport to Breakaway Creek.

~*~

The monsoon season had Central Queensland firmly in its grip. As the train rattled west, Emma realised they were lucky to find the railway line open. The creeks and rivers were flowing fast, their banks piled with fresh silt. Clumps of flood rubbish caught on the bridges attested to the height of recent floods.

When the train reached Clermont, the difference in the town astounded her. In October, hot, dry winds had blown eddies of dust through the streets. Now those same thoroughfares were scarred with muddy wheel ruts and nearby paddocks were covered by a lush growth of green grass that glistened in the early morning sunshine.

After breakfast at the railway station, she left her luggage and walked down Capella Street towards the town centre, feeling vulnerable and very much alone. She stepped carefully around wheel ruts and lifted her skirts to avoid potholes. The lagoon that divided the town was full of muddy water, lapping perilously close to the street. Emma walked onto the footbridge and leant on the rail, staring down at the murky depths.

She remembered her first visit to Clermont, in the company of Lucy and George. They'd bought food at a general store and had seemed to be on familiar terms with the proprietor. Surely he would be able to advise her? Emma turned up Drummond Street, relieved to find it quiet. The hotels that were usually crowded with boisterous gold miners were closed at this early hour. At the general store she was again amazed at the variety of goods on display. The business sold everything from foodstuffs to horseshoes, clothing to fencing wire. Delicate ladies' items like painted silk fans and ivory-backed hairbrushes jostled for space with men's work-boots, sacks of potatoes, cross-cut saws, axes and miners' picks. The storekeeper, a short, balding man with a drooping moustache, remembered her.

'What can I do for you, Miss Watson?' he asked courteously. Emma smiled at him, pleased to encounter a friendly face.

'I've just arrived on the train and I'm wondering about transport to Breakaway Creek.'

He shook his head.

'Miss, the roads are a quagmire. We've had inches of rain over the past few weeks.' Emma's body tensed with frustration and the beginnings of alarm.

'So it's impossible to travel there?' Where did that leave Lucy, she thought? Her baby was due in a couple of weeks.

'Put it this way, it's no trip for a lady. Normally you could have gone out with the mailman, but he won't be doing his run in this weather.'

Emma struggled to conceal her dismay. How could she have come this far, only to have the vagaries of the weather foil her plans? Concern for Lucy made her bite her lip. If the young mother was forced to give birth at Breakaway Creek, she would have no choice but to call on Sarah Baxter to act as midwife. Emma had a feeling Lucy wouldn't appreciate that. And there was no possibility of a doctor's help if things went wrong.

She thanked the storekeeper for his help and left the shop, her mind whirling. She could stay at one of the hotels and wait for the road to dry out. But what if Lucy needed her? She couldn't just sit and do nothing.

She walked back down the street to the livery stables. A man with brown, leathery skin unloaded sacks from the back of a dray, heaving them effortlessly onto his shoulder and carrying them inside the building. A sprinkling of chaff dribbled from the bags and left a trail of dusty gold in his wake. Spotting Emma, he dusted off his hands and removed a blackened pipe from the corner of his mouth.

'Can I help you, Ma'am?'

'I'd like to hire a horse and side-saddle. I need to travel to the Baxter property, Breakaway Creek.'

He regarded her with open scepticism.

'The roads are a boggy mess right now. It'd be a tough ride. Have you got someone with you?'

She smiled.

'I'm afraid not. But it's urgent, so I'm prepared to tackle it.'

'Do you know the way?'

'Yes, I've travelled the road before.'

He shrugged.

'It's your decision. I've got a quiet horse I can lend you.'

She asked him to fetch her luggage from the railway station, and while he did she retraced her steps to the store, trying to remember everything they'd used when she had camped on the road with George and Lucy. The writhing nerves in her stomach seemed to scramble her thoughts. She wasn't the complete new chum of her first trip to Breakaway Creek, but being all alone with the dingoes and the elements was another thing altogether.

The kindly storekeeper helped her put together the essentials: canned meat, tea and sugar, a tin plate, a knife, a quart-pot, matches, a blanket and a piece of canvas. She rolled the blanket inside the canvas to make a thin swag while the storekeeper packed the food and utensils into a split sugarbag. Then he asked his assistant to carry it all to the livery stable while she stopped at the bakery to buy a loaf of bread.

At the stable, the ostler had returned with her trunk. Emma rolled extra clothing inside her swag and begged the use of the man's office to change into a riding habit. Then she made arrangements to store the trunk, before setting off with the swag attached to the cantle of her saddle and the sugarbag tied to the d-rings on the pommel.

The ostler hadn't exaggerated the state of the road. The black-soil flats along Sandy Creek were a gluey mess of deep wheel ruts and hoof tracks that her horse laboured to follow. She urged him onto the grass beside the road, but it was still heavy going. Before long he was blowing hard, his coat steaming with sweat in the humid air. Emma's own face burned under the sweltering sun despite her hat. As they crossed the creek she let the horse drink from the turbid stream. Then she dismounted under a shady tree to rest. Her head ached and the oppressive heat made her ill. At this rate it promised to be a slow trip.

As dusk fell, mosquitoes swarmed around her, settling on any unprotected skin and even biting through the thin material of her blouse. Nightfall found her still a long way from the place they'd camped last time. But at least after all the rain finding water wasn't a problem. Emma made camp beside a muddy pool in a narrow gully and tied the horse on a long rope so he could graze.

Lighting a fire to drive the mosquitoes away was her first priority, but finding enough dry wood wasn't easy. She collected a fallen branch and managed to set alight a bundle of dead leaves, gently fanning the smouldering pile until the flames licked around the twigs and sticks. When the fire was burning properly she added fresh green leaves to make it smoke. Even the horse moved close, seeking refuge from the biting insects.

Later, Emma sat on a log and sipped hot tea from her quart pot, while eating a rough sandwich. Anxiously she watched the western horizon where sheets of lightning flashed in a dark bank of storm clouds. Thunder rumbled, distant at first, but gradually drawing closer until a loud crack reverberated in her ears and made her jump. The rain-scented wind began to whip around her, quickly cooling the humid air. She wrapped herself in the blanket and hunched under the meagre piece of canvas, pressed against a large tree trunk.

As the rain lashed her, it seeped under the canvas and pooled on the muddy ground. Sure she was about to be struck by lightning or a wind-blown branch, she huddled in a trembling ball.

An hour later the storm had passed leaving her damp and cold, her carefully built fire extinguished. She hung her spare set of clothes over a branch, hoping they would at least partially dry, and made a bed on the sheet of canvas with the saddle as a pillow. The air warmed in the aftermath of the storm, but her clothes were clammy and uncomfortable. Thinking longingly of the dry bed she could have had at a hotel in town, she wondered what madness had made her venture out here. Once she was back in civilisation, she vowed, her camping days were over.

She awoke several hours later, as the first fingers of light nudged the eastern sky. Her aching muscles protested as she pulled on damp boots and scrambled stiffly to her feet. As she moved the horse to fresh grazing, the black-soil mud sucked at her boots, clinging to the soles and making every step an effort. Regretfully unable to build a fire, she ate a cold breakfast and lingered as she basked in the sun's growing warmth. She knew it was better to let the ground dry a little before she set off though it might mean spending another night on the road. The thought daunted her, but she'd come too far to turn back now.

It was mid-morning when her horse seemed to sense company ahead. Ears pricked, he raised his head and neighed loudly. Emma's heart drummed in her ears as she stared along the road, conscious of her isolation and vulnerability. Thoughts of murderers and rapists flashed through her mind as she remembered the rough-looking miners she'd seen in Clermont.

As she topped a rise, the travellers came into view. A pair of horses strained into their collars while two men heaved at the rear wheels of a buggy that was obviously stuck in the mud. A lady stood under the shade of a straggly tree, holding the reins of a third horse which dozed with its head hanging.

Emma's pulse leapt. She rubbed her eyes, wondering if her sleepless night was making her delirious. Could the sight be the result of her wishful imagination? Then one of the men shouted at the horses and the familiar voice told her that she wasn't mistaken. So intent were they on the bogged buggy that Emma was almost upon them before they noticed her. Alex looked up first and stopped heaving at the wheel. He wiped his eyes with his muddy sleeve and stared at her. George, at the other wheel, looked across at Alex.

'What –' Then he looked up the road and straightened, his voice incredulous. 'Emma? Is that you?'

She slid out of the saddle without answering. Lucy stared and then moved towards her with ungainly steps, her stomach huge under a loose-fitting dress.

'Emma! What are you doing here?'

In moments she was hugging both Lucy and George, laughing her relief and trying to answer their jumbled questions. Then she looked up at Alex, who still hadn't moved. A rush of emotion flooded her as she took in his mud-spattered shirt and moleskins and his sweaty, frozen face.

'Alex,' she said. 'Oh, how I've missed you all.'

Chapter Ten

While the men freed the buggy, Emma and Lucy sat and caught up with each other's news.

'The rain started just after Christmas. We were hoping for a break in the weather so George could take me to town, but we couldn't wait any longer. Alex offered to come too, and it's just as well.' Lucy looked up as her husband approached and cast an anxious glance at the sky. 'Thank goodness they have the buggy out of that bog. I hope it doesn't rain again tonight.'

George helped Lucy to her feet.

'We'd better be going. I'm worried about the creeks coming up.' Like his wife, he scanned the heavens before looking at Emma. 'Would you like to ride with Lucy in the buggy, Emma?'

'Thank you, but no. Those poor horses don't need the extra weight.' It was true, and perhaps she would find a chance to talk to Alex while she rode.

George gave her a stern look.

'Just what did you think you were doing, travelling out here in this weather?' He eyed her meagre kit. 'You must have been caught in the storm last night.'

'As you were, I imagine,' Emma countered.

'At least we were better prepared.' He indicated some gear in the back of the buggy. 'We have a tent. What did you do when the storm came?'

As Emma explained how she'd sheltered under a tree, a rough exclamation made her turn to a furious-looking Alex.

'You could have been struck by lightning!' It was the first thing he'd said to her and his grim expression wasn't encouraging. 'It's safer out in the open.'

Emma noticed George and Lucy exchanging glances.

'But you weren't struck, and that's all that matters.' Lucy patted Emma's arm, her tone soothing. 'I wish we'd known you were coming, though. We'd have told you to wait in Clermont.'

'It was a last-minute decision.' Emma thought better of mentioning that she'd run away from home. That would keep until she and Lucy were alone.

After they set off, Alex rode on the opposite side of the buggy. He seemed to avoid her gaze, his expression guarded. For Emma it was a bittersweet torture having him close. She'd anticipated seeing him for so long, but it hadn't turned out the way she'd expected. She longed to speak to him, to hear he was glad to see her. But he didn't look particularly glad. There was nothing she could do until she was able to speak to him alone.

They made even slower progress with the buggy than on horseback alone, and dark overtook them before they could reach Clermont. George wanted to forge ahead, voicing his fear that another storm might fill the creeks and strand them, but the tiny sliver of moon that peeked between the scudding clouds and the flickering candles in the buggy lamps were a poor substitute for daylight. The horses were exhausted from hauling the vehicle and Emma knew Lucy was just as fatigued, although she didn't complain.

Eventually George called a halt. The men pitched the tent while Emma collected firewood, watching lightning flicker on the horizon all the while. As she struggled to break sticks into kindling, Alex came to help. He took the timber from her unresisting hands and snapped it effortlessly over his knee. Then he crouched on his heels to light the fire, cupping the match with his hand as the flame sputtered on the damp leaves she'd gathered. Emma ached as she watched him, willing him to speak or flash her that gentle smile she loved so much. But she couldn't think how to crack the wall of silence he'd built between them.

After a quick meal they all retired, the men unrolling their swags under the buggy while Emma shared the tent with Lucy.

'I hope I don't disturb you too much.' As Lucy crouched to unroll her swag, her movements clumsy and heavy, she pressed a hand to her stomach and winced. In the flickering lantern light her face was drawn with weariness. 'The baby's kicking keeps me awake and I have to get up several times in the night. Just now I can feel his foot pressing right against my stomach, and it hurts.'

'But I shouldn't complain,' she said and smiled ruefully, rubbing a spot at the top of her protruding belly. 'I'm well and he seems to be active and healthy.'

Emma watched her in awe.

'George must be proud of you for taking all this in your stride. You're very brave, Lucy.'

'Nonsense! Who rode out from Clermont all by herself?'

Embarrassed, she shook her head.

'I would have gone mad, waiting in town with no news. Last night in the storm I regretted the decision, but now I'm so pleased I did it.' If only Alex would talk to her.

The storms bypassed them during the night and the next morning they packed up at first light. George still looked worried and Emma wondered why.

'What's the hurry?' she asked Alex as he folded the tent. 'Surely there won't be a problem reaching town now.'

He glanced at her quickly, his face unreadable.

'A storm further up Sandy Creek could have brought the creek up again.'

Of course, she thought – why hadn't she thought of that?

When they arrived at the Sandy Creek crossing, no one said a word but the relief was obvious. Her gelding, no doubt anticipating his stable in Clermont, took to the water without hesitation though it was running deeper than when Emma had forded it two days before. She had to hold her foot high against the horse's belly to keep it dry.

Within a few hours they were comfortably settled at the Leo Hotel. The Danish proprietor, a friend of George's, put himself out to make them welcome and even produced a cradle for the coming baby. Emma had the room next to Lucy and George, while Alex occupied the chamber at the other end of the passage. George wasted no time in summoning the doctor to see his wife.

The doctor beamed as he came out of Lucy's room. George had been banished to wait outside and Emma had kept him company.

'She's doing well,' the doctor said. 'The infant's heartbeat is strong and Mrs Baxter is in fine health. She could go into labour at any time.'

That night it rained again in earnest. As the four of them sat down to dinner in the dining room, they watched as water ran off the overhanging roof and beat down on the muddy street. In the glow of the carbide street lamps the thoroughfare quickly became a sea.

'I should have gone straight home. At this rate the creek will flood and I'll be stuck here.' Alex frowned, his usually easy-going face set in bleak lines.

'It won't hurt you to stay in town for a few days,' George told him. 'You can't do much at home when it's this wet.'

Emma looked down at her plate, biting her lip as misery spread through her. She couldn't help feeling Alex's aversion to staying in town had something to do with her. If only she could find a chance to speak to him, but he seemed to deliberately avoid her.

By morning the rain had eased to a drizzle and the sun hid behind a thick veil of cloud. The company at breakfast was as dismal as the weather. George and Lucy made overly bright conversation but Emma was too miserable to respond. Alex looked as if he'd rather be elsewhere and quickly made an excuse to escape as far as the creek, returning with water dripping off his oilskin coat and felt hat.

'The creek's three parts of a banker,' he said. 'Looks like I'm stranded. Anyone would be mad to set off in this.'

In the afternoon the clouds opened with another downpour. Emma and Lucy spent most of the day in the hotel lounge. Emma read while Lucy knitted a woollen baby's jacket in a delicate, lacy pattern.

'I'm making it big enough to fit the baby when he's a few months old,' Lucy explained, holding it up to show Emma. 'He won't need it until the weather cools off in April or May.'

Emma smiled.

'Have you decided it's going to be a boy?'

'I think so.' Lucy moved in her chair, a spasm crossing her face. 'The way he kicks, he has to be.'

Emma watched her apprehensively.

'Are you all right? Would you like me to fetch George?' George and Alex had gone off to test their skill in the billiard hall.

'No, I'm tired of him fussing. It's just the usual aches and pains.' But Emma couldn't help worrying.

That night, after she had gone to bed, a tap on the door woke her from a restless sleep. She was instantly alert.

'It's only me,' came George's voice through the keyhole. 'I've called Doctor Kent. I think her time has come.'

Emma dressed hastily, fingers fumbling on buttons and hooks. She joined George at his wife's bedside, alarmed at the sight of Lucy's white, drawn face and sweat-dampened hair. Emma wrung out a cloth in the basin on the washstand and gently sponged her brow.

'The doctor will be here soon,' she soothed. 'He'll know what to do.'

When Doctor Kent arrived, he seemed unconcerned at Lucy's distress. Immediately he shooed George from the room and assessed Emma with shrewd eyes.

'You can stay, young lady. Keep her company and sponge her face like you've been doing. Give her a drink of water if she wants it.' He washed his hands before examining Lucy with a casual air, which made Emma wonder if she'd ever be able to face the indignities of giving birth. 'It shouldn't be too long. Everything's progressing nicely. Can you rustle up one of the maids and get her to fetch us hot water, towels and clean bedding?'

"Rustling up a maid" was easier said than done, but eventually Emma found a tiny bedroom behind the kitchens and roused the sleeping occupant. Then she hurried back up, faltering when she saw Alex sitting on the top stair. He stood to let her past, his face concerned in the light of the lamp she carried.

'How is she?'

'The doctor doesn't seem worried, but I wish he'd do more to help her. He said it shouldn't be long now.'

His proximity made her feel nervous. She dodged past him to Lucy's room. Outside, George paced the hallway. Lucy moaned, her breath coming in short, sharp gasps as she struggled with the pain. She clutched Emma's hand convulsively.

'Don't leave me,' Lucy begged. She bit off another groan. 'Ah, I can't stand this!'

Lucy's distress made Emma feel increasingly helpless. She was pleased George couldn't see it, although she imagined he could hear enough through the closed door.

'Can't you help her?' Emma looked at the doctor, who didn't appear to be doing much at all.

'She's progressing well. It'll be over soon and she'll wonder what all the fuss was about.'

Emma gave him a caustic look. She hadn't known what to expect, but if Lucy's pain was typical of childbirth, she wondered how women managed to endure it time and again. It was so messy and undignified and terrifying. If Alex didn't want her any more it might be a good thing, she thought; she'd be an old maid and never have to endure this.

Fortunately Doctor Kent's words were prophetic. A few hours later, Emma almost collapsed with relief when he lifted the squalling infant, announcing in proud tones: 'It's a boy!'

Lucy's exhausted face lit up.

'I told you it was going to be a boy,' she said weakly. 'Can I see him?'

'You can hold him in a moment, young lady. Let me tie the cord first.'

In a few minutes the doctor had wrapped the wailing, red-faced infant in a blanket and placed him in his mother's arms.

'Isn't he beautiful?' Lucy pushed aside the edge of the blanket and stared in wonder at his crumpled face. 'Can you fetch George for me, please Emma?'

Emma didn't think the child was beautiful, precisely, but the miracle of the occasion had thickened her throat and her eyes brimmed with tears.

'Of course,' she said. 'It would be a privilege.'

'Just a moment,' the doctor cautioned. 'You may tell him the good news, but don't let him in just yet. I'm not finished here.'

George had heard the infant's cry and was standing just outside the door, his face a study in hope, joy and fear.

'Is Lucy well?'

'She is, and so is your little son.'

'A boy! Thank you, Emma.' He enfolded her in a crushing hug. 'Can I see them?'

'Soon, the doctor said.' As Alex approached she turned to smile at him and in her excitement she forgot the strain between them. 'George, you'd better tell your brother the good news.'

When both mother and baby had been bathed and the bloodied sheets changed, the doctor announced that the proud father could come in. Emma went out to convey the message, smiling after George's retreating back as he hastened into the bedroom. She glanced at Alex.

'I think a cup of tea for us all would be a good idea. Let George and Lucy have their moment of privacy. I know where the kitchen is.'

Acutely aware of him in that dark, confined space, she stoked the coals in the firebox and put the kettle on the hotplate. Holding the lamp up, Alex searched in likely cupboards until he found a canister of tea and some cups.

'Thank God it's all over and they're both well. Poor old George has been out of his mind with worry,' Alex said. He fixed his dark, unwavering gaze on her. 'Lucy was very lucky to have you with her.'

Pleasure surged through her. It was the first warm thing he'd said to her and it was all the encouragement she needed.

'Alex, I've wanted to talk to you, to tell you I'm sorry.' She turned to face him, squaring her shoulders. 'Returning to Brisbane was a mistake. I wish I'd stayed here and braved it out with my parents.'

He swallowed, staring at her.

'Have you changed your mind about us?'

She nodded, nervously biting her lip.

'I love you, Alex. That's more important to me than my parents' goodwill.'

He looked down, busying himself with spooning tea leaves into the pot, still with the shuttered look to his face that she had grown to dread.

'Emma, do you realise how cruel people can be? It's not only your parents you need to worry about. Not many people know who my mother was, but if they ever find out they'll shun me and my family with me. Can you live with that?'

'Do you think I haven't thought of that?' His distant tone stung. Resentment and tension made her voice shrill. 'What do you think has been in my mind, the last few months? I've had plenty of time to come to terms with it.'

He put the lid on the canister and looked up.

'What made you change your mind?'

She twisted her fingers in her skirt, wishing he wouldn't make this so difficult.

'My father was pushing me to marry a man he knew I despised. It made me realise I had no choice but to defy him.' Taking a deep breath, she summoned the courage to tell him what was really in her heart. 'Mr Timms is everything you're not. He is wealthy, successful and recognised by society. He's also selfish and unprincipled and I couldn't bear to be married to him. He made me realise you're ten times the man he'll ever be.'

The silence seemed to echo through the room, punctuated only by the fire crackling in the grate and her pulse drumming in her ears.

'Are you sure of this?' In the dim glow of the lamp Alex's face wore a curious mixture of hope and fear.

'Yes, I'm sure, Alex. I ran away from home to be with you. And even if you don't want me, I'm not going back to Brisbane.'

'Oh, Emma.' He gave a shaky laugh and crossed the room, gathering her into his arms. 'You brave lass. I don't deserve you.'

'I don't deserve *you*, Alex.' Her voice trembled as joy swept through her. The strength of his arms and the closeness of his body sent heat surging through her as she locked her arms around his neck and lifted her face for his kiss.

He murmured deep in his throat and dragged her even closer as she abandoned herself to sensation. Was this really only their second kiss? So much time and grief had passed since that day when she'd fallen off her horse, and so much of her innocence had been lost. In the darkened kitchen she committed herself to him in a way she hadn't known possible all those months ago. There was none of the gentle shyness of their first kiss, just a man's barely leashed hunger and her passion rising to meet it, inflamed by the heat of his mouth and the press of his body.

The kettle bubbled madly and filled the room with steam. The noise brought them to their senses. Alex put her away from him, his reluctance obvious.

'I'm sorry, Emma.' He put his hand to his forehead, breathing heavily. 'That got out of hand.'

'I'm not sorry.' She stretched up on tiptoe to press a quick kiss to his cheek. 'As long as you know I'm serious about marrying you.'

He smiled.

'The sooner the better, after that. Now, don't kiss me again or we'll never get the tea made.'

~*~

Alex sat in a chair in the corner of George and Lucy's bedroom, watching as Emma fussed over the baby. George drank tea while Lucy nibbled on a biscuit with little interest. She looked exhausted, her eyes ringed with dark shadows. George beamed with pride as his eyes lingered on his son. They'd named him Thomas George.

Alex was thrilled for George and Lucy, but in his mind their good fortune took second place to his own. He hadn't expected Emma's change of heart, and he still had trouble believing it. There was a sceptical part of him, a part that had long ago become resigned to settling for life's second-best, and it wondered if Emma was too good to be true.

Thrusting his doubts aside, Alex allowed himself to focus on Emma so he watched her face, flushed and pretty as she settled the infant to sleep. He imagined her with their children and the thought warmed him. After their passionate kiss in the kitchen, it was tempting to imagine her in his bed, but he tried to divert his thoughts to something more suited to present company. At this rate he'd embarrass himself in front of George, who didn't miss much.

When Emma had the baby settled in his cradle, Alex got up and held out his hand to her.

'Lucy needs her sleep. We'll leave you to it, George.'

George flashed him a sudden, keen look, his eyes lingering on the couple's clasped hands.

'I'll see you both tomorrow. Thank you for all your help, Emma. I don't know what we'd have done without you.'

Outside Emma's room, Alex drew her close, but he kept the kiss brief and pushed her towards her door.

'You'd better get in there quick, before I ask if I can come too.'

She looked up at him, her eyes wide with surprise, before hurrying inside and shutting the door behind her. Alex cursed himself as he made his way to his own room. What had possessed him to say that? She was still so innocent, in spite of everything. Perhaps she thought he'd lived a pure life and never done anything shameful.

While he lived at Breakaway Creek Molly's presence was a constant reminder of his guilt. He'd condemned his father's actions, but the way he had used the maid was no better. It was only by luck that his liaison hadn't also resulted in a child. At the time, he'd thought it different, because he shared Molly's Aboriginal blood. But now he wondered if that was really significant. He'd exploited the relationship between master and servant, exactly as his father had. In that he was just as guilty as every white man who used Aboriginal women. He could only hope that Emma would never find out about Molly.

Chapter Eleven

Emma undressed slowly, knowing she should be exhausted. Instead she was wide awake, in both mind and body. The birth of Lucy's baby was a joyous occasion, but her reconciliation with Alex eclipsed everything. Mixed with the delight of their reunion was the excitement his passion had aroused in her, especially his last suggestive words: "before I ask if I can come too". Alex seemed like such a reserved and courteous man, so he had caught her by surprise – even shocked her a little.

He hadn't seemed at all reticent tonight. Instead he'd acted like a man who knew exactly what he was doing and who wasn't hesitant to take that next step. Of course, he was a man of twenty-six, not a young boy. It was probably naïve of her to have imagined he was as inexperienced in such matters as she.

Sleep eluded Emma until the early hours of the morning and when she finally woke she knew it was late. The sun struggled through the clouds and only a few puddles remained of yesterday's deluge. In the dining room, she found find Alex and George at breakfast, lingering over cups of tea. Heat suffused her cheeks as they rose to greet her. Alex pulled out a chair and favoured her with a tender, intimate smile that made her blood rush. She glanced self-consciously at George, who watched them both with unconcealed amusement.

'How are Lucy and little Thomas this morning?' she asked quickly, taking the chair with more haste than grace.

'Tom fed a couple of hours ago and now they're both sleeping.' George looked from one to the other, grinning. 'Are we celebrating more than one event today?'

Alex gave her a questioning look. Emma nodded, smiling shyly at him. Alex's eyes glowed with pride and locked with hers as he began to speak.

'Emma has done me the honour of agreeing to be my wife.' He took her hand and turned to his brother. 'But don't tell anyone, George. Before we make it public I have to write to her father for his permission.'

Emma's head jerked up as alarm shot through her.

'He won't give it, Alex. I can tell you that now.'

Alex's mouth firmed.

'I want to do the right thing, regardless. He can hardly stop us. You're of age.'

Tactfully ignoring their little exchange, George stood up and shook Alex's hand.

'Congratulations, old chap. That's wonderful.' He bent to Emma, kissing her cheek. 'Welcome to the family, my dear. I couldn't think of anyone I'd sooner have for a sister-in-law. Lucy will be thrilled.'

He was right. Lucy's pale, drawn face lit up with excitement when they told her.

'Oh, what wonderful news!' Sitting in bed with the baby in her arms, the greyness of exhaustion seemed to fade from her face. 'This makes everything perfect! Come here, both of you, and let me congratulate you properly.'

She passed the infant to George and hugged and kissed them both in turn.

'This makes you my sister as well as my cousin, Emma.'

Later that day, they went shopping for an engagement ring at the jeweller's on Drummond Street. With respect for Alex's financial circumstances, Emma chose a single diamond in a plain gold setting. It was insignificant compared to what Mr Timms might have bought her, but Emma wore it on her finger with as much pride and excitement as if it had been the most expensive item in the store.

'For now, I'll wear it on a chain around my neck,' she told her new fiancé, removing it with some reluctance. Alex was adamant they should not make a formal announcement until her parents had been notified. Emma had conceded that was the correct thing to do, but it worried her all the same. She was sure her father wouldn't accept her engagement without a fight, regardless of Alex's conviction that he could do nothing to prevent it. Alex didn't know her father.

~*~

Doctor Kent had ordered Lucy to remain in bed for ten days. George decided it wouldn't be worth his while returning to Breakaway Creek in the interval but with the sun shining and the creek passable once more, Alex announced there was no reason for him to linger in town.

'Do you have to leave?' Emma protested privately. 'I'll be lonely without you. I know I can help Lucy with the baby, but she and George are so besotted with him and each other, I feel a bit superfluous at times.'

'Oh, Emma.' He hugged her and kissed her lightly. 'There's nothing for me to do all day, and the nights are worse when I know you're sleeping only a few doors away. For the sake of your reputation you're better off without me hanging around. Especially since we haven't made our engagement public.'

Emma clung to him, wishing he would kiss her again. She had been taught it was the woman's role to be discreet. It was proving much harder than she'd anticipated.

~*~

By the time Lucy was at last allowed to travel home, Emma was tired of the restrictions of hotel accommodation and relieved to be returning to Breakaway Creek. Knowing that her fiancé was waiting for her there had much to do with her impatience. Fortunately the weather had remained fine, making the journey much easier, despite the lurching of the buggy on the rutted track. Some of the gully crossings were washed out, forcing George to repair them with a pick and shovel, which slowed their trip considerably.

Luckily young Tom was a good baby, and managed to sleep even in the jolting vehicle, usually waking just to suckle at Lucy's breast. Only in the late afternoons was he wakeful and restless, and, although Emma's experience of infants was limited, she was surprised at how undemanding he was.

They arrived at Breakaway Creek just before dark on the second day. The rain had transformed the property with an abundance of lush green grass, and Lucy's garden was vibrant with fresh growth. It seemed a fitting welcome for the new infant. The only downside to the beauty were the swarms of flies that had bred in the creeks, forcing them to cover the baby with mosquito netting and burn dung fires whenever they stopped.

Alex appeared at the cottage soon after their arrival and, after duly admiring his nephew, told Lucy she'd have to manage without her cousin for a while.

'Come for a walk with me, Emma. There's something I want to show you.'

Walking hand-in-hand, he slowed his long strides to match hers. Conscious of the grasp of his calloused palm, joy and anticipation bubbled up inside her. She stole covert glances at his profile. He appeared so handsome and happy that just looking at him thrilled her.

Alex led her to their old haunt by the creek, where the once-stagnant waterhole had disappeared, engulfed by a rushing brown flow that reached halfway up the banks. An uprooted tree hung into the water creating swirling eddies in the current. As he drew her into a secluded spot amongst the timber, Emma held him off with a hand against his chest, smiling.

'What were you going to show me?'

He grinned.

'Just how much I missed you.' He pulled her close, kissing her and running his hands down her back, pressing her against his body. Weak with longing, Emma leaned into him, revelling in his strength and the growing boldness of his touch. He was breathing hard when he relinquished her mouth to whisper in her ear, 'How soon will you marry me?'

She laughed breathlessly.

'It was you who wanted to wait.'

'Curse me for a brainless fool. But we should hear from your father soon. You don't want a long engagement, do you?'

Pressed against his warm, strong body, it was difficult to think rationally.

'Just long enough to be respectable. A couple of months, at least.'

He sighed and swatted at a mosquito.

'A couple of months sounds like torture. Especially if we have to fight the insects off every time we take a walk.' He stepped back and tugged at her hand. 'Come on, we'd better go back before they eat us.'

~*~

Lucy had hired a housemaid; a shy, giggling girl from the local Aboriginal tribe. Kitty had been in training for a month or so before Lucy's confinement and still had much to learn, but she was eager to please and willingly tackled the heavy jobs such as the laundry and scrubbing the floors.

Late one afternoon Emma was at the clothesline, unpegging a row of Thomas's dry napkins, when Molly walked up to the back gate. She was a tall, proud-looking girl who always appeared clean and well dressed, but she made Emma uneasy with her arrogant manner. Most of the Aboriginies seemed to share Kitty's deferential behaviour, but Molly almost appeared to look down upon the people who employed her.

'Yes, Molly?' Emma asked over an armful of flannel napkins.

'Is Kitty here, Missus? We always walk to the camp together.'

'I think she'll be out shortly. The new baby's keeping us all busy.'

'White-feller babies make a lot of work.' She nodded at the basket of napkins. 'Black-feller piccaninnies aren't near as much trouble.'

Emma smiled, silently acknowledging the truth of this.

'How's your little boy, Molly?'

'He's down at the camp, playin' with rest.' Molly gave her a sly look. 'Everyone's talkin' 'bout you an' Mr Alex. I never thought he'd catch himself a flash city girl.'

Emma stared at her, a prickling of unease creeping down her spine.

'I don't feel that's an appropriate comment, Molly. Mr Baxter and I are no business of yours.'

'I sure wish ya happy, Missus.' Her flat, hard tone betrayed her words. 'Alex is too good for us black girls now, but he weren't that fussy once. Why don't ya ask him? He an' Molly, we were *good friends.*' She smiled maliciously.

Emma froze. Was she imagining the implication? But that last emphasis, coupled with the suggestively pouting lips, left little doubt to what Molly referred to. The hateful words buzzed in her brain and the prickling sensation turned to daggers, driving into her chest. With an effort Emma pulled herself together, tilting her head proudly.

'How dare you, Molly! I can hardly believe your impertinence!'

Determined to hide her distress from those gloating eyes, she gathered up the basket of washing and hurried inside, blindly grasping the handrail to steady herself as she almost tripped up the stairs.

She could hear Lucy on the front veranda, pacing back and forth as she tried to soothe the restless infant in her arms. Unable to face her,

Emma dumped the basket and hurried to her room, closing the door behind her. She sat on the bed and drew deep, gasping breaths, trying to calm herself. Molly could be lying. It was silly to be upset until she had verified the story.

Surely it couldn't be true. Alex had been so critical of his father's behaviour – how could he have committed the same sin? She didn't know how long she sat there, but when a knock on the door roused her, deep gloom had shrouded her room and the shadows stretched long outside her window.

'Emma! Alex is here to see you.'

Dread swamped her as she dragged herself to her feet.

'Tell him I'll be there in a moment, Lucy.'

She tidied her hair at the mirror, shocked at the wild appearance of her pale face and wide eyes. She didn't want Alex to see her like this, but the sooner she confronted him, the better. Taking more deep breaths, she walked to the veranda where he stood chatting to Lucy, who had Thomas in her arms.

Alex turned to Emma with a smile that twisted her heart.

'That baby must be in a good paddock. He's growing like a mushroom. Come for a walk with me, Emma?'

She nodded without smiling, allowing him to take her arm as they descended the steps. She shrugged off his touch once they were away from the house and watching eyes.

'What's wrong?' The gentle concern in his voice tore at her shredded emotions.

'I saw Molly this afternoon.' She felt him stiffen, saw his expression growing wary.

'What did Molly say?'

She took a deep breath, afraid to put it into words, afraid of his answer.

'She said you used to be "good friends".'

'Oh, hell.' He stopped abruptly and turned to face her. 'I won't lie to you, Emma.'

He looked down for a moment, kicking at a tuft of grass with his boot. When he met her eyes, his were dark with shame.

'I wish I could say I'd never carried on with Molly.'

Emma stared at him, the pressure in her chest making it difficult to breathe. His mouth twisted.

'I know, you're thinking what a hypocrite I am. I was seventeen. She came to my room one night. When I turned her away, she told me who my mother was. Up until then I had no idea my mother was Aboriginal.'

Something in his explanation penetrated through the painful images of him "carrying on" with Molly. She tried to push aside her own feelings and imagine how it must have felt to learn the truth in such a way, how devastating it would have been for a young lad.

'That must have come as a dreadful shock.'

'Too right it was. I admit I went a bit mad for a while.' He took a deep breath. 'I moved into the men's quarters with some rough types we had then. I started drinking and I was in no state to say no to Molly when she next approached me.'

He started walking again, Emma silently keeping pace at his side.

'I'm sorry, Emma. It only went on for a few weeks. Sarah intervened and helped me pull myself together. I was jolly glad when Molly married Mick and moved back to the camp. I swear to God I haven't touched her or any other woman since.'

Unsure how to respond, Emma remained silent, wishing she didn't feel so sick inside. Had she expected Alex to have had led a blameless life? She castigated herself for being a naïve fool.

'Thank you for being honest with me, Alex,' she said at last. 'It happened a long time ago and you were very young. I just need some time to get used to the idea.'

He stopped and turned to face her, catching her hands in his.

'I don't deserve you, Emma.'

She shook her head, miserably torn between her need of him and her repugnance for what he'd done.

'Can I hold you, please?' His dark eyes pleaded. 'Nothing more – I just need to feel you close.'

She acquiesced and he slid his arms around her. A shudder passed through her at the comforting press of his strong body. She laid her face on his shoulder, breathing in the familiar smell of horses and hard work, knowing her love for him was strong enough to forgive him worse than this. She felt his sharply exhaled breath stirring her hair, sensing along with it the flow of tension from his body.

'I love you, Emma. I don't know what I'd do if you left me again.'

'Hush, Alex. I'm not going anywhere.'

~*~

Alex stared blindly down at the top of her head, wondering for the hundredth time if he was asking too much of this generous-hearted girl. What did he have to offer her, when all was said and done? The miracle was that she still seemed to want him, along with all his flaws. He'd always been aware of Molly's spiteful streak, but he hadn't thought she'd have the audacity to carry tales to Emma. Did she still carry a torch for him, after all these years?

Whatever her motives, Alex knew he couldn't afford to let her get away with it, so after he'd walked Emma home, he made his way to the Aboriginal camp.

A group of people squatted around a campfire, roasting a goanna. The acrid smell of charred flesh mingled with the crackling flames and the babble of chattering voices, which ceased abruptly as he approached. Molly's paler skin and neat clothes made her easy to pick out. He knew she considered herself "civilised" and that she looked down on the rest of the tribe, which made it all the more surprising that she'd married one of them. Stopping a little way from the camp, he called her name and waited as she detached herself from the group and hesitantly approached him.

He gave her a hard look.

'You're a bloody troublemaker, Molly. You stay away from Miss Watson, you hear? You've got cheek talking to her like that.'

He must have sounded even angrier than he'd intended, for he saw fear glint in the whites of her eyes before the lids dropped over them.

'Yeah, Boss.' She shuffled her bare feet and looked at the ground, more outwardly humble than he'd ever seen her. 'Sorry, Boss. I won't talk no more, promise.'

He glared at her, pushing down his guilt to press his advantage.

'You've got a big mouth, Molly. It's going to get you into proper trouble one of these days.' He paused for emphasis. 'If you upset Miss Watson again, I'll have you sent away.'

He walked off, wishing he didn't feel like such a bastard. Perhaps there was more of his father in him than he'd thought.

Chapter Twelve

Rockhampton, 2010

At last Luke stopped talking. In the silence, Shelley stared out into the warm night, gripping the stem of her wineglass with unsteady fingers. She felt Luke's presence beside her and knew he was watching her closely. Even now, as stunned as she was, she was aware of his every movement.

'Are you okay, Shelley?' he finally asked.

His gentleness nearly undid her. She wanted to fall into his arms, to feel his reassurance that nothing had changed. She was still the same Shelley Blake, and having a far-off Aboriginal ancestor wasn't such a big deal. Or was it? she wondered – would it change the way he thought of her? Did it change the way she felt about herself?

It shouldn't have come as such a shock. All the clues were there, she realised. Alexander Baxter's dark complexion, her grandmother's aversion to the mention of his name … snobbish Audrey must have hated the stigma of a part-Aboriginal grandfather. Not that attitudes had changed so very much. Shelley thought of the few Aboriginal kids who'd attended her state school and remembered how everyone had looked down on them. Including – shamefully – herself.

She managed a tremulous smile.

'Yes, I'm all right, Luke. But it freaks me out a bit.'

'Does it bother you, having Aboriginal blood?'

Shelley shook her head.

'I don't know. I need to get used to the idea.' She looked down at her arms, which tanned so readily. The brownness of her skin was apparent even in the half-light of the porch. 'The whole story is just so bloody shocking. It all makes sense now, all the letters and Nanna Audrey's stuck-up attitude. Poor Emma, she must have gone through hell! I wonder if the person who shot Alex was trying to stop her marrying him?'

'I suppose we'll never know. It's hard to believe anyone would go so far.'

'Things were so different then. She must have been very brave. Marrying a part-Aboriginal would have been like committing social suicide.'

A car drove past in the street, its headlights briefly illuminating Luke's thoughtful face.

'And she was a city girl, too.'

That just goes to show that not all city girls are like your wife, thought Shelley. But she didn't voice her opinion out loud. She didn't want to risk rekindling Luke's anger by bringing Miranda into the conversation.

She wanted to ask if her Aboriginal blood bothered him, but how could she? It wasn't as if they were in a relationship. She'd offered to help look after his kids, nothing more. Just because they'd got hot and heavy in his Land Cruiser one night didn't give her any claim on him.

'How did your mother know all this?' she asked instead.

'It wasn't really a secret in the Baxter family. My grandfather, Jim Baxter, told her the story before he died. I suppose Alex wasn't our ancestor, so it didn't matter too much to my side of the family.'

'So you're descended from George and Lucy Baxter?'

'Apparently. I've never traced the family tree back that far.'

'I wonder if Alex and Emma kept in touch with them. It must have been traumatic, with the shooting and all.'

'It drove them away from Breakaway Creek.' He swallowed a mouthful of beer. 'I don't think they ever lived there again.'

'Why did your mother inherit the property? Didn't she have brothers?'

'No. She came from a family of four girls. Luckily she married a cattleman who was after a property of his own.' He grinned. 'Dad sure fell on his feet when he took up with Mum.'

As he spoke, an approaching car slowed in the street and turned into the driveway. Shelley straightened.

'My parents are home. Wait until I tell Mum the news.'

'Will she be upset? Is she prejudiced like your grandmother?'

She shook her head.

'She's nothing like Nanna. But if I feel shocked, I imagine she will too.'

When Noela and Peter Blake came in, Shelley introduced them to Luke, trying to behave normally. They responded with the open friendliness they extended to most people, but the whole time Shelley's mind was whirling. She scanned her mother's face for signs of Aboriginal ancestry. But there was nothing. Her mother was fairer than she was. She'd always wondered where she got her olive skin.

At last, over a cup of coffee, Shelley related what Luke had just told her. Her mother stiffened and her face grew pale.

'No wonder Mum never discussed it! She was always trying to distance herself from her family. I think she must have been in some sort of denial.' Noela shook her head, looking dazed. 'I knew she was hiding something, but I never guessed this.'

'Why would you?' Shelley said. 'For Nanna, this must have been her worst nightmare.'

'Poor old Alex got a raw deal,' Luke said. 'He was the oldest son and he got nothing. Just because his mother was Aboriginal.'

'That's the way it was in those days,' Peter said. 'Fairness had nothing to do with it.'

'It's all turned full circle,' Luke mused.

'I need some time to digest this.' Noela was silent for a moment, staring down at her hands clasped in her lap. She seemed to give herself a mental shake and looked up at Luke. 'I'm sorry. What about you? When you rang, Shelley told us you had your two boys with you.'

'Yeah, I sure do. They're asleep now – thank God.'

Luke related the circumstances in which he'd discovered the boys and Noela, always quick to show emotion, exclaimed indignantly.

'The poor little mites! Surely you'll be able to get custody if that's the way she's been looking after them,' she said.

Luke's lips thinned.

'I've got a feeling it won't be that easy. Taking off with them probably wasn't smart, but I couldn't leave them there. She doesn't really want them, but she'll fight me every inch of the way just to spite me.'

They chatted for a while longer until Shelley noticed Luke stifling a yawn and remembered him saying he'd had little sleep the night before.

'It must be time we all went to bed.'

'You're right, dear,' Noela said. 'Show Luke to his room, won't you?'

Shelley led the way and flicked the light on in the spare bedroom, where she'd earlier made up the double bed. The boys were sleeping in her brother's old room. 'I hope the bed's okay. It's pretty old and the mattress is a bit lumpy.'

He paused beside her, smiling, and her skin prickled with response.

'I think I could sleep anywhere tonight.' He reached out and brushed a knuckle across her cheek in a gentle gesture that made her pulse trip. 'See you in the morning, Shelley.'

~*~

Alone at last, Shelley found sleep elusive. Her mind whirled with thoughts of Alex and Emma and their battle against nineteenth-century prejudices. How many people had known of Alex's heritage? Had the couple struggled for acceptance because of it, or had they managed to keep the knowledge within their own family?

Even today, she wondered if people would treat her differently if they knew. She decided it wasn't something she'd make public. It was no one else's business and it had happened so long ago. She supposed it was a bit like discovering one of your ancestors had been a convict. It was vaguely embarrassing – although these days most people seemed to be proud of their convict ancestry – but it didn't change the person you were.

It was only the next day, after Luke had gone, that she told her parents about her decision to return to Breakaway Creek.

'Is that a good idea, Shelley?' Her mother looked at her in concern. Shelley avoided her eyes. Noela was uncomfortably observant and Shelley wondered what she'd sensed about her relationship with Luke.

'It's just until Luke can get a nanny. Besides, I need something to keep me busy until I go back to work.'

'Hmm.' Noela shook her head. 'He seems decent enough, but he's a good-looking bloke and he's still married. With two kids.'

Shelley flashed a quick look at her father. He stared at her intently, saying nothing. With an effort, she met her mother's gaze.

'I know all that. It's because of the kids I'm going. Not because I want to get involved with him.'

Noela shook her head.

'I think you're kidding yourself. I wasn't born yesterday.'

Heat rushed to her face. To avoid replying, she went to the sink where the washing up waited. In retrospect it might not have been the wisest decision, but she'd told Luke she'd go and she couldn't back out now.

~*~

Three days later Shelley once again turned off the highway and drove down the gravel road to Breakaway Creek. It obviously hadn't rained in her absence and the fresh green growth was already withering. The dogs were off the chain and greeted her with a frenzy of barking. Mitch appeared on the veranda, wiping crumbs from his mouth as if she'd interrupted his lunch.

'Hello, Shelley.' He smiled at her, but she sensed a degree of restraint behind it. 'Luke said you were coming back.'

'Hi, Mitch. No more rain, I see.'

'No, worse luck.' He came down the steps and took her suitcase. 'Come on in.'

Shelley rolled her eyes at his back as he turned away. Well, he was obviously thrilled to see her. What had happened to the old, cheerful Mitch?

'Where's Luke?'

'He took the boys to Faradale to stock up on groceries.'

'At least we'll be eating.' She hoped he'd be home soon, and more enthusiastic about her arrival than Mitch. She was beginning to think her mother was right about her coming here.

'Do you want some lunch?'

'Yeah, thanks. It's been a while since breakfast.'

She made herself a sandwich with the bread, meat and salad laid out on the table.

'How are the boys?'

The smile reached his eyes for the first time.

'They're great. Thrilled to be home. I just hope that woman'll let them stay. But I doubt it. I think Luke stirred up a hornet's nest, taking them like he did.'

'I'm worried about that, too,' she admitted. 'Is she the vindictive sort?'

He snorted.

'In my opinion she only took them to spite Luke. Don't ask me what I really think of her – your ears'd burn.' He finished off his sandwich and pushed his plate aside, giving her a sideways look. 'Luke told me what Mum said about Alexander Baxter. So you really are related to us after all.'

'That's true.' Shelley looked at him carefully. She didn't know if his reserved manner was due to his protective attitude towards his brother, or if he was bothered by the old family scandal. The roar of a vehicle pulling up to the house was a welcome distraction. Shortly after, Luke entered the kitchen bearing several bags of groceries, Ben and Jack trailing behind him. He smiled broadly at Shelley, instantly making up for his brother's lukewarm welcome.

'I didn't think you'd be here this early. Mitch, make yourself useful and get the rest of the stuff out of the car.'

Mitch left the room with apparent good grace and Shelley approached the boys, who responded to her greeting with shy smiles.

'You remember Shelley, who we stayed with in Rocky?' Luke encouraged them. 'She's going to help me look after you for a while. Isn't that nice of her?'

Jack nodded shyly and Ben puffed his chest importantly.

'I can show you my pony, Rambo. Daddy took me riding yesterday!'

'Did he really?' Shelley swung an amused glance at their father, who had begun loading food into the refrigerator. 'He's been very busy.'

'Have you seen our dogs?' Ben seemed to be warming to the animal theme.

'Yes, I have. What are their names again?'

'Biddy and Buttons. Did you forget?'

'I must have done,' she lied, smiling at Ben, who was obviously enjoying his little show-and-tell. She turned to the younger boy. 'What about you, Jack? Do you have a pony, too?'

Jack nodded vigorously.

'I ride Rambo, too.'

'I haven't got a second pony for them,' Luke told her from the depths of the fridge. 'If they're going to stay here I'll have to see about that.'

'Have you heard from their m-o-t-h-e-r?' she asked.

'Yeah, I sure have. I'll tell you about it later.'

Mitch came in then, loaded with more shopping bags. Shelley set about making sandwiches for Ben and Jack. It wasn't until that night, when the boys were in bed and Mitch had driven off to see his girlfriend that she and Luke finally had a chance to talk.

'I get the impression Mitch isn't thrilled to have me here,' Shelley commented as they sat over cups of coffee at the kitchen table.

Luke shrugged.

'He's worried about the whole situation with Miranda. But I need someone to help with the boys.'

'So you've heard from your wife?' she asked.

Luke took a swig of coffee and grimaced.

'Have I ever. She abused the hell out of me. They've scheduled some sort of mediation for us, but I don't know if she'll cooperate.' He paused. 'I told her if she doesn't, I'd tip the cops off about her drug habit.'

Shelley put her cup down and stared at him.

'She does drugs?'

'She never used to, but her boyfriend was known around here as a user, and it's a fair bet he's introduced her to them. I found a bag of white powder in a cupboard and they had a pot plant in the laundry.'

'Hell. No wonder you didn't want the boys to stay with her.'

He nodded grimly.

'A fine mother I chose for them. I think that's why Mitch is worried about you – he doesn't trust my judgement about women.'

'But he should know me well enough to realise I'm not like her.'

'He's just being cautious. That's Mitch all over – he's been with Julie for three years now and still hasn't even asked her to move in with him.' He managed a grin. 'He does spend a fair bit of time at her place, though.'

'Do you think Miranda will try to get the boys back?'

'Blowed if I know. Perhaps she'll wake up to what's good for her and leave them be.' He fiddled with a teaspoon, his forehead creased in a frown.

Shelley felt a rush of sympathy for him and had to fight a sudden strong desire to cover those restless fingers with her own. She had a fair idea where that would lead. Instead she pushed out her chair and got to her feet.

'It's been a long day. I'll see you in the morning, Luke.'

He looked up at her with an abstracted smile.

'Righto. Good night, Shelley. Thanks for coming.'

As she lay in bed, she could hear him moving about in the room two doors from hers and then the rushing sound of the shower. She tossed restlessly, trying to distract herself with thoughts of Ben and Jack and how she would entertain them the next day. It was definitely a safer topic than thinking about their father.

~*~

Over the next few days she settled into a routine with the boys. Their energy seemed boundless and keeping them amused without resorting to television was a challenge. They loved being read to, so when tempers became frazzled she found sitting them down with a story was the best solution. She loved the feel of their small warm bodies cuddling up to her as they looked at their favourite picture books.

If they missed their mother, there was no evidence of it. She only wished their father was at home more, but he and Mitch had to finish the work that Luke's trip to Brisbane had interrupted. In defiance of the summer heat they were constructing a new fence, subdividing a paddock to allow for better management of water and grass.

'There are always areas of a paddock where the grass is sweeter and more palatable,' Luke explained to her. 'The cattle tend to flog these spots and we end up with a weed problem. By providing more watering points and dividing the paddocks, we can force the cattle to use the less-preferred areas and spell their favourite patches.'

Each morning they started early to avoid working in the worst of the heat. Mostly they drove home for lunch and rested until the early afternoon before setting out again. But after a few days Ben and Jack had become bored with staying at home and Shelley asked Luke if she could drive them out to see what he and Mitch were doing.

'Why don't you bring lunch out to us?' Luke suggested.

'The boys would love that. But I'll need a map to find you.'

So at twelve o'clock she bundled the boys, a picnic basket and a thermos of tea into the four-wheel drive and set out with Luke's hand-drawn map on the console beside her. As she turned away from the creek and followed a fence line east, the well-worn track reassured her she was heading in the right direction. Accustomed to her little automatic, she struggled with the wagon's unfamiliar gears and clutch, slowing to a crawl as she skidded slightly in a patch of bulldust.

When she came to a fork in the road, she anxiously consulted her map. There were fresh wheel tracks on either route, so that was no help. She tried to work out where she was in relation to the sketch, but because of their slow speed she had no idea how far she'd come. Luke had marked a tank and trough close to the road, but she couldn't remember seeing that.

'Did you boys see a tank?' she asked Ben and Jack, who were squabbling happily in the back seat.

Ben shook his head.

'Are we lost?'

'I hope not. Your father said to turn right after the tank, but if we haven't passed that I'd better keep going.'

She continued down the fence line for another mile or so. The track deteriorated rapidly, with numerous potholes and sections of tree root protruding from the dusty soil. Suddenly she heard a crunching sound and then the vehicle seemed to wobble, with a suspicious rumbling noise coming from one of the tyres.

Her nerves leapt sickeningly. Shelley braked and sat for a moment, unwilling to get out and find what she was dreading – a flat tyre. Castigating her spinelessness, she opened the door and walked around the vehicle, finding the front tyre on the passenger's side already half-deflated and hissing as the remaining air escaped.

'Oh, shit!' she exclaimed, and then glanced guiltily at the boys, who were clambering out to inspect the damage.

'We got a flat tyre!' Jack exclaimed gleefully. It seemed that at his age everything was an adventure.

'I hope you boys are good at changing them.'

Ben shook his head again.

'Daddy always does it.'

'Well, he's not here now.' She drew in a deep breath. 'I suppose I'll have to try. Get your hats on, boys. The sun's hot.'

She found the jack and wheel spanner in a compartment in the luggage area. The spare tyre was bolted onto one of the rear doors and the first thing she did was unscrew the bolts and lift it down. It was heavy and she puffed with exertion. The sun beat down on her back, burning into her bare arms and penetrating her thin cotton blouse.

Once she'd loosened the wheel nuts, she tackled the dreaded jack. Her father had once shown her how to change a tyre but during the years of city driving she'd had no practice.

'You'd think in these days of advanced technology they'd have invented a better way of changing a tyre!' she grumbled, pausing to rest her aching arms. Her hands were filthy and she'd broken one of her fingernails.

'Can I help?' Ben pleaded.

She let him take the jack handle in his small, chubby fist, but after a few half-hearted twists he gave up.

'I can't. It's too hard.'

'I know. It's hard for me, too. Let's have a drink and rest in the shade for a while.'

She glanced at her watch. It was already one o'clock. Would Luke come looking for her if they didn't arrive soon?

The boys, unable to sit still for long, began playing beside the road, using sticks as make-do horses.

'Don't wander away,' she warned them sternly. After a brief rest, she set to work again. Eventually she had the wagon high enough to remove the wheel, but when she tried to fit the spare, she found the fully inflated tyre required more height. As she struggled to wind the stubborn jack handle, she heard a vehicle draw up. She stood and wiped sweat out of her eyes, heaving a sigh of relief as she realised it was Luke in the Land Cruiser.

'I thought you must be in trouble.' He walked over to her, smiling, and cast a shrewd eye over the progress she'd made. 'Looks like you'd have got it done, though.'

'I'm only too happy to hand over to you,' she assured him with a little laugh, trying to ignore the way her heart skipped a beat. 'I don't care if I never have another one of these.'

The boys ran up, their faces red and sweating under over-sized Akubras.

'Daddy, how did you find us?'

'I followed your tracks,' he said, crouching to wind the jack with frustrating ease.

'Oh, yes.' Shelley remembered that he'd come from the same direction as they had. 'Did we take the wrong road?'

'Uh-huh. You should have turned right after the tank.'

'But I didn't see a tank.'

'It was just before the fork in the road.'

'Oh,' she said, feeling foolish. 'I must have been too busy watching the track.'

'That's okay.' He gave her the easy smile that, as always, made her stomach flip. 'It's all strange to you, I know.'

'Mmm, being a city girl and all.'

His smile didn't falter.

'Different to some, though.'

Their eyes locked and he stood up slowly. For a moment that seemed suspended in time he stared down at her, his eyes dark and intense. Her muscles clenched in anticipation.

Then Jack clutched Luke's leg, grasping a fistful of his jeans.

'Hurry up, Daddy. I'm hungry. Wanna go.'

'Righto, Jack. It's past lunchtime.' Abruptly he turned away and squatted to fit the wheel. Shelley handed him the nuts one by one and he took them without looking up. In five minutes he had it all done and everything stowed back in the wagon's boot.

'Follow me,' he said to Shelley. 'Do you boys want to come with me?'

They did, so Shelley was left alone with her thoughts and her frustrated libido as she followed his Toyota down the bumpy track. If the boys hadn't been there, he would have kissed her, she was sure of it. She didn't know whether to be glad or sorry.

Chapter Thirteen

When they met Mitch, Luke led them to a shady spot under a clump of brigalow to eat their lunch. Perched on the top of a rise, they looked down over an open paddock with the new fence at their backs. Shelley rested against a rough tree trunk and handed out sandwiches while Luke poured tea from the thermos. Despite the heat, flies and ants, contentment lulled her senses. Perhaps it was a combination of the fresh air and the delayed meal, but the simple food tasted as delicious as any restaurant meal. Her uncomfortable experience with the flat tyre faded.

Even Mitch was good-humoured, indulging the boys and generally behaving like their favourite uncle. They seemed to like him and enjoy his teasing. If only he was as relaxed with her, she thought.

'Look at that beautiful paddock of grass,' he said, as he sipped at his mug of tea. He swept out his arm, indicating the pasture in front of them. 'If the greenies have their way, it'll be a wasteland of brigalow suckers in a few years.'

Shelley looked at him questioningly.

'Is that because they want to stop clearing regrowth?'

Mitch nodded.

'This paddock was all brigalow before it was pulled, with hardly a blade of grass and very few native animals living here. It's a constant job to keep the suckers under control, with fire and blade ploughing. Spraying's a last resort. If we can't control it, it'll grow back thicker than ever in a few years. Thousands of acres of the best cattle country in Central Queensland will be worthless.'

Shelley was dumbfounded.

'It's not as if you haven't left lots of trees. Some paddocks don't seem to have ever been cleared.'

Mitch shrugged.

'It's hard to convince the greenies. I'm not sure where they think their food comes from. Another big worry is the coal mines. They're taking more and more of the prime farming and grazing land.'

Shelley had heard this topic mentioned on the news and found it personally disturbing.

'The mining companies say they can restore it. Is that true?

Mitch gave short, dismissive laugh.

'Have you seen the land they've supposedly rehabilitated in this area? What was flat land is now steep hills with no topsoil and severe erosion problems. It's barely fit for grazing, let alone farming.'

Ben distracted her then, asking for another sandwich. The conversation changed to other topics. Shelley wondered if it was just her overactive imagination, or if Luke was quieter than usual. But she refused to allow it to spoil her mood, or to let herself wonder if he was regretting that charged moment beside the car.

~*~

Shelley didn't get a chance to be alone with Luke until just before dinner, when she encountered him in the hallway outside the bathroom.

'Shelley…' He hesitated, looking awkward, his eyes not quite meeting hers. 'I'm sorry I came on to you a bit today. It doesn't feel right, now I have the boys here. We have to be sensible for this to work.'

'They're only little,' she countered, keeping her tone cool even as her insides shrivelled. 'I don't think they noticed.'

'No, but it's bad enough seeing their mother … I don't want to set another bad example.' He sighed and shook his head. 'I'm making a hash of this. I probably shouldn't have brought you here, knowing how I feel about you.'

She tilted her chin.

'I didn't come here expecting an affair, if that's what you're thinking.' Brushing past him, she hurried into her room and closed the door firmly behind her. She sank onto the edge of the bed and buried her face in her hands, cringing inside. What she'd just said was a barefaced lie. If she hadn't been anticipating an affair, why had she filled an old prescription of the Pill and started taking it again before she left Rockhampton? She could kid herself all she liked that any liberated twenty-first century woman should be prepared, but the fact remained that Luke was the only man she wanted to get involved with.

Facing him at the table was difficult. She busied herself with the boys and tried to behave normally, striking up a conversation with Mitch because it was easier than pretending she wasn't embarrassed by her earlier conversation with his brother. Mitch watched her with steady, knowing eyes while Luke concentrated on his meal and didn't say much. He looked grim and tired, and as soon as the dishes were washed he disappeared in the direction of the front veranda.

Shelley lingered at the sink, taking her time to rinse it clean and wipe over the stainless steel while she watched Luke through the window. In the faint glow cast by the inside lights, she saw him sit on the front steps. He rested his elbows on his knees and propped his chin in his hands. Although his face was in shadow the hunch of his shoulders spoke plainly of his dejection.

In spite of herself Shelley felt a pang of pity and some other, deeper emotion she preferred not to put a name to. There was more going on here than unrequited lust, she reminded herself. Miranda had been quiet so far, but there was a tenseness in Luke that suggested he didn't expect to win so easily. And he was trying to do the decent thing by the boys – that didn't mean he didn't want her.

She was still lying awake sometime after ten when she heard him go to his room. Shelley sighed and rolled over on the mattress, hugging the pillow to her chest in a futile quest for comfort. From now on, she decided, she wasn't going to add to his worries. She would keep things friendly but cool and try to restore their friendship, communicating with him about the children and work while keeping her personal affairs tucked safely away. For her own peace of mind, she knew she should pack up and go. But if she did, she'd be leaving him in the lurch. And sensible or not, it was the last thing she wanted to do.

~*~

Luke and Mitch were away on the fence line when the car arrived. Shelley watched from a window as a silver Pajero drew up at the gate and two occupants climbed out. A thin, blonde-haired woman in faded jeans and black singlet top walked up the path as if she had a right to be there. The man who followed her was burly, bearded and wore scruffy shorts.

Shelley came onto the veranda, her pulse skittering nervously. As the woman neared Shelley could see she was pretty, in a brittle sort of way, with a row of studs in both ears and a tattoo on her upper right arm. She looked much harder than the woman in the photographs and not the type Shelley would have paired with a country guy like Luke.

'Who are you?' the visitor snapped. Her eyes narrowed suspiciously at Shelley.

Shelley raised her eyebrows at the woman's brusqueness.

'I'm Shelley Blake, the nanny,' she replied, feigning coolness. 'And who are you?'

Not that she needed to ask.

'I'm Miranda, the boys' mother.' Miranda curled her lip. 'He kidnapped them, you know that?'

Shelley didn't respond, fearing anything she said might only fuel the flames. Miranda inclined her head at the man who had come to stand beside her, linking her hand in his.

'This is my partner, Bevan. Where are my boys?'

'They're inside,' she responded, thinking fast. While Miranda was talking to her sons perhaps she could contact Luke on the UHF radio. He had a receiver in his Toyota but he would have to be working close by to hear it.

She led them into the lounge room, where Ben and Jack were playing with a set of Duplo. The boys looked up, wide-eyed, as their mother walked into the room. Their gaze flicked to Bevan and quickly away. Shelley wondered if she'd imagined fear in Ben's round, blue eyes.

'Boys,' Miranda cried, holding out her arms. 'Come and give Mummy a hug.'

For an agonising moment Shelley thought they would defy her. Then Jack got reluctantly to his feet and crossed the room to his mother's embrace. Ben followed with dragging feet. They suffered her kiss, squirming in her arms before pulling away and going back to their game. Miranda's mouth stretched in a smile that didn't reach her eyes.

'They're not much for cuddles, those two. Real little boys.'

Shelley, who found them openly affectionate, bit her lip and said nothing. She resisted the urge to fidget as those cold eyes focussed on her.

'So where did Luke find you?'

'I'm a distant cousin,' Shelley explained, thinking the family angle wouldn't hurt. 'I was travelling through and called to see the old family property. I'm just helping out for a bit.'

Miranda sniffed.

'He's never mentioned you.'

'And he won't be needing you anymore,' Bevan announced, his thick lips pursed belligerently. It was the first time he'd spoken. 'The boys should be with their mother. We're taking them back.'

Shelley's heart tripped.

'You should talk with Luke first. He's their father and he's entitled to a say.'

Miranda's nostrils flared.

'He's not entitled to snatch them from my house. I could have him charged with kidnapping!'

'I'll call Luke. He needs to come home so you can talk about this.' Dread settled around Shelley in a sickening cloud. Even if they waited for Luke, there seemed little chance of any peaceful mediation with this pair.

'Yeah, you call the bugger.' Miranda put her hands on her narrow hips. 'I want to tell him what I think of him, running off with my boys like that.'

Shelley escaped to the kitchen where the UHF radio perched on a shelf beside the refrigerator. She called several times before Mitch's calm voice came over the airways.

'Mitch here. What's the problem?'

'We have visitors from Brisbane.' Shelley was loath to broadcast their identity over the public system. 'They want to see Luke.'

She paused, willing him to understand her message.

'It's important.' She heard Mitch suck in a breath.

'I see. We'll be there shortly.'

She hurried back to the lounge room, where Miranda and her boyfriend sat side by side on the sofa. The boys continued to play with their Duplo, ostensibly ignoring their mother.

'Luke's on his way.'

'I suppose he's at the other end of the place,' Miranda sneered. 'He was never close to home when I needed him.'

'He's only twenty minutes away,' Shelley said, fighting to stay calm. 'Would you like tea or coffee while you're waiting?'

'Sure.' Miranda shrugged. 'Coffee's good.'

It was the longest half-hour she'd ever spent. As Miranda and Bevan silently sipped their coffee, she kept glancing at the clock on the wall. The hands crawled slowly around the dial. The pair seemed little disposed to polite conversation, and in desperation Shelley switched on the television, letting the mind-numbing dramas of *Days of our Lives* distract them from the more immediate conflict at hand. Miranda joined the boys on the floor and made a show of looking at what they'd made with the Duplo, but it seemed like a token effort staged for Shelley's benefit.

As she watched Miranda, Shelley wondered what had drawn Luke to her. A little more flesh would have made her attractive, but her face looked pinched and her movements were quick and nervous. To Shelley it seemed as if Miranda had stretched life to its limits and was now perched precariously on the edge. They'd been so young when they married – God knows what changes the years had wrought.

When Shelley heard the Toyota she hurried outside, relieved to see Mitch alight alongside his brother.

'Is it Miranda?' Luke asked, touching her arm as if in need of reassurance. His eyes were bleak. Shelley nodded.

'She's talking about taking the boys. She has her boyfriend with her.'

'I guessed as much.' He looked at his brother. 'Come on, Mitch. I might need some moral support.'

Shelley hesitated and he must have read her indecision.

'Shelley, can you take Ben and Jack for a walk while I talk to her? They don't need to overhear this.'

Agreeing, she followed them inside. She guessed from the rigidity of Luke's body how much he dreaded confronting his wife and her lover. When he entered the lounge room there was no polite greeting, no attempt to pretend this was anything other than it was.

'Miranda.' His voice was harsh. He didn't acknowledge the man beside her. 'Shelley's taking the boys out while we discuss this.'

Her lip curled again in a way that seemed habitual.

'Do you think that's necessary? How do I know you haven't asked her to drive off and hide them somewhere??'

Shelley bristled.

'I'm not driving anywhere. Don't you think your sons should be spared the arguments?'

Miranda waved her away.

'Oh, just go. All this self-righteous crap makes me sick.'

Shelley bit her lip and gathered the boys to her.

'Come on, Ben and Jack. Let's go for a walk to the creek, shall we? We'll see if we can find any ducks today.'

~*~

Luke watched her hustle them out the door, contrasting her obvious concern with the scornful attitude displayed by the woman on the sofa before him. Miranda had only been gone a few months, but she'd changed so much it was hard to equate her with the girl he'd married.

She'd always had a selfish streak but by the new, hard set to her face, the limpness of her bleached hair and the dark circles under her eyes, it was obvious her life had taken a downward spiral. The tattoo was definitely new. In other circumstances he might have pitied her, but he was buggered if he'd let her stuff up his boys' lives as well as her own.

'I'll tell you right now, I'm not giving the boys up,' he stated flatly. 'I know you're on drugs and you're not a fit mother. I'll fight you every inch of the way.'

'Oh yeah?' she sneered. 'And if I was taking drugs, you would know how?'

He made a contemptuous sound.

'Just look at you. Besides, I saw it in the house.'

Bevan leapt to his feet, that soft, lazy-looking body suddenly vibrating with tension. 'Careful what you say there, cowboy. You can't prove that.'

Luke felt Mitch move up beside him and grasp his arm in a steadying gesture. He took a deep breath, knowing he had to be careful.

'We'll let the courts decide,' he said. 'But until then, the boys are staying with me.'

'I'm their mother! Don't you know the courts always favour the mother?'

'Not if she's unfit.' He glared at Miranda. His belly churned as he silently acknowledged his only hope was to bluster his way out of this.

Miranda flounced to her feet with a contemptuous snort.

'Bevan, this is a waste of time! I'll get onto community services, see what they have to say about this.'

'If you do, I'll tell them about the drugs,' he countered desperately, knowing it was the only thing he had up his sleeve.

'What drugs?' she sneered, tugging Bevan after her out the door. She didn't mention the boys, or seem to care that she was leaving without saying goodbye to them. Not that Luke was surprised. He stood on the veranda and watched as their car roared away in a cloud of dust. He sensed Mitch come up beside him and looked away from the pity in his brother's eyes.

'I know what you're thinking. She's a heck of a lot worse since she hooked up with him.'

Mitch put his hand on his shoulder and squeezed.

'It's tough on you, mate. Surely they can't make you give up the boys to *that*.'

'I was such a stupid prick, getting involved with her in the first place.' Luke thumped his fist against the veranda rail, swearing in pain and frustration.

'Yeah, I know.' Mitch shook his head, as if he was the wise older brother. 'You weren't thinking with your brain.'

Luke looked at him quickly and grabbed his hat from a peg on the wall.

'I'd better find Ben and Jack.'

He sensed Mitch watching after him as he set off for the creek, his mind turmoil of self-loathing and impotent anger. Imagining what an upbringing of indifference and neglect might do to his sons' innocent, happy natures, he clenched his fists until his nails dug into his palms. Normally he didn't feel the need to settle disputes with violence, but right now he wanted to punch someone or something – badly.

Shelley had fetched fishing lines from the shed and the boys sat one on either side of her, reels clenched in their chubby hands, the nylon lines drifting in the still, green water. Ben was asking questions, as usual.

'Shelley, why do the ducks go under water?'

'Because they –' Shelley must have heard his boots crunching on the grass, for she swung around in mid-reply. Her face creased with concern as she looked up at him. 'Is everything all right?'

He nodded, unwilling to say otherwise while little ears were listening.

'Mummy had to go, boys. She said to say goodbye.' He had to pretend, for their sakes. Luke sat down beside them, drawing in a deep breath. He felt a rush of gratitude for Shelley's presence and tugged playfully at Jack's hat.

'Catching anything, buster?'

'Something nibbled!' Jack announced, his chest swelling proudly.

'It was just a turtle,' Ben countered scornfully. 'I saw its head sticking out of the water.'

'Never mind.' Luke willed the tension out of his body and tried to absorb the ambience of the peaceful waterhole, which held such happy memories from his own boyhood. For now, he had everything he wanted just here beside him and he was determined not to let his problems intrude. He'd enjoy each precious moment while he could.

Chapter Fourteen

During the night Shelley was abruptly awoken. She lay still for a moment to listen, until the frightened cry came again. She realised it had to be one of the boys and hastened to their room, almost colliding with Luke in the doorway.

He put out a hand to steady her.

'Ben's having a nightmare.'

In the dim glow of the nightlight Ben was thrashing about, the sheets tangled around his small body. Luke bent over him and shook him awake.

'Daddy's here, Ben. Everything's all right.'

'Daddy!' Ben wrapped his arms around his father's neck, clinging tight. 'I don't want to go with Mummy!'

'Shhh, little mate,' his father soothed. 'You're staying here with me.'

Luke sat on the bed, holding the distraught little boy in his arms. He looked up at Shelley over the child's head, making her glad of the dim light as she remembered the scantiness of her pyjamas.

'Poor little kid,' he muttered.

And poor Luke, Shelley thought. He was suffering just as much.

'It's really tough,' she whispered. 'I wish there was something I could do.'

'It's all right. I'll stay with him.'

But back in bed, she tossed and turned, unable to sleep. Luke had told her the outcome of his "discussion" with his estranged wife and it sounded like he had a battle on his hands.

~*~

The next day Ben seemed his usual bright, cheerful self, but Shelley couldn't help wondering what fears lurked in his subconscious. Both boys already seemed more outgoing and confident than when she'd first arrived. What a tragedy it would be if Luke was forced to return them to their mother. It didn't seem logical that Miranda would have a hope of winning custody, but she knew logic didn't always determine the outcome of such situations. She'd heard some terrible stories of fathers denied the rights to their children.

Luke and Mitch drove off to work on the fence again. Later in the morning, when Shelley was hanging a load of washing on the clothesline, she heard a vehicle draw up. It didn't sound like Luke's Toyota and her senses immediately went on alert. She'd left the two boys playing in the sandpit in the front garden.

She dropped a handful of pegs into the basket and hurried around the house. Her heart plummeted when she saw the silver Pajero. Miranda and her boyfriend were already inside the gate, approaching the boys in their sandpit. Dread squeezing her chest, Shelley called out.

'Hey, there!'

The couple barely glanced at her and continued purposely towards Ben and Jack. The boys had stopped playing and eyed the intruders with anxious faces. She broke into a run, reaching the sandpit only a moment after Luke's wife.

'Come on, Ben and Jack.' Miranda bent down to the boys, lifting both of them to their feet. 'I'm taking you home.'

'But Mummy!' Ben looked about to wail. 'We are home!'

'Your home's with Mummy,' Miranda said firmly. She nodded at Bevan, who moved forward and lifted Jack in his arms.

'You can't do this! You can see the boys don't want to go!' Her outrage gave Shelley the courage to push between Ben and his mother.

'Get out of the way, bitch!' Miranda hissed. 'Who asked you to interfere?'

'I'll handle her.' Bevan's voice was softly menacing. He dumped Jack unceremoniously on the ground and, before she could move away, he'd grasped her arms from behind. 'This is none of your business!'

Shelley's heartbeat accelerated, her body going rigid. Jack was staring at them, his eyes wide with alarm. She realised her mistake. Shelley couldn't physically stop them, and she was only making the situation more traumatic for the children. She shook her head and twisted to look at Bevan's sneering face.

'No, not like this! We're scaring the boys. Just let me go – I won't interfere.'

'Too late.' He poked the small of her back with his finger. 'Come inside with me.'

She paused to look down at the children, too disturbed by their frightened faces to spare a thought for her own predicament.

'Don't worry, boys.' She tried to sound reassuring, despite the betraying quiver in her voice. 'You'll be all right with your Mummy.'

Without further protest she accompanied Bevan into the house, glancing back once to see Miranda bundling her sons into the car. She attempted to swallow down the panic that squeezed her throat.

'Where's the UHF radio?'

Biting her tongue, she led him to the kitchen and indicated the radio. Bevan reached for the mouthpiece and pulled it out of the instrument, then dropped it on the floor and stomped on it. A decisive crunching sound suggested she wouldn't be using it to call Luke.

'Now, the phone.'

She showed Bevan the phone in the office, hoping he wouldn't look further. He ripped the cord out of the handset.

'Is there another one?'

She shook her head.

'Are you sure? I'll check with Miranda.'

'There's one in the lounge room.' She hastened to point it out, realising any further delays would only anger him. It was a cordless phone, so he simply picked up the handset and put it in his pocket.

'What about mobiles?'

'They keep dropping out. And there's no reception where Luke is.'

'Come with me and I'll ask Miranda.'

To Shelley's relief, Miranda confirmed this.

'I told you this was the back of beyond here. I could never talk to Luke when he was out in the paddocks.'

'Right.' Bevan grabbed Shelley's arm and swung her to face him. He pushed his face close to hers. 'Now, you just stand back and let us drive away. If you give us any trouble, I'll tie you up. Remember you said you didn't want the boys frightened.'

His fingers bit into her arm, but Shelley could only think of the poor, confused children.

'Wait a moment.' She looked at Miranda. 'Shouldn't you take some of their clothes and toys?'

Miranda shrugged.

'You pack something for them, then. Go watch her, Bevan. I'll stay here.'

In the boys' bedroom, Shelley gathered up their clean clothes and quickly packed their bags. Bevan's menacing figure lurked in the doorway, making her struggle to concentrate. After adding a few toys from the lounge room floor, she thrust the bags at him with shaking hands.

'Here. Just take these and go.'

She sank onto the front steps and watched the Pajero speed off leaving a long cloud of red dust in its wake. Trembling all over, she fought the urge to burst into tears. Luke had to know; she had to tell him. The only option was to drive.

Shelley lost precious moments struggling to find the wagon's reverse gear and then stalled it as she tried to back out of the shed. Cursing loudly, she over-compensated with the accelerator on the second attempt and the tyres squealed on the concrete floor. Once out of the garage she sped down the road, braking when she came to a fork. For a confused moment she couldn't think which track to take and she thumped the steering wheel in frustration. She took a deep breath, managed to gather her thoughts and turned to the left. When she came to the new fence line she thanked her lucky stars she'd driven the same way before.

Luke and Mitch were sinking postholes when she found them, Luke on the tractor operating the digger and Mitch on the ground with a shovel. Mitch signalled to Luke as she drove up and he turned in the seat to see her. He threw some levers and vaulted off. In a moment, he was peering anxiously in her open window.

'They took the boys,' she told him breathlessly. 'Bevan smashed the radio, so I couldn't call you.'

'Shit.' Under his tan, his face turned pale. He turned to Mitch who stood right behind him. 'I'm going after them.'

Shelley climbed across the seat to the passenger side and Luke slid behind the wheel. He took off up the dirt road at twice the speed Shelley had dared to drive, the vehicle shuddering and lurching over the rough track.

'How long have they been gone?'

'About half an hour. That drop-kick smashed the UHF. Then he ripped the cord out of the phone and took the cordless with him.'

'Bastard!' Luke muttered. 'Were the boys frightened?'

'I made the mistake of trying to stop them at first, but Bevan grabbed me. So I said I'd cooperate. They weren't even going to get the boys' clothes, so I went inside and packed some things for them.'

'Oh, Shelley.' He took his eyes off the road long enough to give her a grateful smile. 'I'm sorry you got mixed up with this mess. Did that bugger threaten you?'

Shelley shrugged.

'He didn't hurt me. I'm more worried about the boys.'

'Be careful around him. I don't know what he's capable of. I'm not leaving the boys with him, that's for sure.'

'So you're going after them?'

'Yep. I'll follow them to Brisbane. I didn't want to dob them in for the drugs, but it's come to that now. They'll get a nice surprise when the police are waiting for them at home.'

Once back at the house, Luke filled the vehicle's diesel tank and hurried off to his bedroom to pack a bag. Shelley threw some things into her suitcase before meeting him in the hallway. He looked askance at the case in her hand.

'I'm coming with you.'

'Shelley, I'd sooner you didn't. You don't need to be involved in this.'

'I can share the driving. Besides, I'm already involved.'

He managed a brief smile, pulling her close for a quick hug.

'Thanks, Shelley.'

She followed him to the car, unable to suppress a ridiculous glow of pleasure.

'There's a telephone book under your seat. Look up Crime Stoppers for me?'

It didn't take her long to find the number. Just before they turned onto the main highway, Luke pulled over and dialled the number she read out. He gave the information in an expressionless voice, citing their names and address and describing the drugs he'd seen. His lack of emotion made Shelley wonder how much it hurt to inform on his own wife.

He placed his phone on the console and turned to her with a grim smile.

'I hope I've done the right thing. It will be frightening for the boys, but I guess the end justifies the means, if it helps me to get them back. They're the only thing that matters now. I'm buggered if I'll stand by and let Miranda screw up their lives.'

'How far are we going today?'

He looked at the dashboard display, which read twelve o'clock.

'We'll grab lunch at Dingo so we should get to Gin Gin or Childers by dark. Might as well pull up then – there's no point getting to Brisbane before they do.'

They ended up continuing to Childers, which offered more choice of accommodation. Luke pulled into a presentable motel and ducked into reception. Shelley watched him through the glass door as he chatted with the receptionist, flashing his quick, courteous smile. A shaft of desire pierced her, along with the first fluttering of nerves in her stomach. He hadn't said a word about their sleeping arrangements, but she was acutely aware that they were alone for the first time in weeks.

'I just got one room, but it has two beds. Is that all right?' he asked and handed Shelley the key.

In the gloom of the vehicle their eyes met. The butterflies in Shelley's stomach took off in full flight. She nodded, not trusting herself to speak – was he going to ask her to sleep with him?

Her hands trembled as they took their bags from the boot. The brush of Luke's arm against hers made her head spin. Inside the room she laid her suitcase on the rack and looked around, taking in the functional space with its queen-sized and single beds, covered in bright quilts. She wished she knew what he was thinking.

She ducked into the bathroom to use the facilities and smoothed her hair in front of the mirror. As she emerged he was taking clean clothes from his suitcase. He laid them on the bed and crossed the room to her, taking both her hands in his.

'Shelley.' His eyes stared intently into hers and he caressed the back of her hand with a calloused thumb. 'What we do is up to you. If you want, I can sleep in the single bed. This is no more right than it was the first time. I just don't have the will to fight it anymore.'

Her heart leapt.

'Do we need to fight it?' she asked. 'If we hurt anyone, it will only be ourselves.'

'That's what I'm afraid of.'

'I'm not. Not anymore.' It had been a day fraught with emotion and fear, and in comparison the perils of a new relationship seemed insignificant. She lifted her hands to his face, framed his stubbled cheeks in her palms and reached up to lightly kiss his mouth.

Luke's clothes smelled of dust, diesel and sweat. Neither of them had taken the time to shower and change. Shelley felt none too fresh. She stepped back even as Luke tried to pull her close.

'Before this goes any further, I want to have a shower.' Luke let his hands fall and drew a ragged breath.

'Good idea. I need one more than you. Why don't we go out for dinner, then? The receptionist said there's a hotel in the middle of town that does good counter meals.'

They'd waited this long, what was another hour or so? She murmured her agreement. Having dinner together first would heighten their anticipation and was definitely a more refined option.

They stepped carefully around each other while taking their separate showers and dressing in more appropriate clothes. Shelley put on a simple wrap dress, delicate, sequinned thongs and applied light make-up. Luke came out of the bathroom bare-chested, a fresh, un-faded pair of jeans snug about his hips. Shelley watched and shivered slightly as he slipped into a casual long-sleeved shirt and proceeded to roll the sleeves up to his elbows. Knowing what they would shortly share she wondered how she would ever get through the meal.

In the hotel lounge, Luke bought a glass of white wine for her and a beer for himself.

'This feels wrong – going out for a meal when I don't know if the boys are okay,' he said, as they sat at a secluded table in the corner

'If you want to change your mind…'

'No. There's nothing more we can do tonight. But I wish our first dinner date was under different circumstances.' He raised his glass to her, then smiled and looked into her eyes. 'To hell with it. To us. And to the night to come.'

She blushed, feeling like a schoolgirl. The heat in his eyes made the pit of her stomach curl and her pulse race. If she had found Luke in denial attractive, this flirtatious Luke was irresistible.

'To us,' she echoed, deciding not to fuel the flames by repeating the rest of it. They made light conversation while they waited for their meals to arrive. Luke didn't mention Miranda or the boys again and they ate quickly, both too impatient to linger.

As they walked out into the dark, deserted car park, Luke took her hand and she moved close, thrilling at the brush of his body against hers. The warm night air caressed her bare skin and her body hummed with anticipation.

Instead of opening her car door Luke spun her to face him and pulled her into his arms. Her blood rushed through her veins, leaving her suddenly weak and light-headed as their mouths and bodies locked together. He pressed her against the side of the vehicle, kissing her as he had only once before – that night beside the flooded creek. It had been weeks, yet she remembered the taste and feel of him. Luke was as familiar to her as if it had been yesterday.

He pushed a thigh between hers, his hand cupping her breast. Shelley tugged the tail of his shirt out of his jeans and slid her hand up his back, delighting in the feel of muscle under her fingertips. He shuddered and groaned, breaking off the kiss.

'Come on,' he said, moving aside to open her door. He was breathing hard. 'We'd better get back to the motel before we get arrested.'

Chapter Fifteen

At their room Luke grabbed her again, pressing her up against the door and kissing her as he fumbled to insert the key. As the door swung open he held her so she wouldn't fall and guided her to the queen bed where they sank in a tangled heap.

Kissing wildly, they tugged at each other's clothes, tossing them carelessly on the floor. At last she felt his hands on her bare skin, caressing her breasts, her stomach, her thighs. She was delighted to finally touch him in return. The rough texture of his chest hair and the ripple of muscle excited her. She took his quickly indrawn breath as a sign of encouragement and slid her fingers over his belly. His voice rasped against her ear when he urgently spoke her name.

Before he pulled off his jeans, Luke slipped a small package from his pocket and tore it open with his teeth. He smiled at her, his eyes glittering and yet tender.

'I came prepared this time.'

~*~

Shelley woke to the sound of the shower and turned to find Luke's side of the bed empty. Sunlight peeked through a gap in the curtains and when she looked at the bedside clock, the digital numbers read 7:15. She'd overslept, but they had been awake until after midnight.

She stretched sensuously, enjoying the delicious sated laxness of her body. She didn't know when she'd last felt like this, if ever. Her face felt as though scraped with sandpaper and her body throbbed in places but, like a starving person who has gorged at a feast, she luxuriated in the sensations.

The running water stopped and a few moments later Luke stepped out of the bathroom, a towel wrapped around his waist. His wet hair stood up in spikes and fresh desire surged in a flush of heat through Shelley's body. She smiled at him and was about to say something enticing when she noticed his expression. He looked every bit as grim as he had the previous day

'Come on, Shelley. We have to get going. We should have been on the road by now.'

Her happiness shrivelled inside her like a flower in a hot wind. She clutched the sheet tight around her and scrabbled for her dress, which lay where it had been tossed. She pulled it over her head and dug in her bag for clean clothes while Luke silently dressed beside her. How could she have forgotten why they were here? Too mortified to speak, she couldn't bear to look at him. Was he regretting what had happened between them?

Ten minutes later as she emerged fully dressed from the bathroom. Luke came in the front door, stowing his wallet in the back pocket of his jeans.

'I just paid for the room,' he said. 'We can pick up some breakfast on the road.'

He grabbed his suitcase and when she hadn't moved or made any response, he paused to look at her.

'Are you okay?'

Resentment spurted through her in a quick hot tide. Clenching her arms to her quivering stomach, she tossed her head and glared at him.

'Oh yeah, I'm fine. This is your usual style, isn't it? Make a move and then back off.' Crossing to the bed, she sat down to pull on her sandals. 'Bloody men!'

The colour ebbed from Luke's face, leaving his tan tinged with grey. He dropped the suitcase and took a step towards her, then faltered. His mouth tightened.

'Shelley, I'm not backing off. But you saw that creep in action yesterday. While we were going at it last night, Ben and Jack were probably scared shitless. And I wasn't even thinking about them.'

"Going at it". Shelley cringed. Was that how he thought of it? Not making love. Was it just a bit of mindless recreation to him, a regrettable distraction from the important task at hand? Like a pressure cooker exploding, all the simmering hurt and humiliation erupted.

'I thought we talked about this! Would worrying about them have helped?' She sucked in a deep breath and clenched her hands, fighting an insane desire to throw something at him. 'I suppose you did try and warn me off, didn't you? You'd better leave me here and I'll catch a bus home.'

'Bloody hell, Shelley.' He shook his head and made a helpless gesture. 'How did we get to this? I'm not leaving you stranded here.'

He stepped closer and pulled her wooden, unresponsive body into his arms. He rested his chin on top of her hair.

'Last night was great. It meant the world to me. But I planned to leave here by six and look at the time! Come on. Please. We can talk in the car.'

Shelley took a deep breath, swallowing hard as she tried to dislodge the heavy, clogging sensation in her throat. Was she being selfish, thinking of herself when his children's welfare was at stake? In the circumstances she could understand Luke's guilt, but surely an hour or two wouldn't make much difference. They had no way of knowing where Miranda and her lover had stayed.

She didn't bother reminding Luke. Shelley moved to the bed and repacked her bag.

'Let's go, then.'

As they drove off, Shelley sat silently in the passenger seat. Remembering her careless words about getting hurt, she wondered what had happened to last night's blithe confidence. His crude description of their lovemaking continued to haunt her. Whatever else he said and did, she wondered if she would be able to forgive for it.

'Shelley, I'm sorry.' Glancing at Luke, she found him looking at her helplessly. 'But can't you understand? The most important thing now is getting the boys back. Whatever's between us has to wait. I don't have the energy to sort things out with you just now.'

You had enough energy last night, she thought.

'I do realise we have to put them first.' She shrugged, pretending indifference. 'Besides, I'll be going back to work before long. I guess our relationship isn't going anywhere.'

'How did I forget that?' Luke's face darkened and his lips tightened.

She'd forgotten it herself, in the heat of the moment. Shelley wasn't in the habit of loving lightly and last night it had seemed they were sharing something precious. But the last thing Luke needed was another city girl.

At Maryborough, they pulled into a fast food drive-through to buy bacon-and-egg burgers and espresso coffee, speaking politely to each other like strangers. Luke ate as he drove as if making up for lost time would assuage his conscience. Shelley nibbled at her burger without appetite, thinking she should have made do with the coffee. Her stomach was so tangled it was in no state to accept food.

They reached the outskirts of Brisbane before noon. Even at that hour the traffic was incessant, making her wonder how she'd ever managed to live in the city. Just a few weeks at Breakaway Creek and she'd turned into a country hick. Much good that was going to do her, she thought.

They finally drew up at Miranda's weatherboard home. Luke stared at the closed curtains, restlessly drumming his fingers on the steering wheel.

'Well, this is it. Looks deserted.'

The carport at the side of the house was empty; there was no sign of the silver Pajero. The cramp in Shelley's stomach tightened. She hated to think they might have lost them. If so, Luke's guilt would be more intense than ever.

'I'll just take a look around.' He opened his door and Shelley hesitated, torn between her desire for action and a determination to not intrude. In the end she stayed put, watching as Luke walked up the path and rapped on the front door. He waited for a few moments before walking along the side of the house and disappearing behind it.

He wasn't gone long, his expression a mixture of anger and anxiety as he returned and spoke to her through the window.

'There's no one at home.' Walking around the front of the car, he slid behind the wheel, slapping it with his palm in obvious frustration. 'Bloody hell! Where could they be?'

When a car pulled up behind them, they both turned to look. Shelley sucked in a breath as she noticed the lights on top and the blue lettering. Her throat went dry as two uniformed men stepped out. Please don't tell us there's been an accident, she thought. She followed Luke as he got out and went to meet the policemen. One of the officers produced his badge and held it up for Luke's inspection.

'I'm Constable Flannery and this is Constable Biddulf. Do you live in this house?'

Luke shook his head.

'My estranged wife and her partner do. I'm the one who rang Crime Stoppers yesterday.'

'Do you know where they are?'

'No, I was expecting them to be here. They left my property in Central Queensland yesterday and I thought they were driving straight here.'

'And your name is?'

Luke introduced himself and indicated Shelley.

'This is my friend, Shelley Blake.'

'We'll have a look at the house before we go. Give us a ring if anything happens.' He scribbled something on a card. 'Here's my number.'

As the policemen walked up the path, Luke went around to the driver's door and slid behind the wheel.

'You know, I do have an idea where they might be. I wanted to check it out before I told the cops, though.'

Shelley looked at him quickly.

'Where's that?'

'At Miranda's mother's. She lives in Redcliffe.' He started the vehicle and threw it into gear. 'Let's go.'

~*~

After seeing where Miranda lived, Shelley wasn't expecting her mother's house to be a comfortable red brick building with a neat garden of flowering shrubs. As Luke opened the car door, Shelley gave him a considering look.

'Do you want me to wait here?'

'Only if you want to.' He sounded distracted. 'You're welcome to come with me.'

She decided to join him. She'd had enough of sitting in the car to last her for a while. Luke rapped on the door several times without result. Through a partially open front window, they could hear a telemarketer loudly extolling the virtues of a miracle anti-wrinkle cream. Luke banged louder

'You there, Carol?' he yelled.

'Hang on a minute!' A few moments later, a plump woman in three-quarter pants and an embroidered T-shirt opened the door. She had a towel in one hand and was briskly rubbing her short, wet hair. If this was Miranda's mother, Shelley could see little resemblance to her daughter.

'Sorry, just got out of the shower.' Her expression changed suddenly. 'Luke! What the bloody hell are you doing here?'

'Nice to see you too, Carol,' Luke responded, his strained face relaxing into a faint grin.

'You gave me a shock – come here, you big hunk.' To Shelley's astonishment she dropped the towel and reached up to Luke, hugging him and giving him a smacking kiss on the cheek. 'I don't care what that ratbag daughter of mine says, it's great to see you.'

His slid his arm around her, giving her an affectionate squeeze.

'It's been a long time.'

'Too bloody long! Come inside and have a cup of tea. I just got home from work,' Carol tugged at his arm. She paused to give Shelley a quick – but not unfriendly – once-over. 'Bring your friend with you.'

Surprised, Shelley followed Luke. She'd imagined Miranda's mother to be a bit rough, but, although she obviously spoke her mind, this woman looked motherly and respectable. And she hadn't expected to see Luke get along with his mother-in-law.

'So who's this?' Carol asked, smiling at Shelley. 'Your new girlfriend?'

Luke coloured slightly, much to Shelley's gratification. After spending the night with her, would he deny it?

But he was too diplomatic for that.

'This is Shelley Blake. Carol Williams, Shelley.' He turned to the older woman. 'Carol, I'd love a cuppa, but we haven't got time. Do you know where Miranda is?'

Carol shook her head.

'I haven't seen Miranda for a week or so. She said you'd run off with the boys. Bloody mad, she was. But if she paid them half as much attention as she does that good-for-nothing bugger she's hooked up with, you wouldn't've had to take them.'

Luke's mouth thinned.

'The trouble is, she's grabbed them back. She and Bevan drove in yesterday and snatched them. We followed them down here, but they haven't turned up at the house. Have you any idea where they might have gone?'

Carol's face creased in a worried frown. Absently she stacked scattered magazines into a neat pile on the table.

'Mmm. I wonder if she's gone to that worthless father of hers?'

'Fred? I didn't know she had anything to do with him.'

'Apparently she's visited him a bit lately. Birds of a feather flock together, they say.'

'Is Fred still living near Beenleigh?'

'Yeah, the bugger. He has a job on the council, but he drinks everything he earns.'

'Miranda must have guessed we were coming after her. Otherwise they'd have gone home, surely.'

'It's hard to know what's going on in that girl's head. I've given up trying to work her out. She left the best thing she had going for her – apart from those gorgeous little boys, of course.' She turned to Shelley. 'Where are you from, Shelley?'

'I'm from Brisbane, but I've been at Breakaway Creek for the last couple of weeks, helping Luke with the boys.' Shelley replied.

'How do you find station life?'

The woman seemed genuinely interested so Shelley answered her honestly.

'I like it. But I'll be going back to work in a few weeks.'

'It wasn't what Miranda expected.' Carol sighed. 'She couldn't handle the isolation. And taking up with Bevan hasn't done her any favours.'

'I hate to tell you this, but I think they're into drugs.' Luke rubbed distractedly at his ear. 'The cops are onto them. I saw a bag of powder and a dodgy pot plant in the house when I was there.'

'The little hussy!' Carol's lips set in a thin line. 'No wonder you took the boys.'

Luke looked to the door, obviously impatient to continue his search.

'We have to get going. Can you give me Fred's address?'

Carol scribbled it on a piece of paper and gave it to Luke, then followed them to the door.

'Let me know what happens.'

'Sure thing.' Luke gave her a quick hug. 'Look after yourself, Carol.'

'And you.' She turned to Shelley. 'Keep this bugger out of trouble, won't you?'

'I'll do my best.' Shelley forced a smile, wondering why Carol's careless assumption of their relationship bothered her so much.

As they drove off, Luke smiled wistfully.

'She's a good old stick. Calls a spade a spade, but her heart's in the right place. Not sure how she ended up with a daughter like Miranda.'

Shelley cleared her throat.

'She's certainly different to what I expected.' Grudgingly she added, 'and she has a soft spot for you. I get the impression Miranda takes after her father.'

He grimaced.

'Yeah, you're right. He's an old alco. Carol kicked him out years ago. She's a nurse – worked long hours to bring up her kids. She deserves better than a daughter who's into drugs.'

Curiosity struggled with her disinclination to make conversation, and eventually won the battle.

'How'd you meet Miranda? She's not the sort I would have expected you to marry.'

Luke sighed heavily.

'I suppose it was a rebound thing. I'd just broken up with a girl. I was down here for the Ekka and a mate introduced us. We had a couple of weeks together and then she rang me later and told me she was pregnant.' His mouth twisted in a faint, self-deprecating smile. 'Of course I had to do the right thing. I was keen enough at the time, but when she came to Breakaway Creek I saw a different side to her. A lot of city girls think graziers are rolling in dough. Miranda found the reality a bit different.'

Shelley observed him surreptitiously, thinking he was selling himself short. Miranda may have had an eye on the money, but it was likely Luke's good looks and sex appeal had bowled her over. Caught in that first flush of passion, she probably hadn't realised that the guy she'd enjoyed a hot fling with was essentially a conservative family man. If she needed excitement on a daily basis, she wouldn't have found it at Breakaway Creek.

Luke drove in brooding silence for a while.

'You know, if I could go back and change things, I don't know what I'd do differently. If I hadn't got involved with her, I wouldn't have the boys.'

In spite of herself, a surge of sympathy warmed her.

'Maybe it's just as well we can't go back.'

They lapsed into silence again as Luke headed towards the Gateway Bridge, driving fast and frequently switching lanes. Several times Shelley noticed the needle on the speedometer nudging over the limit and hoped they hadn't driven through any traffic cameras.

'You know your way around Brisbane,' she commented at last.

'I've had a few trips here, since I took up with Miranda. She always wanted to come back for something.' He glanced at the clock on the dashboard. 'Hope you're not hungry? I just want to find the boys.'

'I'm okay for now,' said Shelley, shaking her head. Her stomach still hadn't settled from this morning's queasiness. In spite of their outwardly amicable conversation, inside she was a seething mess of indecision. What should she do now? Once they'd found the boys, it would be smart to get out. She was getting too involved and she had her own life to go back to. A hot fling with a country guy sounded great in theory, but in real life it wasn't that simple.

~*~

Luke felt like the biggest shithead in the history of man. Shelley seemed to have put her anger aside for the time being, but the coolness in her manner told him she was still upset. He just couldn't afford to put his energies into saving the situation with her. If they got cosy again, he'd be thinking about her and last night, instead of concentrating on the boys. They needed him now. It was tough on Shelley, but he'd tried to warn her.

The familiar feeling of failure rose in him, dragging at his spirits. Miranda had brought him down to the kind of life he'd thought only existed for other people; where lives spun out of control and children were tossed back and forth like pawns in cruel games of petty hatred and revenge.

When Luke contrasted his parents' happy marriage and his own stable, carefree childhood with that of his sons, guilt burned his chest. He and Mitch had never had to watch their parents' relationship deteriorate. They'd never even considered having to leave Breakaway Creek, much less be snatched away. Ben and Jack must be terrified.

~*~

Luke hadn't been to his father-in-law's house before. Realising that they must have taken a wrong turn, he pulled over and grabbed the directory from Shelley, trying hard to conceal his impatience.

'I'm sorry,' she said. 'I know I used to live in Brisbane, but –'

'It's okay.'

'I don't know this area at all.'

He scanned the map quickly and passed it back to her, then put the vehicle into gear.

'I said it's okay. I know where we went wrong.'

He made a U-turn and backtracked until he found the arterial road he was looking for. Steady on, he kept telling himself, as his foot pressed harder on the accelerator. A few minutes either way wasn't likely to make much difference to the boys.

Eventually, they found the house. It was on the outskirts of Beenleigh, at the end of a shabby street of neglected homes. Rotting piles of junk disfigured most of the overgrown yards and Fred's was no exception. As Luke drove slowly by, he noticed several rusted-out cars behind the house, jostling for space with a dilapidated tin shed and piles of lumber. The house's peeling paintwork, broken louvres and drunkenly sagging front steps reminded him of an elderly derelict, abandoned and forgotten by all.

'Look out for Miranda's car,' he said.

Shelley twisted in her seat to look back at the house.

'It's there, parked behind the shed.'

Luke drew in a deep breath.

'Okay. We'll go visit.' As they drew up in front of the house, he looked sideways at her. 'Do you want to wait here? It mightn't be pleasant.'

Her face creased in a worried frown. She reached out as if to put her hand on his arm and then swiftly withdrew it.

'Luke, shouldn't you call Constable Flannery? Bevan's got a violent streak.'

He hesitated. She was right – Bevan had threatened her. Luke glanced back at the house, his attention caught by a shifting curtain at the front window. He glimpsed Miranda's gaunt face and her wide, startled eyes.

'She's seen us. I'll call the cops, but then I'm going in.'

Shelley shook her head, looking exasperated.

'I'll come with you, then. You might need my help with the boys.'

Luke dialled the number the constable had given him and turned to look at her as he waited for an answer.

'You'd be safer staying here.'

She squared her shoulders, her mouth tightening.

'All the more reason for me to come.'

The constable answered before he could argue with her. He spoke briefly and hung up.

'Flannery's alerting the local cops,' he told Shelley. 'They'll be here shortly. Let's go.'

Luke rang the rusty bell and waited, his stomach knotted with apprehension. He was conscious of Shelley's presence and despite his misgivings felt grateful for it, knowing he didn't deserve her unflagging support. He squeezed her hand, but dropped it quickly as a middle-aged man with unkempt, grey hair and distended belly opened the door. Luke hadn't seen his father-in-law in a long time and the years hadn't been kind to him. With rheumy, red-rimmed eyes and sagging jowls, Fred Williams reminded him of a bloodhound that had seen better days.

'Well, look what the cat dragged in. I hear youse've been givin' my daughter some trouble.' Fred peered at him through bleary eyes.

'Where is she?' Luke asked impatiently. 'I want to talk to her.'

'Miranda!' The man turned to yell into the depths of the house. 'Ya got visitors.'

Luke pushed past him.

'Where are the boys? Are they okay?'

The man shrugged and stepped aside, allowing them through the hallway into an untidy kitchen.

'They're all right. They're watching TV.'

After a few minutes Miranda appeared, Bevan flanking her. She gave Luke a hostile look but seemed to ignore Shelley.

'You don't give up, do you?'

'Not when my boys are at risk, no.' Luke's teeth were clenched so tight he felt the veins popping in his neck. 'Why don't you just give me custody and be done with it?'

Miranda rolled her eyes.

'Why the bloody hell should I? I'm their mother. You're too busy to look after them.' She flung Shelley a derisive look. 'Or is *she* a permanent baby-sitter?'

Bevan made a growling noise in his throat.

'Did you set the cops on us, Sherman? They had a car in our street this morning.'

Bloody hell, Luke thought. He'd probably done more harm than good.

'They'll catch up to you sooner or later.' He cast Miranda a pleading look. 'Do you really want the boys to be here when they do?'

'That'll be on your conscience!' she sneered.

'Daddy!' Ben appeared suddenly and ran past his mother to throw himself against Luke and clutch at his leg. 'Did you come to take me home?'

Luke lifted the little boy in his arms, holding him tight as if daring any of them to wrestle him away.

'Yeah, little mate. You're coming home with me.' He thrust past the other occupants of the house.

'Where's Jack?' he asked Ben. 'We have to get him too.'

'He's watching TV. I'll show you.'

Miranda grabbed at Luke's free arm, her face twisted with anger.

'You can't do this!' she shrieked. 'I'm their mother!'

Luke brushed her aside. He hardly registered her desperate strength; he was so pre-occupied with his sons.

'Pity you didn't remember that while you had the chance.' Noticing the alarm on Ben's face, he ruffled the boy's hair reassuringly. 'Let's find Jack.'

In the next room Jack lay on his stomach close to the television, mesmerised by a cartoon. He turned his head when Luke spoke and leapt to his feet, his face lighting up.

'Daddy!' Like his brother, he ran straight to Luke. 'I don't like it here.'

'We're going home.' Luke could hardly talk. A lump was building in his throat. He gathered Jack up with his free arm. 'Come on.'

'What about my toys?'

'I'll buy you new ones. We have to hurry.'

Chapter Sixteen

Shelley waited nervously as Luke disappeared into the house with Ben in his arms. Her stomach writhed as Miranda's face contorted.

'You're not going to let him just walk out of here, are you?' she hissed at her lover.

'Miranda, why don't we cut our losses? Life'd be much simpler without the kids.'

Her sharp, thin face mottled with rage.

'He's got no right to snatch them. Home invasion, that's what it is. He'll be sorry when I put the cops on *him*.'

'Don't worry.' Bevan's fleshy lips peeled back over yellowed teeth. His hand whipped into his pocket and reappeared clutching something. At a flick of his wrist, a vicious-looking blade sprang free. 'If you want me to stop him, I'll stop him.'

For a moment the room seemed to spin. Shelley stared at him in disbelief. She turned to Miranda's father, whose ravaged face had gone slack.

'Don't let him do this,' she pleaded. 'This won't help any of you.'

Fred's wrinkled jowls wobbled as he swallowed and shook his head in silent protest. His daughter's eyes glinted with malicious satisfaction.

'Don't worry, lovey,' she sneered. 'If you're sensible, no one'll get hurt.'

Shelley's heart leapt into her throat as Luke reappeared, carrying a boy in each arm. Bevan advanced towards him, brandishing the knife.

'Put the boys down, Sherman,' he grated. 'Now!'

Luke's face paled. Shelley's mind raced, remembering that the police were on their way. If she and Luke could stall Bevan until they arrived… She tried to signal Luke with her eyes.

'No, Bevan.' Her voice shook in spite of her attempt at calm. 'This'll make things worse for you. You just said you don't want the boys.'

Bevan swung around with a snarl and back-handed her across the face.

'Shut up, bitch! This has nuthin' to do with you!'

Stunned, Shelley jumped back and lifted a hand to her smarting face. She tasted the metallic tang of blood on her lip. Rage flashed across Luke's face. He turned to his wife and thrust the wailing boys at her.

'Take them out of here. They don't need to see this.'

Miranda gathered the boys to her but hesitated. Her earlier cockiness seemed to have vanished.

'Just go!' Luke yelled at her. 'Put them first for a change!'

She turned on her heel and disappeared inside the house.

'Are you all right, Shelley?' Luke's face was taut with concern, his tanned skin tinged with grey. He moved towards her but stopped when Bevan waved the knife. Shelley licked her stinging lips and nodded, retreating until a cupboard pressed into her back. Bevan's eyes flicked between them, his knife poised to strike.

With his fists bunched at his sides, Luke swallowed as if trying to contain his anger.

'Put the knife down, Bevan,' he gritted.

'Stay back, cowboy – or I'll take you!' Bevan spun around and grabbed Shelley, pulling her close and pressing his knife to her throat. 'You can be our little insurance policy.'

Shelley bit off a scream as her all her senses concentrated on the blade digging into her skin. Her body went rigid. Bevan's words registered only dimly as his sweaty odour filled her nostrils. Nausea swamped her. Fighting the urge to gag, she tried to suppress rising waves of panic.

She looked up at Luke, whose eyes were wide with shock and fear. He barely glanced at Miranda when she appeared beside him, her own face white with horror.

'Bevan, no!' Miranda shook her head, spreading her hands in an appeasing gesture. 'Not like this. You'll have us both in jail.'

Luke spoke to her without taking his eyes off Shelley and Bevan.

'Where are the boys?'

'Watching TV. I told them not to come out here.'

The knife pressed deeper into her skin and Shelley fought down a scream. Where were the police? She sensed movement beside her. Fred moved closer, his hands raised in ineffectual protest.

'Come on, Bevan – there's no need for this!'

'Come on, Bevan!' her assailant mimicked, his voice laden with sarcasm. 'Your precious daughter told me to stop him, and now you all want me to put the knife down. Make up your bloody minds!'

All of Shelley's senses seemed heightened and she saw everything happen in slow motion. She was close enough to the front door to hear a car draw up outside, but with the knife biting into her throat she didn't dare turn her head. Bevan moved slightly and his hair brushed her face as he turned to look behind them. Something flickered in Luke's eyes and he rushed at them, grabbing Bevan's arm and pulling the knife away from her. The momentum of Luke's body shoved her back against the wall as the two men struggled. Shelley ducked under their flailing arms and squirmed away from them, casting about for something she could use as a weapon.

She noticed a dirty frypan in the sink and ran to grab it, sloshing its greasy contents on the floor. Luke and Bevan were still grappling, but Luke grimly held Bevan's knife arm. Then Bevan managed to thrust out a foot and tripped him. The two fell to the floor. Bevan landed on top and strained to force the knife down to Luke's throat. Shelley was about to bring the frypan down on Bevan's head when a loud voice made her jump.

'Everyone, freeze!'

Two policemen stood in the doorway. One of them had his gun trained on the men on the floor and the other officer, a red-haired man, moved his gun in a wide arc, fixing Shelley, Fred and Miranda with a hard stare. He motioned to Shelley.

'Put the frypan down.'

Oh yeah, she thought! As if she was the baddie here! Swallowing her indignation, Shelley turned to place the pan on the bench, her hands shaking so much it clattered against the laminate. The first policeman stepped up to press the barrel of his revolver into the back of Bevan's neck. Bevan slowly dropped the knife and the officer kicked it away with his boot. As his partner moved to assist, the first cop knelt on Bevan's back and pulled his arms behind him. Within a few moments they had their prisoner handcuffed. Luke eased himself from under Bevan's heavy body, breathing heavily.

'Don't you move, either!' said the red-haired, freckle-faced officer, indicating Luke with his revolver.

'It's all right!' Shelley put up a hand, terrified he might shoot the wrong person. 'He's the one who called you.'

'And who are you?' said the first officer. He had holstered his revolver and held Bevan still under his boot. He looked ridiculously young, almost like a kid dressed in his father's uniform. Shelley didn't feel much safer than she had when Bevan was holding the knife at her throat.

'Shelley Blake. I've been helping Luke look after his children. He was trying to take them to safety when this man' she indicated Bevan 'attacked me. Luke was trying to rescue me when you came in.'

Cautiously, Luke rose to his feet and Shelley edged closer to him on trembling legs. He reached for her, drawing her to him while never taking his eyes from the policemen.

'Are you all right?' he asked, his voice vibrating with tension. He touched her bruised mouth with a gentle finger and trailed it over her stinging throat. 'Hell, I shouldn't have let you come!'

'I'm okay,' she noticed a trickle of blood on his forearm. 'He nicked you, too!'

Luke glanced down at his right arm.

'It's only a scratch.'

The first officer cleared his throat impatiently.

'I'm Senior Constable Beton and this is Constable Cowdrey. Can you identify yourself, sir?'

'I'm Luke Sherman.' Luke pulled Shelley closer. 'As this lady said, I'm the one who called you. Shelley is my girlfriend.'

He squeezed her waist reassuringly and turned to point at Miranda, who stood stock-still nearby, her face frozen.

'This is my estranged wife Miranda Sherman and the guy with the knife is her partner, Bevan Cahill.' Then he indicated Fred, whose rheumy eyes shifted evasively. 'Miranda's father, Fred Williams.'

'So you're Bevan Cahill?' The officer stared hard at the man on the floor, who had managed to roll to his side. Bevan nodded sullenly, not looking at any of them.

'You and Miranda Sherman are the tenants of number forty-five Navington Street. Is that correct?'

Bevan gave another surly nod.

'Acting on information received, we obtained a warrant and searched the premises. A quantity of amphetamines was found, along with a suspicious plant. We are arresting you both for possession of illegal drugs. Cahill, you will also be charged with assault using a weapon and possibly more, once we've worked out what actually happened here. We'll be taking you both to the police station –'

'What about my children?' Miranda's voice rang with hysteria, cutting across the policeman's spiel. 'I have two little boys.'

'Where are they now, Mrs Sherman?'

'Inside, watching TV.'

'Can I go to them?' Luke interjected. 'They must be terrified.'

The two uniforms looked at each other.

'You're their father?' the senior constable asked.

'Yes, I am. I want to take custody of them.'

'We'll have to call Community Services,' the officer said, throwing a quick glance at Miranda and Bevan. 'Go and see to your kids while we take care of this pair.'

Luke urged Shelley to accompany him as the policeman produced another set of handcuffs and restrained Miranda. Despite Shelley's eagerness to escape Bevan's hostile presence, her legs were almost too weak to carry her and she clung to Luke's arm for support.

In the lounge room both boys sat in front of the television. They swung around, eyes wide and frightened. For a moment they didn't move – it had obviously been impressed on them to stay where they were. Then Luke held out his arms and they ran to him.

Luke knelt down and gathered them close, hugging them tight. Over their heads his eyes met Shelley's and he beckoned to her. She knelt with them and he drew her into the circle, pulling her close with one arm while he held his sons with the other. A warm rush of relief and elation flooded Shelley as she embraced all three of them.

A shudder passed through Luke's body and he pressed a kiss on the top of her head.

'I think I lived three lifetimes back there. If anything had happened to you…'

'Shh. It was my choice to be there.' She drew in a deep breath, trying to calm her still-thudding heart. As she gradually absorbed his words, she pondered the enormous risk he'd taken in coming to her rescue.

'Sherman.'

They both looked up at the red-haired constable who stood in the doorway.

'Back-up's here and DOCS are on their way so I'll wait here with you until they arrive. We'll need you both to come to the station later and make a statement.' He looked at Shelley. 'I assume you want to press charges.'

Shelley nodded. If it helped put that animal behind bars and out of the boys' lives, it would be worth it.

Luke stood up and assisted Shelley to her feet. Her legs trembled and she swayed slightly, using his arm for balance. The constable approached the two boys and crouched to their level.

'Is this your daddy?' he asked them in a gentle tone.

Ben nodded, always the spokesman.

'He's my daddy, and he's Jack's daddy too.'

'Do you want to stay with him?'

Both boys nodded vigorously. Jack moved closer to his father and clutched at his jeans. Constable Cowdrey smiled.

'Looks like you got their vote, Sherman.'

The officer returned to the kitchen where Shelley heard him talking to Fred. Following him to the door, she saw Fred nod dumbly in response to a question. As Cowdrey walked outside, the old man turned to Shelley, his bleary eyes darting to her face and flickering away.

'Are you all right, girlie?' he asked gruffly.

She put a hand to her sore, bruised throat. If there was any blood, it had already dried. She nodded and joined him, watching through the door as another police car drew up and Miranda and Bevan were bundled into the back of it. Fred shook his head sadly.

'I may not be much, but I don't agree with what he did to you.'

'It was none of your doing,' Shelley said gently, turning away from him. She had a feeling Fred wanted to say more, but she didn't feel equal to conversation. As one white and blue car sped off, the two constables walked back to the house. Shelley returned to Luke who was crouched on the floor, holding his boys.

'They've taken them away. I should do something about that cut of yours.'

'You could do with some attention too. There's a first aid kit in my car.' He stood up. 'You wait here with the boys and I'll grab it.'

Since Luke's cut was still bleeding, Shelley insisted on treating it first. While she cleaned and bandaged his arm, he sat on the sofa with Jack on his lap and Ben held close on his other side. Luke did his best to explain the recent events to his boys.

~*~

The social worker seemed to take forever to arrive. At last Shelley heard the policemen greeting someone at the front door and, after a muffled conversation, a middle-aged woman entered the living room. Shelley offered to give them privacy, but Luke insisted she stayed.

The woman's business-like manner was at odds with her gypsy clothing, but perhaps her conversation with the constables had influenced her in Luke's favour; she seemed sympathetic to his case, questioning him at length before cross-examining Shelley.

'The first thing you need to do is go through a dispute resolution process,' she told Luke. 'If that's unsuccessful and your wife contests your custody application, it will have to go to court. But in the circumstances I think you have a good chance of a favourable outcome.'

Even from where she sat, Shelley sensed Luke's sigh of relief. But the smile he gave her was guarded, as if he dare not take success for granted.

'For now, I'm happy to leave the boys in your care.' The woman rose and shook hands with both of them. 'I'll see myself out.'

Luke and Shelley followed the waiting constables to the police station where they were fortified with strong coffee and left to wait for nearly an hour. Luke was called first. Then it was Shelley's turn, and

Luke pressed her hand reassuringly as she walked past him to the interview room.

'Don't worry,' he said softly. 'Just tell them the truth. It's going to be all right.'

It was late afternoon when they were finally free to go, and the boys had long since grown irritable and restless. Luke drove them all across the city, eventually pulling into a motel on the northern side.

'I'm buggered. Let's stay here the night and go out for a slap-up dinner.'

He returned to the car carrying two keys and passed one of them to her.

'I thought you might prefer your own room.'

Shelley certainly hadn't planned on sharing a bed with him in the presence of the boys. A separate room was sensible but she wasn't sure how she was going to sleep after the morning's violence.

They ate at the motel's restaurant. Luke seemed to strive for an upbeat mood to distract his sons, and for their sake she tried hard to put aside her tangled emotions. She could only guess at Luke's innermost feelings, but it was obvious how relieved he was to have his boys back.

Ben and Jack were easily diverted. If the day had left lasting scars, they weren't yet apparent. They applied themselves with gusto to their fish fingers and chips, and when Jack got a little silly smearing tomato sauce on his face and Ben egged him on, Luke merely smiled indulgently. He obviously didn't have the heart to chastise them.

Later, Shelley tried to watch a movie on television, but her mind kept skittering back to the events of the day. It had started badly with her quarrel with Luke and had gone drastically downhill from there. No wonder her stomach was a seething mass of nerves.

She thumbed through the television guide, hoping to find something more entertaining, but eventually threw it down in frustration. When someone knocked on her door, her pulse gave a little leap of alarm. She got up, hesitating.

'Who is it?'

'It's Luke.' She unlocked the door and he came in, closing it behind him.

'The boys are both asleep. I need to talk to you.'

Her pulse tripped again and she took a deep breath, striving for nonchalance. Shelley sank into one of the chairs and waved at the other one.

'Sit down, then.'

For a moment he just looked at her without speaking. He ran a hand through his hair and shook his head, his expression regretful.

'I'm so sorry about today. You must have been scared.' His expression hardened as he studied her face. 'Your mouth's still swollen where that mongrel hit you! If I could get my hands on him –'

Shelley touched her sore lip, self-conscious under his scrutiny.

'But if I hadn't been there, he might have grabbed one of the boys instead. That would have been far worse. The poor kids have been through enough.'

'I know. I'm grateful to you.' He sighed, taking a pen from the bench top and twisting it in his fingers. 'I can't fathom Miranda getting mixed up with that scumbag. She never could settle, but he's dragged her into the gutter.'

His lips compressed into a thin line.

'I just hope she saw the light today when he pulled that knife on you. But she'll still have to face court with drug charges.'

Shelley watched his averted face, her heart clenching as she read the confusion and regret there.

'It could be the shock she needs to pull herself together,' she suggested gently. 'Whatever she does, you shouldn't feel responsible. She's an adult – she made her own choices.'

He gave a rueful grin.

'God knows she was never much of a wife or parent. I'm well rid of her, but the fact remains she's the boys' mother. I hope she pulls herself together for their sakes.' He stood up, stretching his long body. 'I should let you sleep. It's been a long day.'

Shelley wondered if he hoped she'd invite him to stay. If so, he wasn't making much of an effort. Of course, Ben and Jack were alone in the next room and if either of them woke they'd need their father.

'Yes, you'd better get back to your sons.'

'Shelley…' he hesitated, 'I haven't blown it with you, have I? You must've had enough of my problems.'

She wondered what she was supposed to say. Was he talking about their personal relationship, or was he just worried he'd alienated his baby-sitter? In the end she just shook her head.

'I can't think straight now. We can talk about it later. Go back to your sons.'

He seemed to accept that. Moving closer, he pulled her into his arms and held her for a long, comforting moment. He bent to kiss her cheek.

'Okay, I'll go. See you in the morning.'

The door closed behind him and Shelley sat staring at it, feeling suddenly very alone. Part of her wished she had asked him to stay. How would she ever sleep with visions of that vicious knife against her throat, intruding whenever she closed her eyes? But the boys needed him more than she did.

She changed into her pyjamas and climbed into bed, realising she had to distract herself from the nightmarish day. She'd pushed aside any thoughts of the previous night and the intimacies they'd shared. But now, knowing she couldn't have Luke's company, she deliberately opened her mind to the memories.

The night with Luke had been nothing like going to bed with Jason. If she'd been promiscuous, she'd have had a better yardstick for comparison. Was last night really a one-in-a-million, or was thinking that a sad reflection of her inexperience?

Luke hadn't said he loved her, but he'd certainly made her feel that he cared – which was why his abrupt dismissal felt like such a shock. Sleeping with him had only complicated everything and made her feel vulnerable. Her mother was right. The sooner she left this tangle behind her, the better off she'd be.

Chapter Seventeen

Clermont, 1898

It seemed the arrival of the early morning train was something of an event in Clermont. Henry Watson watched the bustle from the station dining room and supposed a town like this offered little else for entertainment. Contented by the knowledge that his dapper three-piece suit set him apart from his fellow travellers, he sweltered in the summer heat as he sat down to a hearty breakfast of steak and eggs. Many of the passengers had already dispersed, except for those who were eating around him. The contents of the goods wagon were still being transferred to an assortment of carts, wagons and drays.

What a backwater, he thought contemptuously, eyeing the roughly clad workmen. Whatever had possessed the girl to run away to a place like this and get entangled with a man like Alexander Baxter? Did she think he wouldn't have uncovered the truth?

Fanny's sister, Lydia, had soon set him straight: "According to Lucy, Alexander's an adopted son. He's older than George, but there's no chance of him inheriting the property. For all intents and purposes, he's just a stockman."

It was enough to make up his mind. Henry Watson wouldn't stand idly by while his daughter threw herself away on a worthless nobody.

He'd force her to see sense if it was the last thing he did. But while he was here in Clermont it wouldn't hurt to ask a few more questions. In his experience most people had something to hide. Perhaps he'd dig up something that would make his task of convincing Emma much easier.

The hotels seemed like a good place to start. The station master directed him to the Leo Hotel, where the Baxters apparently stayed when in town. But the foreigner who ran it was a close-mouthed sort, who seemed to have nothing but good to say about Alex Baxter and his brother George. At North and Co.'s emporium, he had a bit more luck. The storekeeper mentioned a man whom the Baxters had once employed.

'Fred Jenkins was at Breakaway Creek for a good few years. He'll know them as well as anyone.'

'Where can I find this Fred Jenkins?'

'He's a carrier. Drives a dray with a pair of grey clumpers. I imagine he's about somewhere, deliverin' stuff from the train.'

It didn't take Henry long to find Jenkins, but the man was busy hefting casks of beer and rum into the back entrance of the Commercial Hotel.

'If you give me a hand here, I'll be with you all the quicker,' the fellow grunted, effortlessly heaving a cask onto his burly shoulder. Henry eyed the man's sweat-stained shirt and calloused, grubby hands with distaste.

'I'll be waiting in the tea rooms when you're finished. There'll be a quid in it for you.'

'Never say no to an extra quid.'

Henry had finished his pot of tea by the time Jenkins joined him, but he signalled to the waitress to bring another. As they waited, Henry got straight to the point.

'I was told you once worked at Breakaway Creek Station,' he said. · Jenkins looked at him, curiosity glinting in his beady eyes.

'Eh, I did, for a while. What's it to you?'

'I need to find out all I can about Alexander Baxter. Business reasons.'

The fellow smirked.

'Baxter, eh? I can tell you a few things about him, but you'd better hand over the blunt first.'

'This had better be worth it.' Henry said, as he passed over a pound note.

'Oh, it's worth it.' Jenkins's grin peeled over the blackened stumps of his teeth. 'High an' mighty Mister Alexander Baxter Esquire is hidin' a bloody good secret.'

~*~

When the waitress finally arrived with the tea, Henry seized the opportunity to make his exit. He was dammed if he'd give this clod the satisfaction of seeing how rattled he was. He dropped some coins onto her tray and pushed out his chair.

'I'll leave you to your tea, Jenkins. But I wouldn't talk about this if I was you.'

Jenkins grinned.

'I always reckoned it was worth more to me if I kept it to meself.'

Henry had already booked a room at the Commercial Hotel. He hurried down the street, oblivious to the pedestrians he elbowed out of his way. His initial shock had turned to anger, which swiftly built to a towering rage. How dare the girl humiliate him like this! Did she even know what the fellow was, or had she blindly stumbled into it with all her girlish naiveté?

In the privacy of his room he paced back and forth, fuming over the predicament the little hussy had placed him in. He'd be the laughing stock of Brisbane society and all his business associates if word got out. He had to get to the Baxter property and put a stop to it.

Catching a glimpse of himself in the mirror, he stopped short. Fury twisted his features, making him appear deranged. It wouldn't do to be seen like this. Straightening his tie, he drew, deep calming breaths. At last he put on his hat and went to the door, forcing himself to walk sedately downstairs and into the lobby.

'I'd like to see about hiring a horse,' he told the clerk behind the desk. 'I'll need it for several days.'

The skinny young fellow blinked over his spectacles.

'The landlord hires horses to his customers, and there are the livery stables down the street.'

'See if you can arrange it for me, then. I'll need one first thing tomorrow morning. How far is it to Breakaway Creek, do you know?'

'Is that a cattle station? I'm sorry, sir, but I don't know it.'

'Well, find out!' Henry snapped. 'I'll need provisions for the journey, as well.'

'Yes, sir. I'll make sure everything's ready for you in the morning, sir. What time would you like to leave?'

'Seven o'clock. I'll need a decent breakfast first,' said Henry, sharply.

'Bloody mob of yokels,' he muttered to himself as he went back up the stairs. 'Probably wouldn't know a decent breakfast if it jumped up and bit them.'

~*~

Emma was undergoing initiation into another facet of station life. She'd surprised Alex by asking if she could watch the proceedings when they butchered a beast for meat.

'Are you sure you want to see it?' he'd asked. 'There'll be lots of blood and gore – not a sight for a lady.'

'Yes, I'm sure. I won't faint, I promise you. I have a strong stomach and, if I'm going to live in the bush, I need to become accustomed to these things.'

The job was done at the stockyards late that afternoon, in a special killing pen with a stone floor. The stockmen had mustered a small mob of heifers into the yards. As the red sun disappeared behind the treetops and took with it the worst of the heat, George and Alex drove two fat heifers into the killing pen. Alex rested the barrel of his rifle on a rail and sighted along it. From a cautious distance Emma watched, holding her breath as the rifle cracked. Although she'd been expecting it, it still shocked her when one of the heifers dropped instantly, blood welling from a bullet hole between its eyes.

The men worked with quiet efficiency, slitting the dead heifer's throat and standing back as the dark red blood gushed forth, pooling on the stone floor. The hot, sickly smell nauseated Emma, who watched in morbid fascination as the animal kicked its death throes. Alex looked around at her with a concerned smile.

'How are you holding up there, Em?'

She couldn't admit to her weakness.

'I'm sure I'll become accustomed to it in time. We do have to eat, after all.'

'That's the spirit.'

After partially skinning the carcass, the men winched it high on the gallows. Suddenly two dogs that were hovering nearby leapt up and barked frantically. As they raced down the track with hackles raised, Emma spotted an approaching horseman. He was a bulky man who rode slumped in the saddle, as if there under protest. Something about him seemed familiar and as he drew close her throat went dry.

'Who's this?' George said. Then he gave a low whistle. 'Emma, is that your father?'

Emma nodded. Her heart was heavy with foreboding. Henry Watson would not have travelled all this way to wish her well. Mr

Watson reined in and looked at them, his cold glance sweeping over Emma before he removed the cigar from his mouth and nodded to George.

'Good day to you, Baxter.' For a long, drawn-out moment he looked at the swinging carcass, dripping blood onto the stones below. Then his gaze shifted to Alex, who laid down his knife and moved towards him, wiping his bloodied hands on his trousers.

'I'm Alexander Baxter, sir.' Alex looked uncertainly down at his fists. 'My apologies, I can't offer a handshake just now.'

Watson muttered something under his breath and swung his horse aside, jerking viciously at the bit in its mouth.

'Why is my daughter being subjected to this disgusting spectacle?' He pointedly looked away from Alex to his daughter. 'Come with me, Emma. It's time we discussed this ridiculous business.'

Emma stared at him, angry and embarrassed at his rudeness. She hadn't expected her father to welcome Alex as a son-in-law, but she hadn't thought he'd completely dismiss him.

'I'm here because I wanted to be, Father.' She threw her head back in a challenging gesture, her temper flaring. 'But you are right. We do have to talk.'

She led the way to George's house, her father following on horseback. It was nearly a mile distant, but her father's glowering face discouraged her from making small talk.

'Is there anyone who can see to this animal?' said Henry, as he tied his horse to the front gate.

'Out here we tend to our own mounts.' Emma knew her reply sounded short to the point of insolence, but she didn't care. Her father had been unspeakably rude.

'I'll leave it here then.' Henry dropped his cigar, crushed it under his boot heel and followed her through the gate. Lucy appeared on the veranda, untying her apron from her waist.

'Uncle Henry! What a surprise! Come inside.' Her welcoming smile faded as she looked from her uncle's angry face to Emma's anxious one.

'Lucy.' Henry nodded brusquely and accompanied the two women inside the house. He stopped abruptly in the front room. 'We need to talk about this mess you've led my daughter into.'

'Lucy didn't lead me into anything!' Emma looked apologetically at her cousin. 'Please don't blame her.'

'She invited you here, didn't she? You'd think she'd have warned you not to get involved with that character.'

Lucy's face reddened with indignation.

'If you're talking about Alex, he happens to be my brother-in-law and he's a decent, honourable man!'

Good on you Lucy, Emma thought, silently applauding.

'I'm sorry about this, Lucy. Can I take Father into the study to talk?' Humiliation sickened her. How dare her father come here and treat them all like this? His anger was out of proportion to Alex's unsuitability, unless … could he have learned the truth?

'Of course you can use the study, Emma.' Lucy's face was white with distress.

'We can talk here – Lucy's already involved. Besides, there's not much to discuss. Emma is to pack her bags and come home with me. Tomorrow.'

'That, I will not do.' Emma folded her arms across her chest and met her father's glare, though she quailed inside, her stomach leaping with nerves. She mustn't let him see how afraid she was. 'I'm not a child. You cannot force me.'

Henry let out a furious roar.

'Do you think I'd let you stay and marry a blasted black-fellow? I'd be the laughing stock of Brisbane if people knew.'

Lucy gasped and clutched the back of one of the dining chairs for support, her face chalk-white.

'What do you mean, a "blackfellow"?' Her voice quavered uncertainly. 'Alex is George's adopted brother.'

'Oh, Lucy.' Hatred for her father gave Emma the strength to go to her cousin and put her arm around her, easing her into the chair. She thought she could feel Lucy's body trembling, but she was shaking so much herself it was hard to be sure. 'I'm sorry you had to find out like this. Alex's mother was a half-caste.'

Henry looked incredulous.

'Lucy didn't know?' His top lip curled back in a sneer. 'But you did, Emma.'

Lucy looked pleadingly at Emma, ignoring Henry. Her mouth trembled.

'Is this really true? Why didn't someone tell me?'

'I'm sorry. I thought you should know, but it wasn't for me to say. George was trying to protect Alex, I suppose. It was Alex who told me.'

'And that's why you went back to Brisbane.'

'Yes, but once I had time to think it over, I realised it didn't matter.' She looked up at her father. 'As it needn't matter to you, Father. We'll stay out of your life and no one will ever know.'

Henry thumped his fist on the table.

'How can I be sure of that? How do you think I found out? All I had to do was talk to a fellow who'd worked here.'

And the Aboriginies knew, of course. It was a wonder the story hadn't spread further.

'It's been kept quiet this long, and there's no reason why that should change.' Emma took a deep breath. 'So long as *you* don't talk.'

'That's beside the point!' Henry roared. 'You are not marrying him. Did you plan to present me with a black grandchild?'

He looked wildly around.

'Where's your bedroom? You can start packing now.'

He grabbed her arm in a painful grip, propelling her down the hallway. Nauseated and trembling, Emma had no choice but to obey.

In her bedroom she worked with an outward show of compliance, folding clothing and placing it in her trunk while he hovered in the doorway. All the while her mind whirled with furious thoughts of rebellion. It wasn't over, not by a long shot.

George arrived home late for supper. He'd washed his face, hands and arms at the tap outside, but he still wore the blood-spattered clothing from that day. As they sat at the table Henry looked at him in disdain, his nose twitching. Lucy appeared pale and sick, and barely responded when her husband expressed concern for her. Emma supposed she didn't look much better and imagined George wondering at what had transpired in his home. They had no opportunity to tell him.

'Emma's coming back to Brisbane with me tomorrow,' Henry announced baldly.

George looked at her quickly, his eyes shocked and concerned. Emma avoided his gaze. She had no intention of accompanying her father, but she couldn't tell George that. Lucy stared down at her plate, barely fulfilling the role of hostess that she usually performed so well. Emma noticed George watching his wife with a worried frown. There would be fences to mend before harmony was restored to their marriage.

No one made any attempt at small talk. After the meal, Henry retired to the veranda and George, after an uncertain glance at Lucy, followed him. Emma heard the men's voices in heated conversation and the aroma of her father's cigar wafted through the open French doors, making her stomach stir queasily.

As she helped Lucy in the kitchen, Emma tried to put her own distress aside in order to appeal to her set, stubborn face.

'Lucy, I know this has come as a dreadful shock, but please give George a chance to explain himself before you judge him. If you let this come between you, I'll never forgive myself.'

Lucy looked up from washing the dishes, her eyes hard.

'This isn't your fault, Emma. George should have told me. Did he think I wouldn't marry him if I knew?' She shook her head. 'But tell me one thing. Who is Alex's father?'

Emma cringed, knowing this would make it even worse. Her face heated.

'It's Mr Baxter.'

Lucy nodded, not showing any surprise.

'I'd begun to suspect that. It was the only thing that made any sense. To think I've lived with all this depravity under my nose and I had no idea.' A half-sob escaped her. 'It makes me wonder if I know George as well as I thought I did.'

Emma had a fair idea what her cousin was thinking and, in light of what she'd recently discovered about Alex, she hardly dared answer.

'Just talk to him, please.'

As soon as the dishes were done, Emma escaped to her bedroom. She was sorry for Lucy but she had her own pressing problems to deal with. Henry was nowhere in sight and she guessed he'd retired to the room she'd hastily prepared for him. In the glow cast through the French doors, she could see George sitting on the veranda step, his back hunched defensively. But it wasn't her place to interfere, even if she'd had the energy for it.

In her bedroom she retrieved some of the items she'd packed earlier, making a small bundle with toiletries and a change of underwear. She laid one of her riding habits on the bed. Emma counted all the money in her possession, which amounted to only two pounds and ten shillings. Then she changed into her habit and lay fully dressed on the counterpane, listening as Lucy checked the sleeping baby and George took a bath in the deserted kitchen. The tread of George's steps came down the hall to the bedroom he shared with Lucy and the baby. Their voices rose and fell in a conversation that was muffled but obviously impassioned, even though she couldn't make out the words.

Sighing, she rolled to her side and waited for the house to go to sleep. Her father's bed creaked in the room next to hers, and before long he was snoring softly. She heard the clock in the sitting room strike half-past nine. Little Thomas usually woke for a feed around twelve. In another hour, she would have to make her move.

Chapter Eighteen

She had hardly finished her calculations when she heard an urgent whisper at her window.

'Emma! Are you awake?'

Alex! Her pulse leapt with relief. She slid noiselessly off the bed and padded to the open window.

'Thank heavens you came.' As she peered down at his shadowy face, a weight of anxiety lifted from her shoulders.

'Are you all right, Emma?' His whisper was loaded with concern. She shuddered.

'It's awful! Father's determined to take me back to Brisbane tomorrow.' Her voice broke. 'We have to leave, Alex.'

He muttered a word she didn't think she was supposed to hear.

'I'll catch some horses, then, and come for you when I'm ready.'

'No, they might hear you,' she countered softly. 'What if I wait for an hour and then meet you at the saddle shed?'

'Can you find your way? It's dark tonight.'

'I'll manage,' she said. Unless she was prepared to submit to her father's tyranny, she didn't have a choice. Alex reached up to grasp her hand through the window and squeezed it hard.

'I'll be ready for you.'

Emma waited until the clock chimed half-past ten. She pulled on her boots and dropped her little bundle out the window, hearing the soft thud as it fell amongst the geraniums. Nothing stirred in the house, so she took a deep breath and hauled herself over the sill, bundling up the skirt of her habit so she could swing her legs over. She hung there for a moment before dropping six feet to the ground. She felt the woody stems of a geranium crush under her weight and hoped Lucy would forgive her.

Crouching for a moment in the lee of the house, she listened for any movement inside. All she could hear over the thud of her hammering heart was the croaking of frogs and the whirring of cicadas in the garden.

The saddle shed was a hundred yards away. It was a moonless night, with only the bright stars in a clear sky to show the way. Emma was grateful for the long grass either side of the track, which helped keep her on course. Back in November the entire paddock had been bare.

As she neared the cluster of buildings that marked the main homestead, she prayed the dogs wouldn't bark. Finding the saddle shed was proving difficult until she caught the flicker of a lantern swinging inside the doorway. She got close enough to hear the horses snuffle and stamp. Emma had turned her father's mount loose with the night horse and, even though the night paddock was comparatively small, she wondered how Alex had managed to find them in the dark.

He turned from tightening the girth of one horse and moved swiftly to catch her in his arms, kissing her hard.

'Emma, are you sure about this?'

'He knows, Alex. He knows who your mother was.'

'Damn!' His whisper became urgent. 'Em, if we go now there won't be any turning back.'

'I know that.' Her body shuddered with emotion. 'But I couldn't bear to give you up.'

She helped him finish saddling the horses. He'd already collected some food, which he stashed in their saddlebags, and strapped his thin swag to the front of his saddle. Then he hoisted her onto Ranger, the old night horse, and they set off.

Then the station dogs, who had been mercifully silent until then, decided to set up a chorus of loud barks. They heard Frank Baxter's gruff voice yelling at them to "sit down!" and Emma waited breathlessly for someone to come after them. But no one did, and once they were safely away from the homestead they urged their horses into a canter, trusting the animals to follow the shadowy road.

Half an hour later Alex slowed his mount back to a walk.

'I think we're safe now. I'm sure no one heard us go. Tell me what happened with your father, Em.'

She described the dreadful scene that had occurred in Lucy's front room.

'It was a horrible way for the poor girl to learn the truth. She's extremely upset.'

'I'll bet she is.' Alex's voice sounded grim. 'I wonder who told your father?'

'He said it was someone in Clermont who used to work here.'

'Might've been Jenkins. He was working here when I found out. I suppose Molly told him, too.' He drew in a hard breath. 'It's a wonder the whole country doesn't know about it.'

He reached across and gripped her hand.

'Emma, can you live with it if that happens?'

What should she say to that? If she was completely honest, the thought of ostracism scared her. But telling him so would achieve little.

'Of course I can, Alex. The people who really matter will judge us for who we are.'

Soon after sunrise they stopped by a gully for a quick breakfast, dropping the bits out of the horses' mouths so they could graze. Alex lit a fire and boiled their quart pots to make a hot, sweet brew. After riding most of the night, Emma was starving and even the dry bread and meat he'd packed tasted good.

'What will we do when we reach Clermont?' she asked.

Alex's eyes were serious.

'See the minister and ask him to marry us. I know you usually have to apply for a licence, but he can do it in a hurry if he has to.'

Her pulse fluttered and heat crept up her neck. She realised the hurry wasn't only because of her father, but also because of this journey together. Her reputation as a single woman would be compromised.

Soon they were in the saddle once more. All day they pushed the horses as hard as they could, but neither animal was at the peak of fitness. Her father's hired horse had already been ridden for two days and aging Ranger was prized for his placid temperament rather than his stamina. Darkness was closing in when Alex called a halt beside a scrubby creek.

'The horses are knocked up and so are you, I think.' He gently brushed a knuckle across Emma's cheek. 'We'll camp here and set off before daylight.'

The knowledge that her father was probably on their trail remained unspoken between them. Given his state of mind the previous evening, he seemed unlikely to concede defeat so easily.

They made another meal with the bread and meat, and then sat by the fire drinking tea. Though Emma drooped with exhaustion, she found herself watching the firelight flicker on Alex's unshaven face and wondered if she'd ever get tired of looking at him. He sat with a yard of space between them and he hadn't touched her since the previous night, but she didn't feel slighted by his neglect. She knew it was because once they started kissing, it would be impossible to stop.

Alex stood up, tossing the dregs from his quart pot on the fire and then bending to unroll the swag. He spread it carefully on a bare patch of ground. Then he turned to Emma, reaching out to pull her to her feet.

'Are you ready for bed?' he asked huskily.

She nodded and moved into his arms, her weariness forgotten as anticipation sent her pulse flurrying. It didn't matter to her that they weren't married yet. She wanted him with her head as well as her heart. Once she'd given herself to him, her father would surely think twice about separating them.

Embracing and kissing him felt deliciously familiar, but joining him in the swag was fraught with excitement. As he undressed her she felt nervously glad of the dark. She hardly knew what to expect, but Alex was gentle and reassuring and held his own passion in check while he removed her layers of clothing. Immersed in the new and enchanting world of pleasure and desire, Emma grew bold enough to help him slip the buttons on his shirt. As she trailed her fingers over his hard stomach, his sudden intake of breath was all the encouragement she needed.

When he finally moved over her she was more than ready for him and didn't shrink from the pain of their joining. Clinging to him, she rejoiced in the press of his face against hers, the feel of his smooth bare skin under her touch and the wondrous intimacy of his movements within her. She hadn't anticipated the climax: a rush of sensation that built like cresting a wave and then the helpless tumble down the other side. A flood of emotions made her eyes blur with tears as she clung to his hot, sweaty body. She'd never imagined she could feel so complete or so enthralled with another human being.

'I love you,' Alex whispered, brushing her tangled hair from her face and gently kissing her swollen mouth.

Despite the hard ground she slept soundly, curled into her lover's body. When he woke her, a faint glow in the eastern sky signalled dawn and a kookaburra chortled in a nearby tree. When he moved to kiss her, she felt his ardent hunger for her and she was quick to respond. They coupled hurriedly: the menacing spectre of her father hovered at the edge of her consciousness and lent a furtive excitement to their union.

In the half-light he rose and swiftly pulled on his clothes. For an indulgent moment Emma watched him button his shirt and buckle his belt, then bend to pull on his socks and boots. Moving to the fire, he added fresh kindling to the log he'd left smouldering through the night. He knelt beside it to fan the blaze with his hat and the flames flared brightly amongst the dry timber, illuminating his shadowy figure.

As he straightened, a loud crack reverberated in Emma's ears. She sat up in a rush, panic gripping her stomach in a tight ball. Shocked and disbelieving, she watched Alex's eyes widen with surprise. He toppled to his knees and for a moment he seemed to hang there, before slumping face-first to the ground, only inches from the crackling fire.

For one frozen, horrified moment, Emma didn't move. Then she was on her feet, dressed only in her chemise. She pulled Alex away from the fire, rolling his heavy body over and wailing as she bent to feel for his heartbeat.

'No, Alex!' she screamed. A spreading red patch stained the front of his shirt, but his heart still beat under her fingers. Staring wildly around, she tried to see their attacker, but even the birds were silent and the half-light revealed nothing. Would the gunman fire again? She trembled convulsively, thoughts scrambling in her fevered mind. She had to stop the bleeding so she grabbed her petticoat from the pile of discarded clothing and wrenched at the fine fabric, pulling at the seam until it gave way. She folded part of it into a pad and tore the rest into strips to tightly bind the dressing over the oozing wound. Then she waited, crouching low and motionless, listening for any sound.

The silence was absolute. Not even the cracking of a twig or the rustle of a leaf indicated the presence of a lurking assailant. Alex groaned, his eyes flickering open. He stared at her through dazed eyes.

'What —'

Emma suppressed a hysterical sob.

'You've been shot, Alex. I think whoever did it has gone – and I need to get you to a doctor. I'll fetch the horses, but you must stay awake, or I'll never lift you onto your horse.'

She pulled her clothes on anyhow. Haste and fear made her fingers fumble with laces and buttons. When she stood up she knew she presented a clear target in the gathering light, but she had to take the risk. Instinct told her she hadn't been the intended victim.

The hobbled horses hadn't strayed far. With shaking, clumsy hands, Emma unstrapped the heavy chain hobbles and tied them around each horse's neck, before leading the animals back to camp. Deciding Ranger was the most reliable choice to transport her injured fiancé, she heaved Alex's heavy stock saddle onto the night horse's back. Then she put the side-saddle on the hired horse, hoping he was too tired to give her trouble. As she tightened the girth, she breathed a silent prayer of gratitude that she'd learned to do such things for herself.

Her stomach heaved with nausea as she crouched beside Alex and noted with relief that he was still conscious.

'How do you feel?'

'Like hell,' he groaned. His eyes were closed.

'Do you think we can get you on your feet? I've saddled Ranger for you.'

He nodded, grimly clenching his teeth.

'I'll try.'

Emma fetched Ranger close and then helped pull Alex to his knees. A concentrated effort had him on his feet, gasping with pain and leaning heavily against her. She helped him to Ranger's side, where he rested against the horse's body for a long moment, drawing deep breaths. Emma brought him water in his quart pot and he swallowed a few mouthfuls.

'We'd better get this over with,' he gritted.

Afterwards, Emma could never remember how she eventually got him onto the horse. Only the sheer effort of Alex's will had accomplished it. He hung in the saddle and clutched the pommel for support, his face grey and beaded with sweat. Emma found a log to help her into the side-saddle and set off at a cautious walk. Ranger needed little direction from his rider to follow.

Fortunately they were only a few miles from Clermont. Alex told her not to stop, so she didn't although it wrenched at her heart every time she looked back at his sweating, pain-contorted face. When they entered the outskirts of town, people came running to meet them.

'What's happened? Is he hurt?' one man asked.

'Get Doctor Kent, quick!' she retorted. 'He's been shot.'

The man gasped but ran off to fetch help. Another man drove up in a dray and lifted Alex from his saddle. Emma hovered anxiously, trying to shut out his moans of pain as they laid him on the floor of the dray with his long legs dangling over the end.

'We'll get him to the hospital,' the man said.

Doctor Kent met them there. An orderly produced a stretcher and the driver of the dray helped him transfer Alex to it and carry him inside. Alex lost consciousness, but Emma consoled herself with the knowledge that he'd found some escape from the pain.

They made her wait outside while the doctor examined him, with the assistance of the matron. At last Doctor Kent emerged to speak to her.

'He appears to have a bullet lodged in the left side of his chest, just above the heart. I'll have to operate to remove it.'

Emma stared at him anxiously, trying to read his impassive face.

'Will he be all right?'

The doctor hesitated.

'I can remove the bullet, and it doesn't appear to have touched any vital organs ... but there's been considerable damage to the surrounding tissues and he's weak from loss of blood. There'll most certainly be infection. We can only hope and pray for the best.'

Tears stung Emma eyes as she pressed her face into her hands. This couldn't be happening. Only a few hours ago Alex had been full of energy and passion, telling her how much he loved her. She found herself praying as the doctor had suggested, clutching at anything to ease the fear that choked her like a suffocating fog.

God, please don't take him away from me, she thought. I couldn't bear to lose him.

'I'll operate now,' Doctor Kent was saying. 'How was he shot?'

Panic froze her thoughts as she dropped her hands and stared up at him, feeling the blood drain from her cheeks.

'I don't know. He was just stoking up the fire. I heard a shot – he fell...'

The doctor looked at her searchingly.

'Have you any idea who may have fired the gun? Do you think it was deliberate?'

Oh God, she thought. She'd tried not to think about it and refused to believe her own kin could be so evil. Surely her father couldn't…

She shook her head, sobbing.

'I don't know. I just don't know.'

The waiting stretched endlessly, paralysing her with tentacles of dread. When the doctor finally emerged, she jumped to her feet, forced to clutch at her chair for support as her head spun.

'I've removed the bullet,' he informed her. 'He's still unconscious, but you may sit with him now.'

Emma swayed and the doctor moved closer, grasping her arm to steady her.

'Are you all right, young lady? I don't suppose you've eaten. I'll get the nurse to fetch you something.'

'Just a cup of tea, please,' Emma responded, straightening. 'Thank you, but I'm all right now.'

Alex lay on a narrow bed in the austere hospital room. His bare chest was wrapped in a wide bandage and his tanned face was a dingy grey. The sickly smells of ether and phenol lingered in the air. Emma pulled a chair close to the bed and took his limp, unresponsive hand in hers, rubbing it gently.

'Please get well, Alex,' she begged. 'I love you so much.'

A nurse arrived with a pot of tea and a plate of sandwiches.

'Doctor said you should eat,' she said stiffly, putting the tray on the bedside cabinet. She looked Emma over from head to toe and sniffed critically. 'Have you looked in a mirror, Mrs – Miss…?'

'It's Miss Watson.' Emma felt her colour rising as for the first time she wondered what people must have been thinking. 'I'm Mr Baxter's fiancée.'

'Hmphh. I suggest you go to the ladies' bathroom and clean yourself up.'

The woman turned on her heel and left the room, her starched white uniform rustling. Emma remembered the haste with which she'd dressed and looked down at her blouse, which was buttoned all askew. Her hair straggled loose from its braid. But it was too late now to be worried what people thought of her, and Alex was her main concern. She ate and drank before she visited the ladies' bathroom to wash and tidy herself.

When she returned, feeling slightly more respectable, Alex's eyes flickered open. Her heart skittered with relief. She bent over him, clasped his hand and placed a lingering kiss on his brow.

'How do you feel, darling?'

'Groggy,' he murmured hoarsely.

'Doctor removed the bullet. He said there was no damage to any vital organs.' She spoke lightly, preferring not to repeat the rest of what the doctor had said. Alex feebly squeezed her hand, frightening her with his lack of strength.

'Sorry, Em,' he croaked. 'Must have given you a terrible fright.'

'Oh, Alex.' She stroked his stubbled cheek. 'You were in shocking pain.'

The nurse bustled in and fixed them with a disapproving stare.

'So you're awake, Mr Baxter. The sergeant's here to talk to you both.'

All the panic of that morning came rushing back to Emma.

'I can talk to him,' she said, 'but surely he doesn't need to bother Mr Baxter just yet?'

'I don't think you'll convince him of that. He wants to interview you separately. Come with me, Miss Watson.'

Emma followed her into a small room. The police sergeant sat behind a paper-strewn desk. He rose to his feet as the nurse introduced them.

'This is Miss Watson. Sergeant Gunning, Miss.'

The sergeant, a balding man with a drooping red moustache and freckled, pockmarked skin, indicated a vacant chair.

'Please sit down, Miss Watson. Thank you, nurse – you can go.' Resuming his seat, he scribbled something in his notebook and then looked at her with raised eyebrows. 'Can you tell me all the events leading up to the shooting of Mr Baxter?'

Emma swallowed. She squeezed her hands into fists, welcoming the discomfort as her nails bit into her palms. She wondered if she should she be truthful and air all her family's dirty linen. But if her awful suspicions were true, the resulting public scandal, her parents' ruination and the certain exposure of Alex's Aboriginal heritage were enough to prompt her silence.

'Mr Baxter and I were travelling together from Breakaway Creek to Clermont,' she managed, her voice surprising her with its calmness. 'Mr Baxter was stoking up the fire when I heard a shot and –'

Here she faltered, and her throat constricted.

'He fell.'

Sergeant Gunning wrote something in his notebook.

'What is your relationship with Mr Baxter, Miss Watson?'

'He is my fiancé.'

'Indeed. Is it usual for you two to spend time alone, unchaperoned?'

She flushed.

'No, sir. But we were travelling to Clermont so we could be married.' Thinking fast, she added: 'we had an Aboriginal maid with us, but she ran away when she heard the shot.'

'What a pity. Most cowardly of her. And what a shame this has attracted so much attention. I'm afraid people will talk, Miss Watson.'

Emma's flush deepened. The sergeant's tone was insolent, bordering on insulting. She drew herself upright in her chair.

'I believe we are discussing a shooting here, Sergeant Gunning. Not the reputations of Mr Baxter and myself.'

'Ah, but you'd be surprised how often the two things are linked, Miss Watson. Crimes of passion, and all that. Do you have another lover, by any chance?'

'Certainly not!' She glared at him, bristling. 'What sort of person do you take me for?'

He didn't respond to that.

'Why were you staying at Breakaway Creek?'

'I was visiting my cousin, Mrs George Baxter. She was confined recently and I was there to help her with the infant.'

'For how long did you stay at the property, Miss Watson?'

'A couple of weeks. I spent more than a month there towards the end of last year.'

He gave her a sly smile.

'And is that when you became … friendly with Mr Baxter?'

How dare he speak to her in this insinuating manner? Anyone would think she and Alex were on trial, she thought. But she dared not risk antagonising him.

'Mr Baxter and I were courting then, yes.'

He wrote in his book again.

'Do you have family, Miss?'

'My parents live in Brisbane.'

'And do they approve of this match?'

She hesitated. A lie would only make him wonder why she and Alex were in a rush to be married.

'Unfortunately not, sergeant. My father considers my fiancé unsuitable. That's why we were coming to Clermont to be married.'

'Eloping, in other words?' He grinned, displaying yellowed, uneven teeth.

She looked down at her lap, her face hot with mortification.

'If you say so.'

'Do you know of anyone else who may have wanted to stop you? I assume your father is in Brisbane?' he asked.

She was glad he couldn't see her hands, which shook uncontrollably under the desk. She couldn't – wouldn't – answer that last bit. Numbly, she shook her head.

'It must have been an accident. Someone may have been shooting kangaroos.'

'Hmm.' He didn't sound as if he believed her. 'Well, that will be all for now, Miss Watson. I'll speak to your fiancé.'

'Please – he's very weak.'

'It won't take long, Miss Watson.'

Chapter Nineteen

Emma was forced to stay in the hospital waiting room while the sergeant questioned Alex. She fidgeted restlessly in her chair, trying to read an issue of the Peak Downs Telegram and Copperfield Miner that had been left on a table. The words blurred and ran together, making no sense to her. In exasperation, she put the paper down.

There had been no opportunity to speak with Alex to try to match their stories. But she was more concerned about how the stress of the interview might affect his health, than with what he might let slip.

Fortunately the policeman wasn't long. He gave Emma a hard stare as he ambled out the door and she flinched. Somehow he made her feel as if she and Alex were the guilty party, not the victims. She hurried in to see her fiancé, finding him with his eyes closed, his face drained of colour. She sat quietly beside the bed but his eyes opened anyway.

'Are you all right?' she asked softly.

'I didn't tell him anything. About you-know-who.'

Tears stung her eyes.

'I can't bear to think about it. How dare he –'

He shook his head.

'We don't know for sure. Probably a good thing.'

'Sleep now,' she said. 'I want you well, Alex.'

He managed a faint smile before drifting off. Emma sat and watched him, squirming as her back ached in the hard, straight-backed chair. She found herself yawning and realised she'd had only a few hours' sleep in the past three days. But she couldn't leave Alex now.

As the day drew on, he began tossing restlessly in his sleep. His face became flushed and his forehead felt hot under her hand. She went in search of help and found the matron sitting at her desk. A large, mannish-looking woman, her manner was brusque but, thankfully, matter-of-fact rather than judgemental.

'Running a fever, is he?' The woman nodded to herself. 'That is to be expected.'

At Alex's bedside she produced a thermometer and took his temperature, shaking her head as she peered at it.

'I'll get Nurse Graham to sponge him.' She gave Emma a compassionate look. 'Have you anywhere to go, young lady? You look worn out.'

Emma shook her head.

'I'll have to stay at one of the hotels. But I'm not leaving Mr Baxter yet.'

'As you wish.' She bustled off and presently the disapproving nurse came in with a bowl of water and a pile of cloths.

'Miss Watson, I must ask you to leave the room while I attend the patient.'

Bristling, Emma stood up and moved her chair to the far corner where she couldn't be accused of being in the way.

'Mr Baxter is my fiancé, nurse. We are to be married as soon as he's well enough. Surely I have the right to be with him.'

The woman compressed her lips into a thin line. She folded the sheet down to Alex's waist to reveal his heavily bandaged torso and wrung a cloth in the water. Without another word she began the sponging process, her back turned in silent condemnation.

When the nurse was called away, she left the bowl and cloths on the bedside cupboard. Emma shifted her chair back to Alex's side and took over the sponging. Alex tossed and muttered, still feverish despite their efforts. The skin on his flushed face was paper-dry. In fear, Emma talked to him and tried to rouse him from his delirium. At last his eyes flickered open and he looked at her.

'Emma,' he whispered hoarsely. Light-headed with relief, she bent down to kiss his dry lips.

'Oh, Alex,' she begged. 'Please tell me you feel better.'

He raised a hand as if to touch her, but his arm flopped weakly back to his side.

'Emma, get the minister to marry us,' he muttered. 'As soon as you can.'

Her brief moment of hope turned to dismay and her eyes filled with tears as she looked down at his face. His urgency frightened her. Did he think he was going to die?

'Go and ... see him, Emma.' The effort seemed to have drained him. 'Now.'

Trembling, she leaned down to kiss him again.

'I'll go, Alex. Right away.'

In the doorway she almost bumped into the returning Nurse Graham. The woman brushed past without a word, but Emma tried to console herself with the knowledge that Alex wouldn't be alone. She encountered the matron coming out of her office.

'Oh, Matron.' Her voice shook. 'Where might I find the Church of England minister? Mr Baxter wants him to marry us.'

Matron's keen eyes widened and then softened with pity. Emma had the feeling she understood exactly what was happening – how Alex was trying to protect her future if the worst happened. She cut off the thought, refusing to contemplate it.

'Reverend Webster is probably at the manse. It's a bit of a walk.' Matron gave brisk directions and Emma set off, her blurred gaze hardly taking in her surroundings as she forced her unsteady legs to carry her down the street. All she wanted to do was crawl into a corner and weep, but she had to do this for Alex's peace of mind.

It was a long walk, but at last she knocked on the door of the manse. A middle-aged woman opened it and introduced herself as the Reverend's wife.

'He's in his study, preparing Sunday's service,' she said. 'I'll show you through.'

Reverend Webster's jowls creased into a warm smile he welcomed Emma into the shabby, book-lined study. He shook her hand with his flabby one.

'What can I do for you, Miss Watson? How is your fiancé? I'd planned to visit him tomorrow.'

Emma's eyes stung with tears. In the face of kindness it was even harder to stay in control.

'He's not well,' she whispered. 'Reverend, I have an enormous favour to ask. We were on our way here to be married when he was injured. Would it be possible to perform the ceremony now, at the hospital? Please? Alex sent me here to ask you.'

The reverend's smile faded.

'It's most irregular – you'll need a special licence, which is more expensive.' He hesitated, but then seemed to take pity on Emma. 'I suppose it can be done. You'll need witnesses. Do you have anyone in mind?'

Emma tried to sort through the confused fog in her brain. The only person she could think of was Mr Petersen from the Leo Hotel. Possibly the matron would act as the second witness. She mentioned these names to Reverend Webster and he nodded.

'That should do. I'll approach Mr Petersen for you and come to the hospital directly.'

As she walked back up the hill, a man with a delivery cart overtook her weary steps. Perhaps he recognised her, for his face was kindly as he looked at her.

'On your way to the hospital, Miss? Hop in my cart and I'll give you a ride.'

Nurse Graham was still tending to Alex when Emma looked into his room. He seemed little changed and muttered with pain and fever. How would he manage to participate in a wedding ceremony?

She hurried to find the matron, approaching the woman with some trepidation.

'Reverend Webster has agreed to marry us tonight, Matron. Would you be prepared to act as one of our witnesses?'

Matron tutted.

'What goings-on in my hospital! Bedside marriages, indeed!'

Emma's spirits sank, but then the woman's stern face relaxed a little.

'Don't take everything to heart, my dear. Of course I'll act as your witness.' She sighed. 'I only hope this man of yours is up to it.'

Fortunately, when the minister arrived just on dark with Mr Petersen in tow, Alex seemed to rally. Emma had done her best to make herself look respectable, but with her possessions abandoned at the campsite she had no clean clothes. A young nurse had come to her rescue, fetching a fresh gown for her. She couldn't help thinking they made a strange pair when she looked at her bridegroom lying prone in bed with only a sheet covering his bare, bandaged chest.

The brief ceremony hardly seemed real. One look at Alex's face had obviously convinced the minister to reduce it to the essentials. To Emma, everything was blurry around the edges, like an out-of-focus photograph. Alex struggled to make his responses, his face still flushed with fever. All the time Emma clasped his hand, squeezing her encouragement. There was no ring and once they were pronounced man and wife, Emma had to bend to kiss her husband. Instead of the bubbling excitement she'd expected to feel on her wedding day, her chest was heavy with anxiety and dread.

They all signed the marriage certificate, Alex barely managing to scrawl his name. Their witnesses congratulated them both and tactfully left the room. Reverend Webster lingered to give them a blessing. He brushed off Emma's profuse thanks and took her hand in his.

'I hope and pray this night has a happy ending, Mrs Baxter. But regardless, you're his wife now.'

Being called Mrs Baxter induced a little thrill of pleasure that penetrated her anguish. Whatever happened, she'd bear Alex's name with pride.

~*~

Mr Petersen had promised her a room at the Leo Hotel. To Emma's relief he had assured her he would wait in the hospital's front room to escort her there. She'd been dreading the long walk alone in the dark. When she told the matron she was about to leave, the older woman patted her hand and smiled kindly.

'Don't worry, we'll keep a good eye on Mr Baxter tonight. You get some sleep.'

Even so, Emma felt she was deserting him as she kissed her new husband goodbye. Alex had slipped into a deep sleep – or was it unconsciousness? His hot cheek was unresponsive to her lips. With a stab of compunction, she realised the marriage ceremony had drained what little strength he had.

Mr Petersen had his buggy waiting outside. When she tried to step up on the footplate, Emma's strength deserted her and she sagged weakly against the side of the vehicle. Mr Petersen hoisted her up and she rode the few short blocks to the hotel in a daze of exhaustion. Once they arrived at the hotel he called his wife to help her to her room and provide a nightgown and toiletries. Yet when Emma collapsed on the cool sheets, she couldn't sleep. Her mind whirled with tortured thoughts.

When she dozed off, the images she'd repressed all day emerged to haunt her. She and Alex stood on the top of a sheer creek bank, one step away from tumbling over the edge, as her father threatened them both with a rifle. The terror she'd felt at the time of the shooting consumed her again, paralysing her with its intensity. Ignoring her pleas for mercy, her father merely smiled, his face implacable as he levelled the rifle at Alex and squeezed the trigger. She awoke screaming with the sensation of Alex's hot and sticky blood on her hands. The sweet metallic smell of it filled her nostrils in a hideous replay of the previous morning.

At first light she rose and washed, carelessly pulling a brush though her tangled, dusty hair. Weariness dragged at her movements, but concern for Alex prompted her to beg the cook for a cup of tea and something to eat before she hastily swallowed some bread and butter and trudged up the hill to the hospital.

It was long before visiting hours. The building sat quiet and still with the early sunlight slanting onto the wide veranda. She let herself in the unlocked front door and made her way to Alex's room, feeling as if her heart beat right in her throat. What if he hadn't survived the night? Almost afraid to look in, she drew in a sharp breath at the sight of his sheet-covered chest slowly rising and falling. With a heady rush of relief, she crossed to his side. The flush of fever had given way to a frightening pallor, but he appeared to be sleeping peacefully. It seemed his fever had abated, but she was loath to touch him in case she disturbed his slumber.

She pulled up a chair and sat, content to watch and hope. Perhaps she wouldn't be widowed within a day of becoming a wife.

Nurse Graham put her head around the door.

'You! Here already.' She sniffed. 'That farce of a marriage won't stop them talking, you know.'

Alex stirred and Emma hissed at her in anger.

'You'll wake him!'

'Humph!' The woman marched up to the bed and popped a thermometer under Alex's tongue, demonstrating how little she cared for Emma's concerns. She grasped his wrist in her fingers, looking at her fob watch as she took his pulse. Then she read the thermometer and made notes on his chart before walking out without another word. Tears pricked Emma's eyes. How could anyone be so callous?

Alex was now most certainly awake. She leant down to kiss him.

'How do you feel, husband?'

His lips twitched in a weak smile. He tried to move his arm and groaned.

'As weak as a kitten, but better than last night.' His voice was little more than a croak, but, for the first time, she dared hope he'd recover.

'You scared me. Please don't do that again.'

'I was pretty scared myself. Did we get married last night, or did I just dream that?'

She smiled.

'Indeed we did. The Reverend Webster married us. Matron and Mr Petersen were our witnesses.'

'Oh, Emma. I'm sorry. You wanted a proper wedding.'

'I don't mind. In the circumstances, it's a relief to have it over with.' She changed the subject, still reluctant for any discussion about the shooting and her father's opposition. She couldn't bear to talk about Henry Watson. 'Just concentrate on regaining your health, so we can plan our future.'

After managing some bread and milk, Alex slept again. But as the morning progressed, it became obvious he wasn't out of danger. Around midday his fever returned and he was subjected to another sponging.

Matron arranged for the kitchen to send some sandwiches for her lunch, but as the evening approached Emma knew she couldn't impose on the hospital any longer. She'd eaten little in the past three days and she was faint with a combination of hunger and exhaustion.

'You take yourself back to the hotel for a decent meal and some sleep,' Matron told her sharply. 'You look like death. You won't be any help to your husband if your own health fails.'

Alex's condition was unchanged. He was still feverish, but not desperately ill as he had been the day before. Emma decided to do as she was bid and kissed him goodnight. She walked to the hotel before darkness fell.

After freshening up in her room, she timidly ventured downstairs to the hotel dining room. The establishment was familiar to her, but it felt unusual and intimidating to dine alone. Was it just her imagination, she wondered, or did everyone seem to be staring at her?

She hastily found an empty table, hunching her shoulders in a defensive position. When she realised what she was doing she straightened up in her chair, squaring her shoulders and lifting her head high. Were these people so blameless they could sit in judgement of her? She doubted it.

The food was good and she was hungry enough to appreciate it, but the meal was miserable and lonely, nonetheless. As she left the dining room Mr Petersen intercepted her to ask after Alex's welfare.

'He's still battling the fever,' she told him. 'I can only pray he has a better night tonight.'

'Do not worry,' the Dane assured her heartily. 'He is strong man. How do you say…? As tough as old boots?'

Emma smiled, finding his cheerfulness heartening.

'Yes, he is tough, and I'm hopeful he'll pull through.'

Sure enough, when she arrived at the hospital the next morning, Alex was propped up with pillows, eating breakfast. Joy fizzed through her like effervescent soda and her smile seemed to stretch her entire face. When she bent to kiss his cheek, he turned his head to meet her lips with his.

'You must be feeling better!'

'Especially now you're here, my dear. That Nurse Graham's an old battle-axe.' He shuddered. 'I'm flat out feeding myself, but I'm not having her shovelling it into my mouth.'

'Let me help you, then.' She fed him his porridge and poured a cup of tea from the pot on his tray. Obviously even the small effort was tiring him, so once he'd had enough she sat back quietly and allowed him to rest.

Later in the morning, when he'd woken from a restful sleep, she finally said what was on her mind.

'Alex, what are we to do once you leave hospital? I don't want to go back to Breakaway Creek, just in case…' It seemed unlikely her father would still be there, but the possibility frightened her. She felt responsible for everything that had happened and was ashamed to face the rest of the Baxter family. 'Nor do I want to stay in Clermont. I feel like a social outcast, with everyone staring at me and whispering behind my back.'

Alex's face tightened.

'I'm sorry for dragging you into this. You should never have gotten tangled up with me.'

'No, don't say that!' She took his hand and squeezed it, hating it when he spoke so. 'For myself, I have no regrets. But I can't help feeling that I'm to blame for you being shot.'

'The only person to blame is the one who pulled the trigger.' A shadow crossed Alex's face. 'But I don't want to go back to Breakaway Creek, either. We need to make a fresh start, put all this behind us. I'll get a job as a stockman somewhere and save until we can get a place of our own.'

A wave of shame engulfed her. Here she was, thinking of herself, without trying to imagine how Alex must feel. If the experience had given her nightmares, what had it done to him?

'We'll make a new life together, Alex,' she murmured. 'Just the two of us.'

~*~

The next day they had another visit from Sergeant Gunning, who entered the hospital room carrying a familiar swag and a bulging hessian bag.

'Here's everything you left at your campsite, Baxter.' Gunning dumped the lot in the corner and straightened to face them, dusting his hands together. 'The tracker found an abandoned rifle and an empty shell in the scrub about a hundred yards away, along with horse tracks and a man's boot prints. He was able to track the horse nearly into Clermont, before traffic on the road wiped out the trail.'

He looked hard at them both.

'We're still investigating. Do you know anyone who owns a Martini-Henry rifle?'

Alex shrugged.

'They're pretty common. I daresay a lot of men I know would own one.'

'Hmm. One more thing.' The sergeant pulled a brown paper bag from his pocket and dug inside it. His fingers emerged holding the stub of a cigar. 'This was found near the rifle.'

Emma froze. It was identical to the cigars her father smoked, and she didn't know anyone who lived out here who shared the habit. Bushmen preferred pipes.

'Do you know anyone who smokes cigars?' The sergeant's cold eyes bored into her, as if he read her guilty thoughts. Emma shook her head numbly, feeling like a criminal. What else could she do? Implicate her own father?

'What about you, Baxter?' His piercing gaze focussed on Alex.

Alex looked calmly back at him.

'Not from around here. You could ask at the store if anyone's bought cigars lately.'

'I'll definitely do that.' Gunning didn't look convinced. 'Well, if you think of anything else…'

He paused, his glance turning sly.

'I hear you two were married the other day.'

'That's right,' Alex agreed, meeting the officer's gaze with a level one of his own. His eyes held a warning, as if daring Gunning to show his wife disrespect over the hasty wedding.

The sergeant shuffled his feet and returned the cigar to the paper bag before stuffing it in his pocket.

'Well, I'll let you know if we uncover anything more.' He picked up his hat and departed without further ceremony. Alex watched Gunning's retreating figure.

'If we weren't sure before, we know now,' he said. Emma's already squirming stomach gave a sickening lurch. She looked at him anxiously.

'Should I have told him?'

Alex sighed and shook his head, his mouth grim.

'No, it'll only make more trouble. So long as he leaves us alone…'

'I couldn't blame you if you turned him in,' she said softly. 'You were nearly killed.'

'Yes, but imagine what a court case would be like. I hate to think what the papers would make of it. I don't want to put you through that.'

Emma nodded in relief that he hadn't allowed anger to cloud his perspective. A trial would be devastating for her mother. And in the notoriety that would result, Alex's family history was sure to be publically announced. She thought they were all better off this way, even if it meant that a man got away with attempted murder.

The sergeant had not been gone long when they had another visitor. It was George, and he looked as if he'd travelled in a hurry. He'd obviously just arrived in town and his face was anxious as he peered into Alex's hospital room. He quickly crossed to the bed, staring down at his half-brother.

'Are you all right, Alex? They tell me you had an accident.'

'Got myself into a spot of bother,' Alex managed a weak grin. 'But I'm a lot better now.'

George glanced apologetically at Emma.

'Forgive me, Emma.' He bent to kiss her cheek. 'We were worried sick about you both, so Lucy finished packing your things and I got some of Alex's clothes. I have them outside in the buggy. We knew you couldn't have taken much, and I hoped I'd find you here in town.'

'Bless you both!' Emma smiled at him gratefully. 'I wasn't looking forward to purchasing an entire new wardrobe.'

'So what happened?' said George as he looked from one to the other, as if unsure how much he should ask. 'Petersen told me you'd been shot.'

Emma avoided his eyes, uncertain how to answer. Alex came to her rescue.

'Yes, I got hit in the shoulder here.' He gestured to the bandaged area and went on to briefly describe how it had happened, without mentioning their suspicions. 'It could have been someone shooting at 'roos.'

George looked at him hard. He glanced at Emma, biting his lip.

'But you don't really believe that, do you?' He flushed. 'I know he's your father, Emma, but when Watson found you'd gone, he was fuming. I couldn't get a horse quick enough to suit him. And then I noticed my rifle was missing. I set off after him pretty quick but I never really thought he'd use it.'

'Please, George.' Emma rose and put her hand on his arm, pleading with her voice and eyes. 'If it's made public – imagine the scandal. We'll all be dragged through it.'

George's face worked.

'He shouldn't get away with it. How dare he – in this day and age! It's mediaeval!'

'Calm down, George.' Emma marvelled how cool Alex's voice was. 'It'll be on his conscience, and that's enough. As Emma said, it'll be worse for the rest of us if he's charged. And they may not prove it, anyway.'

'The sergeant will want to interview you.' Emma sat down again, mainly because her legs were shaking too much to support her. 'Please don't mention my father's visit to Breakaway Creek.'

'You want me to lie?' George looked as if the idea was an affront.

'We've been lying for a long time now, we Baxters.' Alex's voice was weary. 'What's another one to add to this whole sorry mess?'

For a moment George seemed taken aback, then he let out a long sigh and appeared to crumple, as if all the resistance had drained out of him.

'You're right, old chap. One lie breeds another, as they say. In the long run it all comes back to the sins of our old man.' He pulled up a second chair, his expression critical as he examined Alex's pale face. 'I suppose the main thing is you're getting better.'

'And we do have some good news.' Smiling, Alex reached for Emma's hand and gently squeezed it. 'You'll have to congratulate us. We were married a few days ago.'

George drew in a sharp breath and let it out with a hiss. For a moment he looked stunned, but then his lips twitched with the beginnings of a broad smile.

'You sneaky devil! How did you manage that from your sickbed? But I'm glad to hear it.' He leaned across to shake his brother's hand and stood up to kiss Emma's cheek. 'My felicitations, my dear. I'm only sorry I wasn't here to share the happy day.'

'It wasn't exactly a happy occasion. I thought Alex –' She broke off, knowing she'd be in tears again if she said any more. 'But I'm glad we did it. Surely my father will leave us alone now.'

'I'll make sure he took the train out of here,' George said flatly. 'He'd better be gone, or I won't answer for the consequences.'

'How is Lucy?' Emma asked. 'She was so upset after that awful scene with Father. What a way to learn the truth.'

'Lucy will come around.' George tugged at his collar. 'She hasn't quite forgiven me for keeping her in the dark. And I doubt she'll ever speak to the old man again.'

He looked at Alex.

'But it won't make any difference to how she treats you.'

He left shortly afterwards, and Emma didn't see him again until he returned just before dark.

'I have the buggy outside. I'll drive you to the hotel,' he told her. 'I have good news. Someone answering Mr Watson's description caught the train on Wednesday afternoon.'

Emma did a quick calculation.

'That was the same day Alex was shot.'

'Didn't waste any time getting out of here, did he?' George's voice was bitter. 'I wonder if he knows or cares that Alex is still alive?'

Emma didn't venture an opinion. What could she say? As far as she was concerned, she no longer had a father.

'Have you seen Sergeant Gunning?' she asked, when her thoughts quietened.

'Yes, he caught up with me in the main street. We went to the police station for a lengthy interview and he showed me the rifle he found. It looked like mine but I didn't say so. Since I can't claim it back, looks like I'll have to buy a new one.' George made a wry face. 'I doubt if Gunning will bother with the long ride to Breakaway Creek, but I'm going home in the morning and I'll talk to everyone. I'll make sure they keep quiet.'

'I'm so sorry about all of this.' Emma pressed his hand gratefully. 'I'm blessed to have you for a brother, George.'

George's ruddy complexion heightened.

'No, my dear – the good fortune is all mine.'

~*~

Over the next few days, Alex grew steadily stronger. Finally Doctor Kent pronounced him well enough to be discharged. Mr Petersen came by with his buggy and drove them to the hotel. As Alex walked slowly and carefully down the hospital steps to the waiting vehicle, Emma realised how weak he still was. He stopped to lean against the buggy, his face pale and damp with sweat. Mr Petersen got him on board, and, at the hotel, helped him up the stairs and into their room.

At last they were alone, really alone, for the first time since their marriage. Emma fussed with Alex's few possessions, unpacking his brush and razor and setting them on the top of the duchess next to her own things. Alex lay silently and watched her, resting after his exertion. Finally he spoke.

'Emma.' When she looked at him, he reached to her with his hand. He was smiling. 'Come here, Mrs Baxter.'

She returned the smile, a combination of shyness and anticipation making her lips tremble. She still wasn't accustomed to having him call her that.

'Don't you need to rest?' she asked softly.

'I've been resting for days. Now I need you.'

She flushed. Surely he didn't mean…

'Alex – it's eleven o'clock in the morning! Besides, you're not strong enough.'

His eyes glinted.

'I wouldn't put money on that.' He seized her hand and pulled her close, surprising her with his sudden vigour. 'At least let me hold you. It's a nice change not having that old battleaxe of a nurse glaring at us.'

Emma sat beside him on the bed. He pulled her face down to his and kissed her lingeringly.

'In sickness and in health,' he mused. 'Isn't it a wife's duty to entertain the invalid?'

Chapter Twenty

Brisbane, 2010

When Shelley eventually slept, nightmares claimed her. A heavy weight pressed her down on the bed and strong hands brushed away her flailing arms. Then a knife pricked her throat, the sharp blade slicing her skin until blood gushed forth, flowing down her chest and pooling obscenely on the white sheets. She screamed and struggled, fighting her way to consciousness through layers of horror.

She lay panting, heart hammering, her pyjamas soaked with sweat as she battled to shake off the oppressive dream. A knock on the door made her body go rigid until she recognised Luke's worried voice.

'Shelley! Are you all right?'

Untangling herself from the twisted sheets, she scrambled out of bed. Her legs trembled and her hands shook as she fumbled in the dark to find the doorknob and slide the chain. Luke stepped inside and pulled her into his arms.

'You were screaming! Did you have a bad dream?' He ran a caressing hand over her hair. 'You're shaking.'

She nodded, hardly able to frame the words.

'It was awful.'

'Don't worry, you're safe now. I'll stay awhile if you like.' He squeezed her tight.

She nodded again and clutched at him as if he were her only chance for salvation.

'It was Bevan,' she mumbled, shuddering. 'I keep remembering the knife.'

'I'm so sorry, Shelley.' He flicked the light switch and pushed the door closed then reached for a chair and sat down. He pulled her onto his lap. 'You've been through hell, all because of me.'

'We've all been through hell.' She burrowed into his shoulder, finding comfort in his strength and the warmth of his body. Luke bent his head and she lifted her face for his kiss, a gentle caress that skirted the broken corner of her mouth. She slid her arms around his neck and ran her fingers into the waves of his hair. With the nightmare fading, her body began to stir and she lifted her lips for more.

Then he really kissed her and the pain in her mouth was something to be welcomed and embraced. It wasn't fear that made her heart race now. After several minutes he eased her off him and stood up, switching off the light. With only the faint glow of the bedside clock illuminating the room, he slid his hands under her singlet top and cupped her aching breasts. She ran her hands down his back to the waistband of his boxer shorts and pressed against him in a desperate need to be closer. When he began to edge her over to the bed, it didn't even occur to her to protest.

~*~

Later, as the tingling feeling eased out of her toes and the heated flush faded from her body, his words from earlier that day came back to make her squirm: "While we were going at it last night, Ben and Jack were probably scared shitless. And I wasn't even thinking about them." Beside her, Luke's breathing was loud in the silent room and his heart thudded under her cheek. His damp skin smelt faintly of soap and sex and that particular essence that belonged to him alone. They'd just done it again and if he had been thinking of his boys, she certainly hadn't.

'Hadn't you better get back to your boys?' she said, suddenly ashamed. She moved away from his encircling arm and sat up against the pillow, tugging the sheet to cover her breasts.

She really hadn't meant to sound so abrupt. She sensed him stiffen and roll away from her. He swung his legs over the side of the bed. In the dim light, she saw him search for his boxers and she tried not to watch as he stood to pull them on. In spite of herself, his shadowy figure tugged at her gaze. Then he turned to look over his shoulder at her.

'The boys were sound asleep when I left them. I thought you needed me more.'

He left the room without another word. She slid down on the bed and buried her face in the pillow, tears squeezing past her eyelids. What had happened to her resolution to be strong and sensible? This situation seemed only to be hurting them both. It was little consolation that he'd managed to distract her from her nightmare.

Sleep took its time to claim her again. When she awoke to broad daylight, an instant recollection of her fractured relationship with Luke swamped her with misery. Fighting the urge to burrow back under the sheets, she dragged herself out of bed and ran a hot shower. The water flowed over her, removing the lingering traces of his scent from her body. If only the ache of uncertainty could be as easily erased.

She dressed and applied a generous layer of make-up, trying to hide the dark shadows under her eyes and the marks Cahill – she preferred not to think of him as Bevan anymore – had left on her. Then she steeled herself to knock on Luke's door. He answered, giving her an uneasy look even as he spoke into the phone held to his ear. The boys ran to her and grabbed her hands, dragging her over to the table in the corner.

'Look, a lady brought us breakfast!' Ben announced. 'Are you having some?'

Shelley hugged them both and forced herself to respond to their enthusiasm, eyeing the cereal, fruit and toast without much interest. Being around Luke wasn't doing much for her appetite. It struck her as ironic that the boys, whose mental welfare she'd worried over, seemed so resilient and happy while she seemed to have been shredded into emotional tatters.

At last Luke disconnected his phone.

'That was Uncle Mitch.' He smiled at the boys as if determined to pretend there was nothing wrong, using a hearty tone that was totally unlike him. 'Grandma and Granddad rang him last night. They'll be home from overseas next week.'

'Can we see them?' Jack asked.

'Soon,' Luke replied. 'They're not back yet.'

'Are we going home today?' Ben's big eyes looked up at his father pleadingly.

'If we get that far.' Luke ruffled his son's hair. 'You'd better be good. No fighting in the car.'

Shelley's stomach lurched. He still hadn't looked at her beyond that first fleeting glance. She took a deep breath and tried to sound casual.

'Can you drop me in Rocky on the way through, please?'

He looked at her then, with a puzzled, anxious frown that made her flinch inwardly.

'What about your car?'

'Oh, of course. I'll go back with you to pick it up, but I won't stay.' She felt herself flushing. She'd completely forgotten about it. How stupid was that? Seeing a shadow cross his face she added: 'I don't like to leave you in the lurch with the boys, but there are things I need to do.'

Like get on with her life, she thought.

He shook his head and turned away.

'The boys aren't your worry. It's time I looked for a nanny.' He paused and there was a moment's silence. 'We'll stay in Rocky tonight. I'll drop you at your parents' and the boys and I will stay at a motel. We'll go the rest of the way tomorrow.'

In less than an hour they were on the road again, heading north for Rockhampton and the Capricorn Coast. As Luke drove, Shelley rang her parents. She hadn't been in touch with them since leaving Breakaway Creek. She deliberately played down yesterday's drama, omitting that Cahill had held her hostage. Her lip was still swollen – Luke's kisses last night hadn't helped – and a red line on her throat marked where the point of his knife had pricked her skin, but she'd wait to tell them more when she saw them face-to-face.

'I'll see you this afternoon,' she told her mother on the phone.

'I'm looking forward to it. Have a safe trip.' Her mother sounded concerned. Shelley had never been good at fooling Noela, but she wasn't sure how much she felt like sharing.

~*~

It was a long drive, fraught with the challenge of keeping two small boys entertained. At last Ben and Jack drifted off to sleep and Shelley found herself nodding against the headrest. Since Luke had declined her offer to give him a break from driving, she made herself comfortable and attempted to catch up on some of the sleep she'd missed the night before.

She awoke as they entered a roundabout on the outskirts of Rockhampton. Was it only two days since they'd driven south past that statue of the grey Brahman bull? So much had happened since then, she thought, it seemed like weeks ago.

Her parents came out to meet them as they drew up in front of the house. Her mother kissed her, but then stepped back and eyed her face.

Her gaze flashed to Luke as he slid out of the driver's seat, and back again to Shelley. Noela frowned.

'What happened to you? You didn't say you'd been hurt.'

Shelley's hand went to her mouth in an involuntary movement and she looked away from Noela's worried gaze.

'Someone objected to us taking the boys.' She glanced at Ben and Jack, who were still in the back seat unbuckling their seatbelts. 'I'll tell you all about it later.'

As she greeted her father, Luke came around the vehicle and shook first her mother's and then her father's hand. He'd removed the bandage from his arm and stuck Elastoplast over the knife slash. Shelley noticed her parents looking at it.

'I must apologise for letting Shelley get mixed up in my dramas,' he said, visibly bracing himself as if for some form of reprimand.

'Don't blame Luke, I insisted on being involved.' Shelley said quickly. She opened the rear door and stood aside as the boys scrambled out. 'Ben and Jack, you remember my mum and dad? Mr and Mrs Blake?'

'Hello,' Ben said shyly. He looked up at Shelley's parents and took a deep breath. 'D' you know, Bevan had a knife?'

Noela gave a little gasp and Luke moved quickly to his son's side, encircling the boy with his arm and pulling him close.

'That's enough, Ben. We'll talk about Bevan another time.'

'Bevan's bad man!' Jack announced. Luke flinched visibly.

'Looks like a debriefing session is in order,' he muttered to no one in particular. Then he looked up at Shelley's parents. 'I'd explain if their ears weren't flapping.'

'Luke, would you like a cup of tea?' Noela asked with forced brightness. 'Or a cold drink? The boys must be due for a break.'

'Thanks. Just a cold drink and we'll be on our way.'

When Shelley returned from taking the boys to the bathroom, Luke was sitting on the front porch with a glass of water in his hand, deep in conversation with her father. Noela passed plastic tumblers of cordial to the boys.

'Sounds like you had an eventful time,' she said over their heads.

'To put it mildly, yes.' Tired of sitting from all the hours in the car, Shelley leant against the railing. Luke's gaze flicked up to her face.

'I hope that mongrel spends a long time in jail for what he did,' he said.

'Knowing the legal system, he'll be out in no time,' Shelley's father offered. 'If he even gets locked up at all.'

'You're probably right. But I'm going to apply for legal custody of the boys, so I only hope they'll take the drug charges and Bevan's violence into account.'

Ben and Jack had taken their drinks to sit on the porch step, hopefully out of earshot.

'Do you think he mistreated your boys?' Peter asked in a lowered voice. Luke's face tightened.

'They were scared of him and Ben's been having nightmares. But I don't have any evidence that he's abused them physically.' As he spoke he looked at Shelley and she turned away, not meeting his eyes. She wondered if he was thinking of her own nightmare the previous night. And what had happened afterwards.

Luke cleared his throat and stood up, placing his empty glass on the outdoor table.

'We'd better get going. Thanks for the drink.' He looked at Shelley, his green eyes dark with confusion and regret. 'I'll pick you up in the morning, Shelley.'

Stepping closer, he clasped her shoulder and bent to lightly kiss her cheek.

'Thank you – and sorry.'

After he'd gone, she felt her parents silently watching her.

'Well, you sure got mixed up in something,' Noela said. 'Just how involved are you? Luke seems a nice fellow, but he's caught up in a rotten situation.'

Shelley flushed. He'd said "sorry" – but for what, she wondered. Sorry for getting her into danger? He'd apologised for that enough already. Was he sorry because it was over between them? She wasn't sure it had ever really begun. She couldn't admit any of this to her parents.

'I'm just going back to pick up my car. I told him I wasn't staying.' She sank into a chair with a heavy sigh. 'I don't think it would ever work between us anyway.'

~*~

If Shelley had been more miserable than this, she couldn't remember when. She'd thought it was bad when she kicked Jason out. Because she'd been living with him, her whole life had been disrupted and she'd been hurt and angry. But her heart hadn't felt as if it had been torn out of her body and left hanging by a thread, as it did now.

As promised, Luke had collected her the next morning, and she'd accompanied him back to Breakaway Creek. She had stayed only long enough for a quick snack before leaving in her car. Luke had said he'd be in touch, but a week had passed and there'd been no word. Surely that was a good thing, she thought. Hadn't she decided it wouldn't work between them?

Shelley tried to focus her mind on other things. But mental images of Luke kept intruding. It was easy to picture him in the yards with his cattle or cuddling his two little boys, but most of all, kissing her, touching her and making love to her. Pain lanced her chest each time, choking her until she could hardly breathe.

If only she hadn't taken so long off work. She needed to keep busy. She recommenced her search for a unit, determined to fight the numbing sense of loss before it strangled her.

Eventually she settled on a small, one-bedroom unit not too far from her work. The details were finalised quickly and it would be ready for her to move in after Christmas. She would drive to Brisbane a few days before she had to start work again, to give her time to fetch the things she'd left in the flat Jason still occupied.

Feeling energised at the accomplishment, she decided to drive to the mall to find some Christmas gifts. Forced to park in the next street, she was walking to the mall when her eyes fixed on the man on the footpath in front of her. He was tall, slim and wore faded Wranglers and a checked shirt. An Akubra hat covered most of his brown hair.

Her heart leapt. Could it be? It had to be! Was it Luke?

She hurried to catch up with him, wanting to call out but afraid to, just in case. He turned into a shop selling western wear and she followed, breathing shallowly. As she entered, he stopped to investigate a shelf of high-topped boots. She drew level with him and saw him from the front.

His face was smooth and unlined, with a large nose and receding chin. He definitely wasn't Luke. It was as if her subconscious had superimposed his image onto the other man's form.

Her heart plummeted and she turned away, slinking into the furthest corner of the store and taking deep breaths to calm herself. She feigned interest in a row of checked shirts to cover her confusion. Her buoyant mood had entirely dissipated. Suddenly she had no interest in shopping, but she forced herself to continue on to find gifts for her parents.

Once home, she went to her room and looked dispiritedly at the shirt she'd bought for her father and the bright, floral scarf she'd found for her mother. Christmas was only two weeks away and she'd never felt less like celebrating.

She thought of Ben and Jack and how excited they would be about Santa Claus and the other trappings of the festive season. It hurt to think she wouldn't be there to share it with them. For their sakes, and Luke's, she hoped Miranda had the sense to leave them be.

Chapter Twenty-One

'Are we there yet, Daddy?'

Waves of heat shimmered off the bitumen in front of them and danced over the brown paddocks beside the road. Luke blinked against the glare and glanced at his son in the rear-view mirror.

'Won't be long now, Jack.'

'Will Grandma and Granddad have presents for us?' Ben cut in, full of eager anticipation.

Luke sighed. Today's kids were so materialistic.

'I don't know. Maybe, if you're good.' He turned up the music, hoping the Adam Brand CD, which the boys loved, would distract them for a few more kilometres. If only it was as easy to distract himself. With every kilometre that brought him closer to Rockhampton, the knot in his gut tightened. Driving to Rockhampton brought him closer to Shelley.

He was supposed to be interviewing a girl who'd answered his ad for a nanny, but he couldn't seem to focus on the task. He had this vague sense of unease. The girl was only eighteen – how would she cope with the boys when he and Mitch were out working? Would she be able to handle the isolation?

Recalling how great Shelley had been with them and how well she'd fitted into their lives, he sighed again. He couldn't stop thinking about her, missing her. But most of all he remembered the time they'd spent together at the motel in Childers.

But after a night of the best sex he'd ever had, he'd totally stuffed up. He hadn't done much better the following night, either. She'd actually let him near her again but it hadn't ended any better. Was she really sure that she belonged in the city, he wondered, or was it that he hadn't tried to persuade her to stay?

At the time, he had been so preoccupied with Miranda and her dead-beat boyfriend that he hadn't been able to handle the situation with Shelley. Maybe he could have tried harder.

He'd been close to ringing her a dozen times, but a niggling thought had always stopped him. When Miranda took off, he'd envied his friends with their settled country wives and had vowed he'd never get mixed up with another city girl. Not that Shelley was anything like Miranda. She fitted into bush life in a way Miranda never had. She was good with the boys and they loved her. Yet, when she'd had a go at him that morning in Childers, it had been like the same old thing was happening again. Perhaps he didn't have it in him to keep a woman happy.

With that miserable thought, he drove straight through Rockhampton and turned towards Yeppoon. He hadn't seen his parents for several months and was looking forward to their company.

After his marriage to Miranda, Diane and Barry Sherman had found it a bit crowded at Breakaway Creek and had bought a small property north of the seaside town. His father had started a small Droughtmaster stud, which had kept him occupied until they decided to travel to Europe. Now they were home again, they were eager to see their grandsons. Perhaps, he thought wryly, they'd even missed *him*.

~*~

Later that afternoon, after he'd dutifully looked at his parents' photos and reluctantly confessed all that had happened with Miranda, his father took the boys outside for a game of footy. Left alone with his mother, he looked up to find her studying him.

'So, how's our long-lost relation? What's her name? Shelley, isn't it?'

A tide of heat crept up his neck and he looked down, rubbing his hands on his jeans. He had a feeling his mother remembered her name perfectly well.

'I haven't spoken to her for a while.'

'It sounds like you owe her for helping out the way she did.'

Yeah, he thought, and look how he'd screwed her over. He flinched inwardly, hating the kind, concerned way his mother was looking at him. Things were really bad when you became an object of pity to your own parent.

'Shelley's a great girl,' he said, at last. 'I should ring her. But she was talking about going back to her job in Brisbane.'

'So what? You don't expect her to drop everything and move in with you at a moment's notice, do you?' His mother stood up and walked briskly to the television cupboard. Kneeling down, she pulled out a cardboard box and sat beside him on the sofa. 'Speaking of city girls, I have something to show you.'

She took a tattered, leather-bound book from the box.

'Remember you were asking about Shelley's ancestors? Alex and Emma Baxter?' Luke's pulse leapt.

'Yeah.' He tried to sound nonchalant. 'What about them?'

'Your questions got me thinking,' she explained. 'When we left Breakaway Creek I packed up some old stuff of my mother's, including some diaries I'd never read. I thought I'd have more time once we left.'

She gave a little, dismissive laugh.

'That spare time never seemed to eventuate. But your questions aroused my curiosity. So once we got home, I dug them up.'

She opened the book at a marked page and passed it to him.

'This one is fascinating. It belonged to Lucy Baxter, my great-grandmother. She was Emma's cousin.' She looked at him as if trying to gauge his reaction. 'My father told me a bit about Alex and Emma. But I didn't know all of it. Reading about it first hand was enlightening. This section in particular.'

The handwriting was an old-fashioned, copperplate style and painstakingly neat. Luke glanced at it curiously, wondering if his thudding heart had anything to do with the age-old mystery, or more to do with him being a sucker for anything that reminded him of Shelley. With growing fascination, he silently read the words that had been penned more than a century before.

You won't believe the uproar we have had in this house! Emma's father, my Uncle Henry, arrived yesterday. To say he was displeased about her engagement to Alex is an understatement. He let drop something that came as a terrible shock to me, and I am not sure I can forgive George for deceiving me. Alex's mother was a half-caste and worse, Mr Baxter Senior is his father! Suffice to say, it is a scandalous state of affairs, and I cannot believe the family I thought decent and respectable has all along been harbouring this dreadful secret.
There was a terrible row. Uncle Henry was determined to take Emma back to Brisbane with him and have her marry his business partner, whom I know she despises. But this morning, we found Emma and Alex have fled! My uncle has set off after them, vowing to bring her back. I'm so worried about poor Emma — and poor Alex! He is the innocent party in all of this, after all. I cannot think any the less of him for something that was none of his doing. What will come of it, I dare not imagine!

Another entry, several days later, said:

We have heard nothing from Emma and Alex, or even from my uncle. We are positively frantic with worry about them. George set off for Clermont today, to find out what has happened.

Four days later she wrote:

George arrived home from Clermont today. I was beyond shocked when he told me Alex had been shot. Thank goodness he is recovering, but it sounds as though it was a near thing. What an ordeal for him and Emma! But of course, the wonderful news is that they are married! Well, I hope it is wonderful, because I really fear the repercussions for Emma. What if Alex's secret becomes generally known? What if there is a problem with their children? I think my cousin is far braver than I am.
George told me something else which disturbed me even more. He went to see the police and they showed him a rifle they had found abandoned in the vicinity of the shooting. It was George's own, which has been missing from our house since Tuesday last. He recognised a scratch on the butt, so he knew without a doubt that it was his. But he had promised Emma that he would not betray the culprit, so he pretended ignorance.

Luke let out a little whistle of surprise, but kept on reading.

This is diabolical! Imagine shooting another in cold blood, and for no better reason than to protect the family name! Imagine the slur on the family name if that person's actions became known! Surely a marriage to someone of mixed ancestry is a minor scandal in comparison. I have to say, I sympathise with Emma's desire for silence, but my blood boils with the need for justice. Apparently Uncle Henry took the first train out of town and it is doubtful he will ever have to answer for his actions.

Luke lowered the book, deep in thought. Emma had been a city girl, and look at everything she'd gone through. Racial intolerance aside, life in the bush had been much harder in those days. If she could handle all that, why wouldn't Shelley?

'Fascinating, isn't it?' His mother leaned closer. 'I wasn't sure if they knew who'd shot Alex, but this makes it pretty clear.'

Luke sucked in a deep breath.

'It's hard to believe Watson would go to those lengths to stop his daughter marrying the wrong bloke. Sounds like he got away with it, too.'

'They were different times,' she said. 'I doubt the word "racism" existed in those days. Daughters were supposed to do as they were told and marry to improve the family fortune. It wasn't considered cold or calculating as it would be now.'

'And they talk about the "good old days"! Shelley would love to see this.' He closed the diary with a snap. He should contact her, ask her to come and meet his parents. Assuming she still wanted anything to do with him.

His mother put her hand on his arm, her eyes soft with concern.

'I know I shouldn't interfere, but Mitch said you had something going with her. He also said you've been like a bear with a sore head the last couple of weeks.'

'Mitch should keep his bloody mouth shut.' But then he looked up and met his mother's eyes. 'Mum, she's a great girl, but I don't want to be like Miranda: neglecting the boys for my latest lover. And I don't want to put them through another messy break-up if it doesn't work out.'

His mother sighed.

'It's all a bit soon, I know. But if it feels right, you have to take that chance. Mitch said she was brilliant with the boys. She could be the best thing for them.'

It was true, but he was surprised that Mitch had said it. He slid his arm around his mother's shoulders and gave her a quick hug.

'You're a nosy old woman, but full of good advice, as always.' He smiled ruefully at her. 'You're probably right. I should go and see her.'

~*~

Desperate for something to fill her time, Shelley had spent a couple of days helping her mother in the office of the family business. There was plenty to occupy her during the pre-Christmas rush. Then, with the time they'd saved, she took her mother for a drive to the coast for the day. They ate fish and chips on the beachfront and drove north of Yeppoon, where they visited a pottery in the midst of the rainforest. Shelley bought her mother a pretty soap dispenser for her bathroom and, for a few hours, she didn't think about Luke and his sons.

The next morning the doorbell rang as she helped her mother with the breakfast dishes. Noela left to answer it and promptly returned to the kitchen.

'It's for you, Shelley.'

'Who is it?' Her mother's expression made her wonder. Noela merely shook her head and resumed drying dishes, a funny little smile playing about her mouth.

Shelley's throat went dry. A sudden surge of hope pierced her and sent her hurrying to the door. All the while she scolded herself for being a silly fool. She must be going crazy, anticipating him at every turn. But there he stood, holding a large bunch of red roses. He smiled uncertainly at her, as if unsure of his welcome. Shelley stared at him, wondering if her demented imagination had conjured him up again.

'I just had to come and see you, Shelley,' he said. The husky catch in his voice sent little tremors down her spine. 'I'm sorry I didn't ring you.'

His mouth twisted and he thrust the bouquet at her.

'I'm sorry for a lot of things. These are for you.'

'Oh, Luke.' Clutching the flowers, she bent to breathe in their heady scent. Tears pricked her eyelids and her throat felt choked. 'I don't know what to say.'

'If you want to tell me to bugger off, I probably deserve it.'

Shelley shook her head.

'I'm not going to tell you that.'

He took a deep breath and flashed his old, charming smile.

'It's been crap at home without you. It's taken me a while to realise just how much I missed you. I know you want to go back to Brisbane, but can we keep in touch, see if we can work things out?'

She nodded, a happy little laugh mingling with her tears.

'I've been so miserable these past two weeks. I have to go back to work, but it won't be for ever.'

He stepped closer and pushed the flowers to one side so he could kiss her.

'It's not the same at home without you, Shelley. The boys have been asking for you, too.'

'I've missed them – and Breakaway Creek.' She brushed his rough cheek with her lips, inhaling the seductive scent of his skin. 'But most of all I've missed you.'

He kissed her again until her head spun and her knees went to water. At last he lifted his head and tipped her chin up with his fingers so he could look at her. He was breathing unevenly and she sensed the tension in his body.

'Shelley, are you busy today? I advertised for a nanny and I have to interview someone. After that, will you come away with me?' His fingers played with her hair, combing it away from her face. 'Mum and Dad have the boys and they're happy to keep them for a couple of days. We've never had any real time together.'

He looked so earnest and intense that she didn't have the heart to refuse him, even if the prospect of spending time alone with him had been possible to resist.

'No, I'm not busy at all,' she said, smiling up at him. 'Where did you have in mind?'

~*~

Two mornings later Luke took her to meet his parents. They followed a narrow bitumen road that wound through a remnant patch of sub-tropical rainforest before emerging into cleared grazing country. They turned off the main road at a sign that read: Briar Gully Droughtmasters. A modern brick home appeared, built on the side of a lush, grassy hill. Red, Brahman-cross cattle grazed in the paddock in front of the house. A shed and a set of stockyards nestled close by.

'What a beautiful spot,' Shelley exclaimed. 'How long have your parents lived here?'

'They bought it soon after I was married,' Luke said with a smile. 'When they decided it was time to leave Breakaway Creek to the younger generation.'

He looked relaxed and happy, free from the tension that had once accompanied any mention of his marriage. When they drew up at the house, Shelley put her hand on his forearm, needing to touch him. She loved the feel of his firm muscles under her fingers.

They'd spent two nights at a local resort, away from the shadows that had followed them over the past weeks. Together they'd been able to unwind and relax for the first time. Their relationship was new and thrilling. There had been no discussion of the future, but she no longer doubted they had one.

Luke leaned over the console to kiss her.

'Mmm,' he murmured. 'Now you're getting me all hot and bothered, and here comes the welcoming committee.'

Shelley drew back hastily, running a hand over her hair. As they got out of the car, Ben and Jack ran up, their little faces lit by excited smiles. Luke hoisted them up, one in each arm, and then set them down so they could greet Shelley. She bent to hug them both, gratified that they seemed pleased to see her again. Luke's parents followed more sedately.

Diane Sherman was a tall, slim woman in her late fifties. She was still attractive with sleek, chin-length dark hair. The likeness to Luke was unmistakeable. Barry Sherman was fair and of a stockier build. His cheery smile instantly reminded Shelley of Mitch.

Luke put his arm around Shelley and drew her close as he made the introductions. To her surprise, they both greeted her with a kiss.

'So you're our long-lost relation!' Diane exclaimed. 'We're so grateful for the help you've given Luke with the boys.'

'I've enjoyed it,' Shelley said happily, taking an instant liking to her warm, friendly manner. 'They're beautiful boys and they've been through a rough time.'

'All three of them, I'd say.' Diane's eyes twinkled.

Shelley flushed, laughing.

'That wasn't what I meant, but I guess it's true.'

Luke's father winked at Shelley.

'Come in, both of you. Time for a cup of tea.'

They passed a pleasant hour on the breezy front porch, talking over coffee and homemade scones. Diane showed Shelley photos from their trip to Europe while the boys played with the Sherman's border collie in the front yard.

'Ben and Jack seem happy,' Shelley commented. 'It's amazing how resilient children are. You wouldn't think they'd recently been through such a horrible experience.'

Diane and Barry exchanged glances.

'I think it left its mark on all of you,' Diane said quietly. 'We all react to things in different ways.'

'Yes.' Shelley looked thoughtfully at the silent man beside her. 'You're probably right.'

Later, Luke took her into a large, comfortable lounge room with a deep pile carpet and burgundy leather armchairs.

'You have to read Lucy Baxter's diary,' he said.

Shelley drew a deep breath as he passed her the book. Her hands shook. In the anxiety of the past few weeks, she hadn't spared a thought for Emma and Alex, but now it all came rushing back: her initial curiosity; her shock when Alex's secret was revealed; and her empathy for the city girl, Emma. She read the words aloud, conscious of Luke sitting close by.

At last she looked up at him, shuddering.

'People talk about the "good old days", but I'm glad I was born in the twentieth century. We have our problems, but it must have been hard for women back then.' She skimmed over the next couple of entries which seemed to record mundane activities. There were no further mentions of Alex, Emma or Mr Watson. She turned to Diane who had just entered the room. 'Do you know what happened to Emma's father?'

'No, I don't.' Diane sat on the armchair opposite. 'He deserved a sad end. That could be your next project, Shelley.'

'With your permission, I'd love to read all of this.'

'Of course. There's a lot of stuff about Emma and Alex that you'll enjoy.'

'I'd like to know what happened to them after they were married. I gather they didn't return to Breakaway Creek.'

'No.' Diane's smile faded. 'I think they had a fairly hard life. Alex took a job on an isolated property north of Clermont, partly to avoid the gossip in town, I think. He worked there for a few years and was promoted to manager. Eventually he saved enough to buy land of his own, but it was only average cattle country and I don't think they made a fortune on it.'

'Do you know if they had more children? Only one birth was registered in Clermont.'

'Yes, Lucy mentions more in the diary. Three, I think it was.'

'I wonder if Emma ever regretted marrying him,' Shelley mused.

Diane shrugged.

'Who can know for sure? From what I learned about her, I doubt it. I'm certain her family was more important to her than a life of luxury in the city.'

'I agree. It sounds like she was a brave, generous person, and she would have known that Alex didn't have money.'

~*~

In the afternoon, Luke took Shelley for a walk down to the gully that ran in front of the house. A corridor of virgin scrub had been retained on either bank and they stopped in the shade of a sprawling eucalypt, sitting close together on a log that had been weathered smooth. The air smelled different here; it had a hint of tropical spice and musty damp that was so opposed to the crisp, dusty dryness of Breakaway Creek.

Luke stared pensively into the scrub-tangled depths of the gully.

'You know, Shelley, reading those diaries a few days ago made everything fall into place. After Miranda, I thought I must be mad getting mixed up with another city girl. But your ancestor, Emma, came from the city and look what she went through. She risked becoming a social outcast to marry Alex.'

Shelley was silent for a moment. She could understand his thoughts, but it was unfair to compare her to Miranda. Perhaps Luke read her mind. He took her hand in his, rubbing his thumb over her palm.

'I know I shouldn't have let my experience with Miranda cloud my judgement. You've proved time and again you're nothing like her. It took me a while to realise how stupid I was being.'

Again, she said nothing. A lump had lodged tight in her throat. He turned to face her, his eyes apologetic, pleading.

'Shelley, it's still a few months before I can get a divorce, and I've probably got a custody battle ahead of me.' He grimaced. 'I know I'm not much of a catch and I come with a ready-made family. But I love you. Can you see yourself living at Breakaway Creek? Or am I rushing you, asking that?'

'Oh, Luke.' She shook her head, giving a broken little laugh as emotion welled up inside her. 'I loved being at Breakaway Creek. And I love you and your boys. So yes, I think I can see myself living there. Eventually.'

Smiling, he slipped his arm around her waist and hugged her.

'That's good enough for now. Looks like the wheel has turned full circle. I reckon there was always meant to be another city girl at Breakaway Creek. I just had to find the right one.'

Heather Garside grew up on a cattle property in Central Queensland and now lives with her husband on a beef and grain farm in the same area. She has two adult children and two beautiful granddaughters.

She has published five novels and has helped also to write and produce several compilations of short stories and local histories. The Cornstalk was a finalist in the 2008 Booksellers' Best Award, Long Historical category, for romance books published in the USA. Breakaway Creek was a finalist in the QWC/Hachette Manuscript Development Program and was first published by Clan Destine Press. Morgan's Road is her latest novel.

Heather works at home on the farm and for many years has helped produce a local monthly newsletter, amongst other voluntary activities. She enjoys patchwork and sewing and regularly attends a local craft group.

For more information about her books, please visit her website at www.heathergarside.com